THE midnight carnival

step right up, don't be shy ...

erika mcgann

**Winner of the Waverton Good Read
Children's Award 2014**

THE O'BRIEN PRESS

DUBLIN

First published 2015 by The O'Brien Press Ltd,
12 Terenure Road East, Rathgar, Dublin 6, Ireland.
Tel: +353 1 4923333; Fax: +353 1 4922777
E-mail: books@obrien.ie
Website: www.obrien.ie

ISBN: 978-1-84717-740-7

8 7 6 5 4 3 2 1
19 18 17 16 15

Layout and design: The O'Brien Press Ltd.
Cover and internal illustrations by Emma Byrne
Printed and bound by CPI Group (UK) Ltd, Croydon, CR0 4YY
The paper in this book is produced using pulp from
managed forests.

THE midnight carnival

Praise for

THE demon notebook

'a spookily bewitching story' *The Irish Times*
'the teen dialogue is sharp and realistic, an excellent read'
Irish Examiner

Praise for

THE broken spell

'the multi-layered plot bounds along breathlessly, with crisp schoolgirl
dialogue… the eccentric new characters make for an Irish Hogwarts'
Irish Examiner

'a very exciting read that offers young readers something to think about
as well as something to make them jump'
Books for Keeps

Praise for

THE watching wood

'chockfull of dilemmas and dramas that any young reader from Detroit
to Delhi can enjoy reading … a touch of Hogwarts – but with half
a dozen girls in the foreground … in short; quirky, spooky fun with

'once : SP   : turner
… Ho   ds and

ERIKA MCGANN grew up in Drogheda and now lives in Dublin. As a kid she wanted to be a witch, but was no good at it, so now she spends her time writing supernatural stories, and living vicariously through her characters. She hopes, in time, to develop the skills to become an all-powerful being. She has written three other books about Grace and her friends, *The Demon Notebook*, *The Broken Spell* and *The Watching Wood*.

dedication

For Kunak,
the best big sister a little sister ever had.

acknowledgements

Thanks, as always, to my wonderful editor, Marian Broderick. To my gorgeous friend, Rachel Mungra, for far too many favours. To Emma Byrne for her brilliant designing. And finally, thanks to Helen Carr and everyone at O'Brien Press.

Contents

PROLOGUE

The sun beat down mercilessly, parching soil that had already turned to dust. Strong winds swept dirt across the valley, billowing terrible sandy clouds, revealing nothing underneath but more cracked, useless earth. A caravan of trucks and trailers surrounded a red-and-white striped tent and, nearby, roustabouts assembled a ferris wheel, hauling it upright with pulleys and ropes. There were lightbulbs at every join of the wheel's flaking frame, in the shape of a giant star, but no-one lit them in the daylight. A man rested against a 1928 Chevrolet, a pickup truck with oversized mud-flaps either side of its narrow bonnet. He wore a red-tailed coat, high-waisted trousers and black knee boots. There was a permanent crease across his forehead where a top hat usually sat, and his cheeks were ruddy and red. He twisted one end of his thin, waxed moustache and watched intently as a woman stepped inside a trailer with dirty net curtains at the window.

'Earn those pennies, Grigori,' he growled, though no-one was close enough to hear. 'She may be the only customer we get in this good-for-nothin' town.'

✳ ✳ ✳

Inside the trailer, an elderly man sat at a fold-out table. He wore a crimson housecoat, his grey hair smoothed against his neck. He smiled at the woman sitting opposite, revealing a single gold tooth. She stared into the whiteness of his eyes – no pupils, no irises.

'You are blind, old man.'

'I am Grigori,' he replied, 'and I have only sight that matters. Many peoples claim gift, but I have gift.'

'A true seer,' she said, pleased.

The man took a large deck of cards from the pocket of his housecoat and placed them in front of her. She looked with distaste at the dust blowing in from outside, and piling on the floor beneath the filthy curtains.

'Shuffle, and I will tell you past, tell you future,' he said.

'It is the future I seek, Grigori.'

She shuffled the tarot deck, caressing the cards with her long fingers, then handed them back. Splitting the deck in three, the man turned over the top card of each pile, one by one. Staring straight ahead, his fingertips lightly danced over the cards.

'Great power, I see. Like can of petrol that will explode. So much power inside one person.'

The woman's dark eyes lifted in a satisfied smile.

'Go on.'

'I see great effort, much work. Holding flame to petrol,

waiting for great boom.'

The woman nodded.

'And then?'

The fingertips danced again.

'And then... nothing. No explosion, no boom. Petrol leaks from can that is old, turning to rust.' His voice was sympathetic. 'There is no greatness for you.'

The dark eyes narrowed.

'Look again,' she said. 'Check your filthy cards again.'

'I see only potential,' the man stroked the tarot cards gently, 'and failure.'

Her mouth, sticky with ruby-red lipstick, quivered and grimaced.

'Do not play with me, old man. I have done things you could not dream of. I will do more...'

'These things you will do, power you have. But in the end... it come to nothing.'

Her breath rasped quick and shuddering. She snatched him by the wrists and he cried out under her grip.

'Curse you and your kin!' she hissed.

A sandstorm erupted in the tiny confines of the trailer, and the woman's grip tightened on the old man's wrists. A realisation came through the screeching darkness, like a shark through dirty water, and a name escaped his lips.

'*Murdrina*!'

When he awoke the woman was gone. On the fold-out

table sat a wooden box, curling petals carved into the lid. He clutched a silk scarf to his mouth, coughing up the remains of the sandstorm. Feeling the box on the table, his wriggling fingers tipped the lid open and grasped what was inside; a straw doll, crudely made with thin wires pinching the neck, waist, ankles and wrists. He snatched his hand back as if it had bitten him.

Grigori's woeful howls echoed through every soul in the valley, but the damage had already been done.

1

Leaping Goldfish

Grace was underwater, battling a hideous sea creature that she couldn't quite see. The current swirled and spun, but she held fast to the tip of the monster's tail, twisting and turning as it fought to shake her off. Then suddenly the depth was too much. There was a weight on her chest, not enough air in her lungs, and miles of ocean above her. She let go of the creature and bolted for the surface, but the pressure remained the same. No matter how hard she kicked she got no closer to fresh air. She squirmed and weaved against the tide but it only dragged her further and further into the darkness until...

Grace started awake to a pair of grey eyes staring straight into hers. They were shaded by a bob of black hair, and the little upturned nose beneath them wrinkled.

'Morning. There's a carnival.'

'What? Where... What's going on? Una? What are you doing in my room?'

'Your mum let me in. There's a carnival.'

Una lay across Grace's bed, her arms resting on her friend's chest, propping up her chin. Grace wriggled against the weight.

'Why are you on my bed?'

'I told you, your mum let me in.'

'Then why are you cutting off the circulation to my arms?'

'Oh,' Una said, springing back onto her feet, 'whoopsie. Sorry about that.'

'You could have just knocked on the door.'

'I was going to, but then I looked in and your face was all twitchy like you were having a dream and I thought it looked interesting, so I was just gonna watch until you woke up. Then you woke up.'

Grace sat up, rubbing her eyes and shaking out the pins and needles in her arms.

'Great. Well, thank you very much for waking me. It's the weekend, you know.'

'Yeah, but your mum said *you should wake her up anyway, or she'll miss the best part of the day*. There's a carnival.'

'You said that.'

'In the park.'

'I didn't hear anything about a carnival coming to town.'

'Nobody did, but they're here. There's a ferris wheel, and a giant tent and lots of stuff. So we're going. Now.'

'I'll get up in a minute.'

Una went to leave, but stuck her head around the door.

'You'll miss the best part of the *day*, Grace.'

'Get out of my room!'

Una disappeared downstairs, where Grace knew her mother would ply her with toast and orange juice. She dropped back onto her pillow and groaned. It was so *early* for a Sunday.

It was a fresh autumn morning. Grace loved this time of year. She didn't like starting back to school after the summer holidays so much, but she loved the change in the air; when everything was still sunny and bright but there was a chill creeping into the weather. The trees looked beautiful too, especially the ones lining the streets of Dunbridge. They were turning red and golden and making the town look kind of supernatural and gorgeous. She made the mistake of telling Una all of this.

'You mean the way leaves turn brown and fall off, right before they turn to mulch on the ground? You know we're going to be slipping on that stuff from now until Christmas.'

'It's still pretty.'

'It's mulch. Ooh, look! You can see the ferris wheel.'

From the small hill at the top of North Street they had a great view of Dunbridge Park. There was the distant hum of harpsichord music, and the ferris wheel, with a star of lights inside its circular frame, was turning slowly. Right in the middle of the park there was a giant red-and-white striped tent – at least it might once have been red and white, it looked so old and battered now that the white stripes were stained a dirty cream colour, and the red had faded to pinky brown – and there were loads of stalls with more music that clashed, making the whole thing sound brash and loud and full of life. At the entrance hung a curved sign that read 'LE CARNAVAL DE MINUIT'.

'The Midnight Carnival,' Grace whispered to herself, smiling. 'And look, there's Rachel.'

Leaning against a post and filing her nails, Rachel's face was shielded by layers of chestnut-coloured hair, but Grace would know those clothes anywhere. Since her swashbuckling adventures on the magical island of Hy-Breasal, Rachel's taste in fashion had taken a decided turn towards the piratey. She wore skinny jeans a lot, with black boots over them and a wide leather belt. She sometimes wore a flowy blouse, sometimes a short-sleeved top with braces, but today it was a shirt and leather jacket. Grace had to admit she always looked really good, but she also looked really *grown-up*.

'Don't censor her, she's becoming a woman,' Una had once said when she voiced her concerns, and that had made

Grace blush like crazy.

Now, to avoid thinking about it and blushing again, she called out, 'Hey, Rach, where's Jenny? Una said you were collecting her on the way.'

Rachel tucked the nail file into her back pocket.

'She told me to get the hell out of her room and, if I ever wake her up on a Sunday again, she'll shave my head. I'd say she'll be along later when she's had a proper lie-in.'

'Coola boola,' said Una. 'I've texted Adie as well, and she's going to call to Delilah's house on her way here.'

'Mrs Quinlan still won't buy Delilah a mobile phone?'

'Nah, Old Cat Lady fears technology. She prefers the pongy smells of potions and magical stuff.' Una slipped and pointed angrily at the grass. 'See, Grace? Mulch.'

'Step right up, step right up, ladies, don't be shy.' The man wore tattered cord trousers, with black braces over a dusty shirt. His hair looked unwashed, and the shirt was patched in several places with poor stitching. But his charming smile and bright eyes were impossible to ignore. 'Throw a hoop and win a fish. And what spectacular fish!'

He bounced between several stalls, but directed the girls towards one with rows and rows of goldfish bowls. The fish swimming around inside were not your average goldfish – they were varying shades of violet, with tall tails that undulated beautifully in the water.

'Wow,' gasped Una, 'look at those. One of them would look deadly in my room.'

'I'm not playing this one,' Grace said. 'It's cruel. Those fish have horrible lives and they never live long after you get them home.'

'Aw, come on. They're really happy. Look at them, swimming around like they haven't a care in the world.'

'The bowls are too narrow. Look, there's hardly any surface area on the top. That means they're getting very little oxygen from the air.'

Una looked at her like she was an idiot.

'Fish don't breathe air, they breathe water.'

'They breathe oxygen in the water that *comes* from the air. It's cruel, Una.'

'They don't look unhappy to me,' said Rachel, picking up a couple of hoops.

'Fine,' said Grace, 'then go ahead and play.'

She stood back with her arms crossed, and blushed when she saw the game operator watching her with a smile. Grace urged herself to make her case about animal cruelty but, though she was a girl of strong convictions, she was also a girl that embarrassed easily. She gave the operator what she hoped was a disapproving look and stayed quiet.

'What? No way!' Rachel pointed at a bowl in the centre of the stall. 'That fish jumped.'

Her red hoop sat perfectly around an empty bowl.

'Sorry,' the operator said, 'you hooped an empty vessel.'

'But it wasn't empty. There was a fish in it, and he jumped! Look, there's two in the bowl next to it.'

'Ah, the rare double win. Hoop *that* bowl and a magnificent pair of Indigo Daega is yours.'

Rachel wasted her last go trying to hoop the pair of fish, then sulkily made way for Una. Una's first hoop clattered to the back of the stall, her second skipped off to one side with the ringing clink of wood hitting glass, but her third landed neatly around one violet fish. That jumped. Grace saw it, it definitely jumped. The hoop landed, there was a flash of purple in the air, a plop of water, and the fish was in the adjoining bowl.

'Hey!' cried Una. 'No fair.'

'Nice try, nice try, ladies, you very nearly won, how lucky. Another go? The Coconut Shy, perchance?'

'Yeah, right,' Rachel muttered, 'the coconuts are probably glued on.'

Grace, who meant to add some parting comment about surface area and oxygen levels in water, was too distracted by the idea of jumping goldfish to say anything. As they walked away, Una shrieked and grabbed hold of the others. Something lumbered through the grass at their feet, about three metres long with squat legs and nobbled brownish skin that looked like armour.

19

'That's Legba,' the game operator called after them over the noise of the stalls. 'We picked him up in Louisiana. Ain't he a beauty?'

The alligator pushed through the crowd with its broad snout and seemed unperturbed by the occasional scream it elicited from those caught unawares. Excited whispers spread through the mass and people sprang out of the reptile's way, leaving a clear path. It meandered on, like a king in procession.

'A freaking alligator,' Una said, clutching Grace's top. 'This place is deadly!'

'Adie! Delilah! Run. There's two seats left.'

Grace frowned at Una, who leaned against the bar of the ferris wheel car, yelling at the girls on the ground far below. Una had convinced the operator to let herself, Grace and Rachel squeeze into one car, even though it was only really meant for two people at a time. They were at the very top of the wheel, held stationary while their friends got on at the bottom. Grace waved down at the girls – Adie was already looking queasy, and the wheel hadn't even moved yet.

Grace couldn't blame her. From afar the wheel looked pretty and elegant; up close it was covered in flaking rust, the joints looked battered, and some of the lightbulbs that made up its star of lights had blown and turned black. The cars were wooden and very basic in shape. There was a safety bar that sat across their laps, but it rattled and felt loose, and there was ample room to slide out underneath it if you felt the sudden urge to jump.

'Adie looks like she's going to barf,' said Rachel.

The car rocked disconcertingly as Una leaned over to look straight down.

'Una, don't rock it!' said Grace.

'Why would she be scared?' asked Una. 'Even if she fell out, she could cast a spell and fly. We all could. There's no danger for *us*.'

'Somehow that doesn't help.' Grace jumped as the ferris wheel lurched suddenly into motion.

'She's probably just forgotten. I'll remind her.' Una twisted between the other two girls to look back and shout, 'Adie, if you fall out, just don't hit the ground!'

Grace could see Adie's face turn pale green as she grabbed on tighter to the bar in front.

'I think that worked like a charm, Una, well done. And would you mind not yelling to the whole town that we're witches?'

'I spoke in code. No-one will know what that meant.'

'It's a wonder the CIA haven't hired you yet.'

After a dozen creaking turns, the wheel stopped and the girls climbed off. They were shortly joined by Delilah and Adie, who still looked a little wobbly.

'Wanna go again?' said Una.

'I'm good for now,' said Grace, noting the relief on Adie's face. 'I *am* hungry, though.'

'There's candy floss somewhere around here,' said Delilah. 'B-brr pokes me in the ear every time he smells it.'

At the mention of his name, the little wood nymph stuck his face out between strands of the small girl's hair. He was about ten centimetres tall, with brown grainy skin, and a faint whiff of dried leaves clung about him. Delilah adored the creature – he was devoted to her – and Adie found him very cute, but the mischievous little faery gave everyone else the creeps. The girls knew they would never have escaped the dangers of Hy-Breasal without him, but he still wasn't a favourite among them. Knowing B-brr wanted candy floss somehow made Grace want it less.

'I wouldn't mind some popcorn or something. I'm sure they've got other stuff at the stall.'

'Or,' Una said suddenly, 'we could visit the fortune-teller.'

She pointed to a weather-beaten trailer with a sign out front. There were stained net curtains in the windows and the outside of the vehicle was filthy.

'I don't know. Maybe food first. I could–'

'Fortune-teller.'

'–maybe a drink too, and–'

'Fortune-teller.'

'What does everyone else–'

'Fortune-teller.'

'*Fine*, Una. We'll go to the fortune-teller first.'

'Ha! I knew I could annoy you into it.'

2

Painted Faces

There were three steps up into the trailer and even at the bottom Adie could pick up the powerful and musty scent of incense.

'It smells really strong in there.' Tugging at her dark curls, she willed the colour to return to her cheeks, still pale from the death-ride on the rusty ferris wheel.

'That'll sink into your clothes,' Rachel said in warning. 'Seriously, you'll stink of it all day, it's like cigarette smoke. I'm not going in.'

'Adie, you wanna go in with me?' asked Una. 'It'll be great craic.'

Adie nodded, wishing she had the guts to say 'no thanks'. She didn't mind funfairs, as long as she didn't have to go on the scariest rides, and she didn't mind dusty old flea markets, as long as she didn't have to haggle with the eccentric people that ran them. But this place seemed to be an eerie mix of both – scary rides, weird stalls, and way too many strange characters.

Una pushed Adie up the steps into the darkness of the fortune-teller's trailer. Adie didn't admit it, but the heavy incense made her feel claustrophobic. It was like being trapped by an invisible wall of scent.

'Welcome, young peoples. I am Grigori.'

The old man sat at a fold-out table, his hands flattened next to a set of tarot cards. He wore a collarless shirt, dark waistcoat and a long, crimson dressing gown. His grey hair was smoothed down over his neck, and his perfect smile boasted a gold tooth. Adie shivered as he turned his pure white eyes toward them – no pupils, no irises, just blank white eyes.

'We... um... we were wondering if you could read our fortunes.'

'That why I here.' His accent was very strong, and Adie couldn't place it. 'Sit. I tell you past, I tell you future.'

Adie took the seat opposite and felt Una grip her shoulders behind.

'Ask him the future,' she hissed in Adie's ear. 'Who'd bother asking about the past? You know that already, you were there.'

'Um... I'd like to know the future, please.'

'Cross palm with silver,' the man said.

'Huh?'

'Money,' Una said. 'Give him money.'

Adie rummaged in her pocket and placed a €2 coin in the fortune-teller's hand.

'Good,' his gold tooth sparkled. 'We begin. Shuffle, please.'

Adie shuffled the tarot cards awkwardly, and handed them to the man, who split the deck in three and turned over the first top card.

The image was of a stone tower being hit by lightning. Flames burst from the windows, and two men were falling to their death from the top. The fortune-teller didn't look down at the card, but touched it lightly with his fingertips.

'Ah, the tower. Great upheaval, disaster comes. The men fall, yes? Because there is no control. You cannot prevent.'

'Oh.' Adie shifted uncomfortably in her chair. 'Okay.'

She didn't ask any more about her impending doom. She thought it might lengthen the session and she wanted this over as quickly as possible. The man turned over the second card. This one had a big, red heart in the centre, with three swords piercing it.

'Three of swords,' he said sadly. 'Separation, sorrow. You have time of great grief.'

Lovely, Adie thought, but she smiled politely. Even Una had gone quiet.

The third card showed a woman in a white robe, with an infinity sign above her head. She petted a smiling lion at her feet, and the roman numerals VIII were at the top of the picture.

'Strength,' the teller said. 'This card mean strength, but not strength from outside. From inside. Great power, great control. See how woman tame lion? She persist, survive. Make great trial seem small.'

'Oh, right,' said Adie, intrigued in spite of herself. 'But why is that one upside down?'

The teller's fingertips stroked the card.

'Inverted, so it means opposite. Weakness, failure. No strength from within, no power. This not good card for you.'

A cold feeling rippled down Adie's spine. *It's just nonsense,* she told herself. *I'm not weak. This teller doesn't know how many dangers me and my friends have faced. And how many we've beaten.* But a little knot in the pit of her stomach made her repeat the words in her mind, *me and my friends.* Her friends. She was nothing without her friends. She was brave only when they were brave. She fought back only when they fought back. All their adventures flew through her mind and she wondered, would she have survived any of them without her friends?

The fortune-teller suddenly gasped and grabbed her hands. His white eyes gazed upwards as if he heard a voice from above.

'I see...' he said, 'I see...'

His eyes lowered to Adie's and a smile crept across his face.

'Friends you have. Great friends. And they are special.

27

Indeed, they are special.'

It was as if he had read her mind. Frightened, she pulled her hands from his grip, but he didn't seem fazed.

'So long waiting. And then, something special...'

Adie had had enough. She got up, grabbed Una's hand and stumbled from the trailer.

'Well, that was all kinds of creepy,' said Una.

'Horrible. That was horrible. All that stuff about...'

'Hey, don't worry about it. What does he know? You're a certified superhero in an actual superhero gang. And *this* superhero's hungry. Let's go get some food.'

Adie let herself be led away, but couldn't help taking a glance back at the spooky trailer. Behind one of the net curtains, she could see a pair of white eyes staring blankly in her direction, and the glint of a single gold tooth.

✹ ✹ ✹

'Oh, my God, you got it in my hair!'

Jenny had finally arrived, and Rachel was glaring at her.

'That's not candy floss. That's that mousse, or whatever stuff you put in it,' Jenny sniffed.

'It is not. The stuff I put in my hair makes it silky.' Rachel pulled a few strands through her fingers. 'This is sticky and – yuk, there's more of it!'

'Relax, it'll wash out.'

Rachel's nostrils flared as she took a deep breath. Adie

imagined she was silently counting to ten, so as not to flip out and whack Jenny on the head.

'Just keep it away from me.'

'Alright.' Jenny took an exaggerated step backwards, then waved to Adie and Una with the ball of pink wool in her hand, nearly getting Rachel again. 'Heard you were having your palms read. How was it?'

'It was a tarot reading,' said Adie, 'and it was terrible.'

'Nah, it was cool,' said Una. 'You should try it out, it's well freaky.'

'Will do.' Jenny tossed the candy floss into a nearby bin. 'Who's on for the ferris wheel?'

'We already did that,' said Rachel.

'Without me? Why didn't you wait?'

'Maybe you should get up earlier.'

'Maybe you should go mousse your hair.'

'Come on, knock it off,' Grace said, nibbling on a bag of popcorn. 'Why don't we go on those flying chair things? They look pretty dangerous.'

Adie smiled at her friend munching on popcorn. Grace was great at diplomacy. She knew Jenny would rise to the challenge of danger, and Rachel would like the idea of perching elegantly in a seat that flew through the air. It came so naturally to her, thought Adie, that Grace probably didn't even know how essential to their group she was. But Adie knew. Grace was the glue.

Adie wasn't the glue. She wasn't the adventure. She wasn't the elegance and she wasn't the fun. The girls were about to start their third year in secondary school, and she still didn't know what – if anything – she brought to the table. Opting out of another rusty carnival ride, she watched the others climb on and felt blue. Even Delilah, although she was the quiet type, like Adie, she was daring. They all were. Her friends were fearless and always ready to try new things. Look at how they were all reacting to the carnival. It just felt icky to her – the people, the noise, the eerie weirdness – but her friends felt right at home. Adie didn't like new things, she didn't like change. As the breeze from the flying chairs made her blink, and her friends shrieked with laughter above, all she could think of was that she was scared. She frowned and tucked a stray curl behind her ear. She was the scared one.

'Hey there, little bunny.'

A man's smiling face loomed out of the twilight. At first, all she saw was a mouthful of brown teeth and a top hat. Then a pair of ruddy cheeks, and an icky, skinny, greasy moustache. His breath smelled of something rotten, she wasn't sure what, and he was standing way too close.

'I'm Felix,' he said, touching the brim of the hat and grinning. 'This here is my carnival.'

She mouthed 'excuse me' and walked away. To her dismay, he followed. She was uncomfortable, but wasn't sure at what point she was allowed to be impolite. After walking a lap around the flying chair ride, she decided it didn't matter, and rounded on him.

'What do you want?!'

The man laughed heartily. His red tailed jacket nearly burst at the buttons with his chuckles.

'Only to give you these, honey.' He held out a bunch of pale pink tickets. 'For the main event tonight. Aerial acrobatics, the Melancholy Clowns, and much more. You and your friends will have a whale of a time.'

'No, thank you.'

'Now don't go having kittens, little lady, I'm just offering some free tickets. That's just the kind of operation we got here. We take care of the customers.' His accent was American – one of the southern states, she guessed – and he flitted unnervingly between sweet smiles and sad frowns. 'You don't want your friends to miss out, do you? These are the last tickets I got left. You don't want them missing out just cos you were a scaredy cat, now do you?'

That hit where it hurt. Snatching the tickets, Adie backed away.

'Thank you.'

'You're welcome, little lady.' He tipped his top hat again. 'Enjoy the show now.'

And with a swish of his coat-tails he was gone.

Music pumped through the main tent, reverberating through the tarpaulin walls. The air was heavy inside with so many people crammed into the space, and the tiered seating surrounded a circle of dry dirt in the centre. Grace wondered if the town council would go mad when they found a big chunk of Dunbridge Park reduced from green grass to dusty soil.

'Ladies and gentlemen!' The ringmaster, complete with top hat and red coat, materialised before the bustling audience. 'My name is Felix Renaud and I welcome you to the *Carnaval de Minuit!*'

People rushed to take their seats. The show was about to begin.

A small, dainty figure descended from the ceiling on a thick, white rope.

'I won't bore you by flattering my own performers. I won't give you the hard sell. I'll just tell you this,' the ringmaster's eyes darkened, 'the Minuit experience is one you will never forget. To begin, *la belle Justine!*'

In a flash of red he was gone, and the figure on the rope tumbled, apparently out of control. The audience gasped, until she stopped abruptly, only a metre off the ground. Balancing on one foot, still wrapped in rope, the girl grinned wickedly. She was no more than thirteen or fourteen years old, and dressed in ballet pumps and a pink leotard with shorts. But it wasn't her outfit that made Grace stare – it was her face. For the lower half of the young girl's face was completely covered in a thick beard of soft, brown hair, ending in one twirling curl beneath her chin.

Some nervous chuckling rippled through the audience as people began to notice, but the girl seemed unaffected. She tipped backwards and climbed the rope feet first, like Spiderman, then wrapped one leg and spun around with alarming speed. Grace and the others joined in the 'oohs' and 'aahs' as the bearded ballerina curled herself into impossible positions, arching her back to press the soles of her feet against the back of her head, stretching into the splits with only one leg entwined by the rope.

Grace hadn't seen the tightrope positioned two-thirds of the way to the ceiling until Justine somersaulted onto it. The girl then performed a beautiful tightrope ballet – pirouettes and turns, elegant arches with one foot raised in the air – all the while balanced on the thin cord suspended many metres above the tent floor. It was stunning and terrifying at the same time, and it wasn't until the girl snatched the rope and slid to the ground for a bow, that Grace realised she had been holding her breath.

'That was amazing,' Rachel breathed.

'Yeah, holy cow,' said Jenny. 'She could have fallen and broken her neck. That was awesome.'

'Why does she have a beard?' asked Adie.

'Don't know,' replied Grace. 'Maybe it's genetic.'

'Maybe it's fake,' said Jenny.

'It looks pretty real to me.'

A number of acts followed, including a strongwoman with rippling muscles, who threw an anvil like it was made of cardboard; a mystical sorcerer whose light display was like fireworks inside the tent; and two brothers, conjoined twins, who sang such a haunting melody that Grace swore her heart was breaking. But as the end of the show drew near, the lighting dimmed and the ringmaster re-appeared.

'Ladies and gentlemen,' he said solemnly, 'they make you laugh, but may also make you cry... the Melancholy Clowns!'

Grace disliked them instantly. They were unlike any troupe of clowns she'd ever seen, creeping into the ring like furtive creatures, and tumbling silently towards the audience. Their tattered silk suits, even when brand-new, would not have been jolly. They were mostly grim shades of grey, purple and brown, with some muted red and yellow stripes. Their make-up was so heavy that their eyes disappeared into their faces, and their large fake grins stood out horribly.

The Melancholy Clowns cartwheeled and somersaulted, crashing into each other in the way clowns usually do, but there was nothing fun about this performance. They didn't laugh uproariously and point at each other, and when they fell it was like slow motion; they drifted mournfully to the ground. They rolled and jumped, but their slippered feet were completely quiet. There was no music either, and Grace couldn't fathom how there wasn't a single sound from the six performers. There was an air of discomfort, and the audience seemed reluctant to break the silence.

In the final sequence, three clowns tiptoed around the front row, each holding a finger to their lips, as two of their companions wheeled a huge canon from behind the back curtain. Grace shuddered as one silent performer crept past her. Up close his white make-up was dry and cracked, his eyes too deep, and his grin unfriendly. The canon was aimed at the final unsuspecting clown who stood distracted, breathing in the scent of a wilting lily in his hand. The fuse was lit and the fizzing, hissing sound was all that could be heard, until–

BANG!

The awful crack of the canon made the spectators shriek with fright. As the smoke cleared, a clown lay lifeless on the ground, his crushed lily beside him. The painted face nearest to Grace turned slowly and smiled.

3

ROTTEN FEET

'Creepy, creepy, creepy,' Una huffed. 'I did not care for those creepy clowns.'

'Me neither,' said Grace, 'but the rest of it was amazing.'

'Seriously amazing,' said Rachel. 'Did you get a weird feeling when those twins were singing? The song was... I don't know, but I felt the saddest I've ever felt. Smudged my freaking eyeliner.'

'Yeah, I did get that. The sadness, not the eyeliner.'

Rachel nudged her as the girls ambled through the maze of tents and trailers. They weren't really heading for the exit, more wandering in a circle, but no-one pointed it out. There was something so wonderfully strange and eerie about the place, they didn't want to leave. At least, five of them didn't. Adie's feet dragged in the muddying grass.

'I'm going to head home.'

'Are you sure?' said Grace.

'Yeah, I've to – I told my mum I wouldn't be late.'

'I'll come with you.' Delilah allowed B-brr to perch on her shoulder now there was nobody about. 'I need to feed him anyway.'

'He ate dirty great big mouthfuls of my candy floss,' Jenny snarled.

'Proper food. When he just eats sugar he gets terrible wind.'

'That is delightful. Thank you for sharing.'

B-brr let out a little squeal and stuck out his tongue – Grace could never be sure how much of their conversation he understood – then willingly stepped onto Adie's outstretched hand. She smiled.

'See you all later.'

'Okey-doke,' said Grace. 'See you tomorrow. And thanks for the tickets.'

'Yeah, cheers,' Jenny called after them as Adie and Delilah jogged away. 'And hey, you guys, three days of freedom left. Make the most of 'em!'

Grace watched her two friends disappear into the night-time.

'Do you think it'll be different?'

'What?' said Jenny.

'Third year. Do you think we'll be different?'

'You won't. Exam year; exams are your thing. You'll be more *you* than ever! It'll be exhausting for the rest of us.'

'Funny.'

'Oi! Get over here.' Una was ahead of them, peering through a gap in one of the tents, a plain one, not draped in lights.

'Una, don't. I think people live in some of these.'

Una just frowned and waved at them to hurry. A kerosene lamp dimly lit the crack in the tarpaulin – the tent was indeed somebody's home, but Grace found herself peering in with the rest of them.

The bearded ballerina, Justine, sat on a long upholstered stool, with one leg outstretched. She held a slim length of wood in one hand, and her pointed toe was pressed onto the curved end by a strip of material. When she stretched out the leg, the wooden implement forced her foot to arch unnaturally high, so much so that the top of her foot rounded like a ball. It looked very painful.

'You can come in, you know,' the girl's voice startled them all, 'if you wanna take a closer look.'

She dropped the leg to look up at them and smile. Grace had been so distracted by the foot, she'd forgotten about the girl's soft, curly beard. Up close the curls were so neat and shiny, it felt strange to think it, but it kind of suited her.

'I'm really sorry, we didn't mean to –' Grace had never been caught spying into someone's home before, and didn't think there was any way to apologise. 'We're so sorry for bothering you.'

'I don't mind.' The girl's accent was like that of the ring-master, American with a southern stretch in the vowels. 'You're welcome to come in. Come on, get out of the chill air.'

It wasn't chilly, but the girls trooped happily inside. They perched where they could, between the small dressing table and chair, a couple of stools, and the single cot bed.

'Doesn't that hurt?' Jenny asked.

'Loads, but you gotta do it. These feet won't destroy themselves.'

'Does it really wreck your feet?' asked Una. 'How come you do it then?'

'For that ballet arch.' Justine demonstrated by elegantly pointing one toe. 'It looks real nice when you get that foot good and bendy. All ballerinas have to do it. Otherwise you'd be good for nothin'.'

'I've heard ballet people can get arthritis from all the exercises,' said Grace.

'Yup. And that's not the worst of it. Take a look at this.'

Justine whipped off her light cotton socks and the girls gasped in horror. Her toes were calloused and bright red at the joints, and there were flaking scabs everywhere. Two of her toenails were turning black.

'Holy fudgeballs, that's rotten!' Una caught a look from

Grace. 'Oh sorry, I mean it looks really sore.'

'Painful?' Justine said. 'It sure is. That's mostly from *en pointe* stuff – you know, when you walk around on top of your toes – and it hurts like hell. Gonna lose this one soon.' She picked at one blackened nail. 'It's almost better when they fall off.'

'Ewww, gross... oh, sorry again.'

Justine laughed – a lovely, ringing sound – and shook her head.

'That's okay. I like shocking people with 'em. Looking all graceful when they're in shoes and then whipping them out. It always gets a reaction.'

'That rope stuff was amazing, by the way,' Jenny said. 'Where'd you learn that?'

'From my mama, before she passed away.'

'I'm sorry,' said Grace.

'It was a long time ago now. Got no family left but the carnival, and I'm alright with that. The bonds you make here run deeper than blood.'

The conversation felt suddenly serious and Grace wasn't sure how to respond. The others didn't seem to know either so, after a long pause, she said,

'Well, we should let you get back to your... stretching thing. Thanks for the show, it was really great.'

'Yeah,' said Jenny. 'It was awesome.'

'Then please come back again.' Justine pushed her foot back into the band of material on the wooden stretcher.

'And you're welcome to my tent anytime, you hear? I enjoy the company.'

The girls took their leave with smiles and thanks, stepping out into the night air.

'Think she meant it?' asked Una.

'About going back?' Grace replied. 'She seemed to.'

'Cool. I am going to live here until these people leave. I'm gonna live in the carnival.'

'But sleep at home, I hope. You might look a bit weird curling up on the grass.'

'Sleep at home, then back to the carnival. The last three days before school are going to rock.'

Grace waved to the others when she turned off towards her street. She grinned at the little nugget of excitement growing in her tummy. It had taken over the gloomy anticipation of going back to school, and she was really glad she and her friends would have something to distract them this week. It wasn't that she disliked school – she didn't – but Jenny had hit the nail on the head when she mentioned it was their exam year. Grace was a good student at school, as well as in witchcraft, and in the grand scheme of things the third year exams weren't a big deal, but they made the months ahead seem very serious; not like the previous two years of mischief and magic that the girls had shared so far. She sighed deeply and pushed the thoughts away, reminding herself of the red-and-white striped tent and three days of

41

proper fun.

She didn't notice the hunched figure of a teenage boy walking to her right until they almost crossed paths. She was a little startled and stepped back to let him go ahead of her. But when he lifted his head she nearly shrieked in fright. She could clearly see in the moonlight that the skin on his face was dark green with fine cracks all over it. His teeth looked yellow and his mouth too pink against the green. She was reminded of the lizard her cousin kept in a tank in his front room.

'Sorry. Didn't mean to scare you.'

He hunched his backpack higher on his shoulders. His accent was like that of Justine and the ringmaster, but softer, and his voice was low and warm. It was friendly too, but Grace's heart was pounding with shock.

'Are you from the carnival?' she stammered.

It was a bit abrupt, but her fright was still wearing off.

'Heading out from there, yeah. Is this the way out of town?'

'There's just a little village in that direction. Where are you going?'

'Anywhere.'

That wasn't much help. After thinking, Grace told him how to get to the bus station.

'Don't need no bus. I'll walk it.'

'Well... that road to the left leads out of town. It eventually takes you to one of the motorways, towards Dublin. But it's really far. You couldn't walk it.'

'I'll try it out and see how I go.'

'You really should take the bus. Or the train. It'd take days walking.'

'Nah, I'm good. I don't mind the walking. Thanks for the help. Much appreciated.'

He turned and walked away, and Grace felt a pang of guilt. Despite his unusual skin, she could tell he was no older than she was; he shouldn't be walking to Dublin on his own at all, let alone at night. She looked anxiously towards the carnival. Should she tell someone? Maybe she'd get him in trouble if she did. Maybe she *should* get him in trouble. But the confidence with which he'd moved made her think it was none of her business and she would be prying to get involved.

In the end, she turned back towards her house and said nothing to anyone, unconsciously gritting her teeth against the notion that she had done something wrong.

As the bulbs of the ferris wheel flickered and went out, a tall man with a wide-brimmed hat and dark coat entered the ballerina's tent and took a seat on the cot bed. The ballerina stopped rolling her hair into curls and glared at the man in her dressing table mirror.

'What do you want, doctor?'

'You're making friends,' he said.

'What's it to you?'

The man lit a skinny cigar and smoked it slowly.

'I don't like it.'

'It ain't none of your business.'

'Oh, but it is, Justine. We both know that.'

'I like 'em, that's all. I'm allowed to have friends.'

The man made a hissing sound, a strange kind of laugh. He stood, loomed over Justine and stubbed his cigar out on her dressing table, scraping scorched black across the white paint.

'We'll see about that.'

✳ ✳ ✳

Adie had suggested a movie. She had suggested practising spells in the woods. She had even suggested browsing the shops and trying on every single make-up and perfume tester in town, thinking that Rachel at least would go for that one. But no such luck. In the carnival, the others had found something to amuse them for days, and they weren't going to miss a minute of it. Except Jenny. It was 10.30 a.m. but she wouldn't get up before noon unless her bed was on fire.

After getting chapter and verse of the visit to the bearded ballerina's tent, Adie and Delilah broke off from the others. Delilah liked to wander in amongst the tightly packed trailers away from the carnival stalls, where B-brr could safely peek out from beneath her collar.

'I can tell he likes it,' the small girl said, 'he keeps wriggling his toes. He usually only does that when he smells apple pie in the oven.'

'Mrs Quinlan bakes?'

'No, she buys those frozen ones. I tried making muffins once from scratch, but Mephistopheles doesn't like ingredients.'

'Doesn't like ingredients?'

'Flour and sugar and things. I think they make him angry. Anyway, he pushed them off the counter and made a huge mess. Vera threw him outside and banned all baking in the house. Now we get the frozen stuff.'

Mephistopheles was one of Vera Quinlan's cats. Adie found him temperamental and obnoxious – he hissed at the girls whenever they were in the house – and it seemed fitting that he was Old Cat Lady's favourite.

The girls passed by a grey trailer, with its door swinging open in the breeze. There were dozens of ageing postcards pinned to the inside of the door. Delilah suddenly tripped up the wooden steps and pointed to one.

'Soroca!' she said, running her fingers over the pencilled image.

It was a drawing of a stone tower, with no windows but one door at the bottom. There was an arched panel above the door and, above that, a dark cross. At the top of the structure was a stand with a hoop.

'What a strange building. It looks like a candle,' said Adie.

'It's called the Thanksgiving Candle. It's in a place called Soroca, in Moldova.'

'Where you're from?'

'My uncle's farm was further up the river, but we went to Soroca loads of times. It's pretty, isn't it?'

'Verrry prrretty,' said a deep voice from within.

Delilah leapt off the steps like a scalded cat. A woman now filled the doorway of the trailer. She was so tall she had to duck under the frame, and her sleeveless shift showed off rounded arms with huge biceps. Adie was about to run when she recognised her as the strongwoman from the show the night before.

'Sorry, we didn't mean to bother you.'

'No, no, mein kinder. Es ist okay.' The woman pointed to the postcard. 'Soroca. You know?'

'Yes,' Delilah replied.

'Is good, ja? Soroca. Good people, ja?'

'Yes, it's a lovely place.'

The woman jabbed her finger into another postcard, and named a place in a language neither of the girls recognised.

'And dis, ja?'

'No, I don't know where that is. Sorry.'

'Ah, is okay.' The woman waved her hand, as if she had been silly to ask. She smiled. 'My name is Agata.'

'I'm Delilah, and this is Adie.'

Adie waved shyly.

'And dat boy is Drake.' Agata pointed behind them at a figure curling onto a tree stump at the very edge of the park. He was just within earshot. 'Say hallo, Drake!'

The boy raised his hand in a reluctant half-wave, and Adie was shocked to notice the green shade of his skin was not because of the shadow of the trees. There were lines and cracks that made it look like he was covered in scales, and she felt a little queasy. As if he knew what she was thinking, the boy buried his gaze in the backpack on his lap, and said nothing.

'He is shy today,' Agata said smiling. 'Have some tea?'

The boy looked more cross than shy to Adie, but she smiled warmly and accepted Agata's offer.

4

Tea and mooning

'Kohl. Cabbage, ja?' Agata swirled her fingers in the air as if to suggest something rolled up. 'And meat inside.'

'Sarma!' Delilah said. 'Minced meat in cabbage leaves.'

The strongwoman nodded, raising her eyes and hands to the sky like the mere thought of the food was divine. Adie thought it sounded gross. She hated cabbage, and she was no fan of minced meat either.

'Yummy,' Delilah sighed.

'Ha!' Agata slapped her knee, grinning. 'Yummy! Das ist gut. Yummmmy... I use dis word now.'

Adie sipped politely at her black, unusual-tasting tea, and watched the small girl clapping her hands and exclaiming every time Agata mentioned something that she missed about Moldova. Delilah had never been so boisterous in the whole time that Adie had known her. She was like a different girl. And the light in her big, brown eyes made Adie feel guilty – by avoiding asking about her past, had the girls kept Delilah quiet and shy? She had certainly never opened up about life with her wicked mother, and Adie was sure she didn't want to. Meredith Gold had been a blonde beauty, a talented witch, and the most evil person Adie had ever met. She treated Delilah like a slave, and the small girl never showed a moment's regret when she was banished forever down the demon well.

Still, thought Adie, perhaps the girls should have asked about the rest of her family. Delilah had fondly mentioned a grandmother, aunts, uncles and cousins, but Adie and the others still shied away from quizzing her about them. They had asked about her father once, but Delilah didn't know where he was, and the subject was dropped like a hot potato.

'Drake, tea!'

Agata yelled with all the strength of her great lungs, though the boy wasn't that far away, and still he didn't answer. He remained curled on the tree stump, focussed on whatever was in his backpack.

'Drake, TEA!'

Adie jumped at the bellow that nearly burst her eardrums, and a little hot tea spilled on her legs.

'Ah.' Agata waved her hand and laughed. 'He is shy.'

Just call a spade a spade, Adie thought. *He's rude.*

Something pushed against the back legs of her chair and, when Adie looked down, there was the famed alligator, like a dark brown monster with lifeless eyes, its short snout full of terrible, pointed teeth.

'Okay, that's it. I'm going,' she said.

'Now?' Delilah said. 'But it's early. We said we'd meet the others for a go on the ferris wheel.'

Adie had no intention of taking another ride on that rusty death trap.

'Sorry, I promised my dad I'd clean out my wardrobe before school starts and... well, I don't want to get stuck doing it tomorrow. It's our last day of holidays.'

'I could help you do it tomorrow. Or this evening. It wouldn't take long with the two of us, we–'

'No, really, that's okay. Thanks though. I'll see you tomorrow, yeah?'

'Are you sure? Okay. See you tomorrow then.'

'Gut to meet you, ja.' The strongwoman beamed over her teacup.

'Nice to meet you, Agata. Thanks for the tea. Goodbye.'

As Adie stepped delicately out of the alligator's path, she knew the others were watching her leave. Their conversation only started up again when she was out of sight behind a trailer, and she heard the voice of Delilah squealing with excitement about something. But Delilah never squealed. She was the quiet one.

Not any more, Adie thought as she picked her way through the muddied grass. *I guess I'm the quiet one now.*

'Grace! Jenny, over here!'

Grace did a double-take when she saw Delilah on the steps of a grey trailer, waving wildly at them.

'You have to meet Agata,' the small girl said breathlessly, smiling. 'She's so nice. We've been talking about Soroca, and lots of other places the carnival's been to. They travel all over.'

Delilah pulled a fold-out chair from inside the caravan, and propped it open next to three others on the grass.

'Agata.' She called into the trailer like it was her own home.

Grace recognised the large woman that appeared in the doorway with a teapot in hand.

'New friends. So nice! Tea, ja?' She leaned past the door-frame and shouted to her right, 'Drake, dis time you have tea, okay? Meet nice new friends.'

Following her gaze, Grace spotted a boy sitting cross-legged on a tree stump at the edge of the park, and caught her breath. It was the strange-skinned boy she had met the night before. Smiling in recognition, he uncurled himself from the stump and made his way over.

'You didn't make it out of town then?' Grace kept her voice low as he passed.

His smile was weary, but his eyes twinkled.

'Never do.'

Agata's English wasn't great, but she managed to communicate so many funny and wonderful tales of far-off lands while the girls drank tea and laughed. The boy, Drake, parked himself on the steps of the trailer, taking it all in and occasionally interrupting to correct details in Agata's stories, which would result in the woman flapping her hands and nodding her head earnestly, saying,

'Ja, ja, ja, dis I know. I forget. Is correct, ja, ja.'

Delilah was more lively than Grace had ever seen her, and was becoming a little reckless with the wood nymph that remained hidden beneath her collar. She pulled at her jumper when he shifted into an awkward position, and one time she even scowled at him, scooping her hair over one shoulder and sharply tapping her back. It wasn't long before the strongwoman noticed something was amiss. Prodding the bump on the girl's shoulder, she said,

'Is moving. Dis? Is moving, see?'

She jammed her finger into the lump, wriggling it roughly, until B-brr's face burst from Delilah's neckline and bit down firmly.

'Aaaaaaaghh!' The woman leapt from her chair, sending teacups flying, and bounced from foot to foot. 'Owweeeee! Ow, ow, ow, ow, ow!'

Aghast, Delilah cupped the nymph in her hands, but Drake was already in front of her, gently prising her fingers apart.

'Agata,' he said, 'come here, you gotta see this.'

'Is rat,' the woman declared. 'Is nasty rat. It bite.'

'No, no, it's not. Look. It's a little guy. A tiny little guy.'

The woman crept over and her eyes went wide. The girls were too panicked to speak and, in the silence, Agata reached out her finger again. B-brr snapped.

'No!' she said. 'No bite, little man. Is bold.'

She tapped him on the head in punishment, and quickly withdrew the finger before it could be bitten again.

'Where'd he come from?' asked Drake.

Delilah seemed to be struck speechless for the moment, so Grace stepped up.

'We, eh... we found him. Delilah did, anyway, and he kind of... he just kind of latched on and... and now he's just here permanently, I guess.'

Drake didn't seem at all satisfied with the answer, but he didn't push. He just smiled and looked closer at the nymph, laughing out loud when the little brat bent over and mooned Agata. The woman didn't seem too bothered.

'Is not polite, dis little man.'

'I'm so sorry,' Delilah said finally, and blushed bright red.

Strange as it seemed, the tea party went back to normal after that. Grace couldn't grasp why Drake and Agata weren't freaking out about the faery hiding in Delilah's long, black hair. The strongwoman went back to telling her stories, and Drake resumed his seat on the steps.

'So how much can you actually lift?' Jenny asked.

'You want to know?' Agata winked. 'You see show.'

'I saw show. I mean, I went to the show. You threw an anvil right across the tent. Was it fake? Was it made of polystyrene or something?'

'Ha! Fake? Is no fake. Look at dis.' The woman curled one arm and the rounded bicep swelled until it was the size of a football.

'Woah.' Without asking, Jenny reached out and squeezed the giant muscle. 'It is real.'

'Ja, is real. You lift weight?'

She was asking all of them. Grace smiled and shook her head.

'I'd love to learn, though,' said Jenny. 'Could you teach me?'

A wide grin spread across Agata's face. She went inside the trailer and emerged with a large dumbbell in each hand.

'Ja!' she said. 'You start vit dis.'

She dropped the weights in front of Jenny and they thumped to the ground, denting the grass.

'Are you serious?' Grace said to Jenny.

'I've never been more serious in my life.'

✷ ✷ ✷

The discordant music from all the different stalls was like a cheese grater on Adie's ears. It must be torture to listen to that racket all day. She passed under the carnival entrance and relaxed as the noise faded behind her. She thought she might take the long way home since she had time to kill. She didn't really have to clean out her wardrobe – well, she did, but she had no intention of doing it anytime soon.

The sound of a snapping twig made her spin around. But there was nobody there. Just the carnival in the park and the empty road in front of it. Must have been a cat or something, playing in the trees that lined the street. Adie shivered, and she walked a little faster.

It was never this quiet on the main road – she couldn't see a single person – and the wind was picking up leaves and swirling them in a way that somehow looked deliberate.

Great, she thought, *the whole town is catching the creepy vibe from that carnival. Even the weather's joining in.*

Another snapping twig. But when she turned this time, she saw him.

The brim of his silk hat sagged to one side, and the long, black crosses painted over his eyes made him look forlorn. His suit had sombre stripes of grey and pale purple, and she could see the cracks in his white make-up from where she stood. He was some distance away, but closer to her than he was to the carnival. He leaned out from a tree on one side of the road, tilting his head, his mouth pulled down into an exaggerated frown. Lifting one arm, he opened and closed his hand in a mournful kind of wave.

The fear came like a punch in the stomach. Frozen at first, Adie just stared, until his frown lifted and spread wide in a grin while his curled fingers continued that weird wave.

She took off at a run, not looking back to see if he was following. She didn't want to know. She'd just keep running until she saw someone else, anyone else. There wasn't a single soul until she reached her own street. By then her breath felt like knives in her chest, and the tears were streaming down her face. Not wanting to enter the house crying, she slipped through the side-gate into the back garden, headed for the treehouse at the end of the lawn, curled up and buried her face in her hands. It wasn't until dinnertime that she finally went inside, her face dry and wiped clean with a tissue. She said nothing to anyone about the Melancholy Clown.

The air in the main tent was still humid and thick with the breath of the last audience. It had been packed, as usual, and now, with the seats virtually empty, the ghostly scent of the absent crowd made for a gloomy atmosphere.

Felix Renaud, the ringmaster, stood centre-stage, whipping his riding crop back and forth through the dust at his feet. It was a sign of impatience, and the seats were quickly filled by performers and roustabouts as the whipping got quicker and quicker.

'Eighty years.' The light voice he saved for the customers

was gone, replaced by a deep, throaty growl. 'Eighty years enslaved, imprisoned. Eighty years...'

He stared into the distance for a long time, but no member of the carnival dared to break the silence. He whipped the riding crop again and smiled, baring his blackened teeth.

'However, hope is on the horizon, friends. Hope comes to us all, and you better be ready.' The riding crop pointed feverishly at random faces in the audience. ''Cos this time we're getting out. And no soul is gonna stop us!'

The crop lingered on a boy sat at the very back of the bleachers. His green, scaly face showed no expression, but the muscular woman in front of him reached back and patted his arm protectively.

'This time we're getting out,' the ringmaster repeated.

He walked the line of performers in the front row, receiving encouraging nods from the group of grim-faced clowns.

At one end of the front bench, where Felix had placed it, sat a wooden box with curling petals carved into the lid. It shuddered at the sound of the crop whipping once more, so much so that its lid popped open and snapped shut again. Cool air filled the space as Felix's laughter echoed around the tarpaulin walls.

5

THE DOCTOR

Grace felt sick. In her hurry to join the girls at the carnival again that morning, she had gone without breakfast. It was after five o'clock, and all she'd eaten all day was candy floss, popcorn and a bagful of sugared nuts. She had wanted to visit Drake and Agata's tent much earlier, but the others had such a long list of performances they wanted to see and carnival rides they wanted to go on that she had had to wait until late afternoon. She had wondered why Drake wasn't part of the main show in the evening, and she was eager to see what he could do.

Adie was missing from the group that day. Oddly, she had told two different stories: Rachel that she had to help clean out the garage at home, and Delilah that she wasn't feeling well. Grace suspected she was bored with the carnival, and didn't want to go on any more vomit-inducing rides. It was the last day of the holidays; she couldn't blame Adie for wanting to chill out at home and do nothing.

As they made their way through the packed stalls, Jenny seemed eager to see Agata again. She had been very taken with the idea of weightlifting, and Grace was sure she had seen the tall girl flexing her muscles beneath her hoody more than once during the day. Delilah was also keen to see the strongwoman's show, but Una and Rachel had to be dragged along.

'That tent is teeny,' Una complained. 'How good can it be?'

'So what if it's small?' Jenny snapped. 'Agata was awesome during the main show. You saw her.'

'Yeah, the one with the weights, I remember. It was okay, I guess.'

'Okay? That stuff weighs—'

'Let's just go, Una,' Rachel interrupted. 'It won't take long and then we can go get some hotdogs.'

The tent was a fraction the size of the red-and-white striped spectacle and, with only a few kerosene lamps to light it, it was quite gloomy inside. There was a small platform in the centre that looked homemade, just planks of uneven timber nailed together, and Grace didn't think it could fit both performers at once.

It didn't have to. Agata was up first. Confined to the tiny

stage, she couldn't do the tremendous anvil-throwing that had startled them during the main show, but she had a selection of dumbbells that looked progressively heavier. She did some poses first, flexing her enormous biceps, and showing off the massive chiselled muscles in her calves. At first, she just lifted the weights, then threw them in the air and caught them, then got some gasps from the audience as she juggled three of the largest. To finish off the performance she invited six kids to sit on a low wooden bench next to the platform, then lifted it clear above her head. She grinned widely at the girls, holding the bench aloft like it was no trouble at all, the kids squealing and laughing as their feet dangled in the air.

There were whoops and cheers as Agata took a bow, then Drake quietly replaced her on the stage. Some sitar music started up from offstage, and the twanging notes of the guitar-like instrument created a mysterious atmosphere. Drake's blue eyes scanned the crowd, and Grace found herself checking her chin for any traces of candy floss, and sweeping a few loose strands of hair off her face. The boy didn't engage the audience with big smiles, like Agata had, but he was hypnotic nonetheless. He opened his arms wide, as if to welcome them, then bent backwards into a crab position. His feet lifted slowly off the ground to point forwards, then his back curved so tightly he was able to raise his head and look straight at those in front. Lowering onto his elbows, his feet then pulled back to rest under his chin.

Grace was transfixed, but also aware of the junk-food discomfort in her tummy. Watching Drake twist and turn into improbable shapes made her feel all the more queasy. She hoped it didn't show in her face, especially when he caught her gaze and flashed a barely there smile. It didn't quite fit with his super-cool performance, but she liked that he did it anyway.

As his performance continued, the green-skinned boy appeared to have bones made of jelly – he turned to the side, making a c-shape with his whole body, then did some push-ups where his back was arched allowing him to tuck his feet into his armpits. But the big finish came when Agata brought out a glass box and rested it on the stage with a door open on one side. It was perhaps big enough to fit a child half Drake's size. But he crouched down next to the open door and slid one bent leg inside until the knee was lodged firmly in the top corner opposite. Then, hunching his shoulders and ducking his head, he pushed most of his body into the box. With his one free arm he shunted his head along the glass front, further and further, until it rested almost against his far knee. With one final flourish, he kicked out his free leg, pointed the toe, and curled the limb inside. Agata reappeared, beaming brightly, and closed the glass door.

There was a flurry of clapping and cheering, and Grace couldn't believe that that ball of tangled limbs was a boy, bigger and taller than her, squashed inside that tiny box. Una turned to her, her hands clapping furiously, and an expression of pure delight on her face.

'That was really gross!'

Grace laughed. 'Okay.'

'Seriously. Totally gross. So glad we came to this.'

The applause continued as Drake unfurled from the glass box and took a sweeping bow. He looked for Grace again and smiled at her.

'You're gone all red.' Rachel was watching Grace with narrowed eyes.

'No, I'm not.'

'Yes, you are.'

'It's warm in here.'

Rachel turned back to the stage, still clapping and smirking slightly.

'It's not that warm.'

✫ ✫ ✫

The girls couldn't get tickets for the main show that night, but they hung around the emptying park anyway, playing a few games at the stalls that were still open and wandering around the red-and-white striped tent listening to the cheering of the audience. It was officially a school night, and Grace knew they would all be in trouble for getting home late, but these were the last precious moments of summer and they wanted to cherish them. When the crowd finally filed out of the big top, and the lights went out, the girls drifted towards Justine's tent, hoping to get a glimpse of the bearded girl before they all went home.

'Hey there.' She strolled towards them, pulling hairpins out of her soft, brown curls so they tumbled to her shoulders. 'Didn't catch you guys at the show tonight.'

'We couldn't get tickets,' Rachel replied.

'Well, goodness, you shoulda come to me. I'd have got you in.'

She smiled as she ducked under the tarpaulin door of her tent, and held it up for them. They followed her inside and sat on the cot bed and stools, watching her wipe off her stage make-up.

'Something the matter? Y'all seem a little down in the dumps.'

'School starts tomorrow,' said Grace. 'We should really get going. It's late.'

'How about we feed you a little something first? Can't be sending you home with empty bellies now, can we? That wouldn't be neighbourly.'

Grace grinned with the others as Justine led them out of her tent to a large marquee, sheltered behind a line of trailers. It was filled with long, fold-out tables and chairs, and every performer the girls had seen in the past few days sat gobbling up bowls of delicious-smelling stew.

'Take a seat. I'll go rustle you up some grub.'

Across the tables Grace spied Agata and Drake. She waved at them; Drake looked at her but only Agata waved back, and neither of them got up to join the girls.

'I guess they're wrecked after all the shows today,' Jenny said.

She sounded as disappointed as Grace felt. 'Guess so.'

'Beef strew with all the trimmings.' Justine had arrived back with a large tray. 'Eat up.'

The stew of chunky beef, carrots and potatoes, tasted as good as it smelled. The girls ate as much as they could stuff in on top of all the hotdogs, candy floss and popcorn they had eaten that day, but they couldn't ignore that everyone was taking sly glances at them as they ate. *Maybe they don't have outsiders for dinner very often,* Grace thought.

'We saw a great show today,' Una said, breaking the silence.

'Is that right?' said Justine.

'Yeah, with the strongwoman. Agnes, is it?'

'Agata.'

'Right. She was cool, but the boy with the green skin was amazing. He squished himself into this tiny box, it looked like he had no bones.'

'Uh-huh.'

'How come he's not in the main show? You should put him in, he's fantastic.'

'It's not up to me, that's Felix's decision. You know, the ringmaster.'

'I'll say it to him if I see him. He's missing a trick there.'

'You gotta be a tight group for the main show, you know? It's a fast-moving thing and you gotta work together.' Justine picked at her dinner. 'Drake doesn't work great with others. He likes to do his own thing.'

'He seems to get on well with Agata,' said Grace.

'Sure, she's like a mom to him. But everyone else...'

Grace noticed then that Agata and Drake sat alone. All the other tables filled up, but theirs remained strangely empty, except for one tall man that now joined them. He wore a long, dark trenchcoat and a hat with a brim that shaded his eyes, fingerless gloves and heavy, leather boots. He sat one chair away from Agata, nodded slowly at her, then set his gaze at Grace and her friends. Grace recognised him as the sorcerer from the main show, who had created a mini-fireworks display inside the tent with a mix of chemicals and weirdly shaped instruments.

'Who's that?' asked Delilah.

'That's the doctor,' Justine replied. 'At least that's what they call him.'

'Why?'

'He was a medical doctor once. Lost his licence though. There were rumours going round... Anyway, he joined the carnival after that.' The ballerina shook her head. 'You don't concern yourselves with him now, you hear?'

'What you do mean?' said Rachel.

'He's not... He doesn't like outsiders. You give him a wide berth and you'll be fine.'

The man raised a skinny cigar to his lips and lit it.

'He's looking at you now.'

'Yeah,' Justine said, stacking their empty bowls onto the tray. 'He doesn't like me neither.'

The bearded girl got them toffee apples from the dessert table, and they all strolled back towards her tent chewing on the sticky fruit.

'I hope this won't be your last visit, just cos you're starting back to school.'

'No way,' said Una. 'We'll be back here every evening as long as the carnival's here. How long are you staying?'

Justine delicately picked at her apple, avoiding getting her beard stuck in the toffee.

'Couldn't say. We don't stick to no schedule. But I think we're gonna be here for a while.'

★★★

Grace's mum was cross when she finally phoned for a lift home.

'Do you know what time it is? You've got school tomorrow.'

'Sorry, mum, we just forgot the time.'

'Did you even get a proper dinner, or have you been eating sugar all day?'

'We had some beef stew.'

The was silence, then her mum sighed.

'I'll be there in a few minutes. But this is the last time, okay? No more late nights.'

Grace waved goodbye to the others and waited by the entrance of the carnival in the dark. The stars twinkled above her, and the whisper of the wind through the leaves of the trees made her smile. She'd had a really good last day of freedom.

Then another whisper caught her attention. It came from behind her. Creeping back into the park Grace could make out the silhouette of two figures by the first trailer. One voice rose in anger, but not loud enough for her to make out what they were saying. Tiptoeing closer, she ducked behind a tree and strained to hear.

'Patience. It's out of your hands for now.' The first voice was deep, forceful.

'But it's not out of yours.' The second voice was Drake's, Grace was sure of it. 'You could strike now if you only had the guts.'

'Ah, the petulance of youth. Only a fool attacks who knows he'll lose. Bide your time, lizard boy.'

There was a growl and one of the figures stalked off. There wasn't much light from the stars, but Grace saw the hint of green skin. In the shadows the second figure stood in silence, an ember glowing in the dark.

A cigar, thought Grace.

She inched her way back to the entrance, making sure her feet made no sound. She tried to put it out of her mind, but she couldn't help wondering who this doctor was, and what Drake wanted from him.

6

ask old cat lady

The strongwoman hauled weights to the stage, the muscles of her arms swelling with every lift, and shrinking with every drop. Every now and then she balanced a dumbbell on her forearm, letting it roll back and forth before she bounced it to the other hand. She didn't see the clowns enter the tent, creeping like spiders on a string of gossamer, silken suits in drab colours blending too easily in the dim light. One crept up behind her and pulled at a lock of her hair. She gasped and swung a fist, missing the painted face that moved too fast. He smiled and dropped a deep bow.

'Is bold,' she said, her breath fast. 'No playing now, I have show.'

The painted faces in silk suits didn't move.

'I do not vont you here. Understand? You leave now. I

have show.'

The silk suits filed into line and sat in the front row, crossing their legs in unison. There were more weights behind the small stage, but the woman seemed reluctant to turn her back to retrieve them. Instead she stood, her shoulders hunched, watching the front row as if it were filled with coiled vipers. Eventually, one silk suit raised his hands and clapped. Soon they were all applauding as the woman stood trembling. She didn't budge from her spot on the floor until all of them had blown kisses, stood up from their seats, and filed out of the tent.

Shaking, the woman wiped sweat from her brow and slowly bent to her work.

✼ ✼ ✼

'Feel that.'

Jenny curled her arm in Grace's face.

'Why?'

'Just feel it.'

Grace pinched her bicep. 'Okay.'

'That's muscle.'

'Doesn't feel like more muscle than I've got.'

Jenny slumped into her chair.

'That's cos I've only just started. Wait a couple of weeks and I'll have biceps the size of Agata's.'

'Might take a little more than two weeks, Jenny.'

'Why would you want muscles like Agata's?' said Rachel. 'You'll get all bulky and won't fit into your clothes.'

'That's the plan, Dan,' said Jenny. She growled and pulled a body builder pose, making Rachel grimace.

They'd just finished their first day of third year, and now they were waiting patiently for Miss Lemon in her empty classroom. The teachers had gone easy on them the first day back, but the mention of end-of-year exams already had Grace's stomach in a knot. The whiny hum coming from the back of the room wasn't helping her nerves.

'Una, give it a rest, will you?'

Una cupped her hand to her ear.

'Hmm? You want more, you say? Sing it loud, you say?'

'Oh, God,' moaned Jenny as Una kneeled up on her chair. 'She found some album of power ballads belonging to her dad, and fell in love with them. It's been like this all day – "I can't live without you, you are my everything," blah blah blah.'

'It's Heart, baby!' Una yelled. 'They're classic.'

'You only heard of them yesterday.'

'*You're the voice and the something soomethi-ing, something else and some other stuuuuuuff. Woah-oo-woah-ooo-woah-oh-oh.*' Una wailed with her eyes squeezed shut.

'Oh, my God.' Rachel stuck her fingers in her ears. 'At least learn the words if you're gonna be screaming it at–'

'*IIIIIII can't learn the wor-or-ords, there's waaaay to maaaany wor-or-or or-or-ords.'*

'Good heavens, girls. It's you making all that racket?'

Miss Lemon shut the door behind her, straightening the bun of dark hair at the back of her head, and set a pile of books on her desk.

'Sorry, miss,' Grace said. 'Una's discovered music.'

'Is that what that was.'

'How are you, miss?' Una was a little out of breath as she took her seat.

'I'm very well, Una, thank you.' The teacher fixed them with a steady look. 'And I trust you girls are ready to work hard on your craft this year?'

Miss Lemon, along with Delilah's guardian, Vera Quinlan, had taken charge of the girls when they became interested in witchcraft, and she had now been teaching them secretly for two years.

'But we kept up with our magic lessons during the summer,' said Grace. 'We're not behind, are we?'

'No, you're not, but Vera and I took it easy on you during your holidays. Now the real study begins.'

The teacher was smiling, but Grace felt uneasy as she pulled what looked like timetables out of a folder and handed them out.

'Every day, miss?' asked Delilah as she scanned the sheet she was given.

'Every day, including weekends. And we're introducing tests once a month, too. Vera agrees with me that you need regular assessment to ensure you're keeping your skills honed.'

'But we've the Junior Cert this year,' Grace said. 'How are we going to fit it all in?'

'Don't worry, you'll manage.' Miss Lemon beamed as she handed her a timetable. 'And I'll be here to help.'

Grace's heart sank as she looked through the jam-packed schedule, until she suddenly felt something was wrong. She glanced around and realised Adie was sitting alone in the back row. Had she been there all along? She caught her eye and smiled. Adie smiled back but quickly dropped her gaze to her timetable.

I'll catch up with her on the way home, Grace thought, *and make sure everything's okay.*

But Grace did not catch up with Adie. For one thing, she became so absorbed in lessons and timetables that she completely forgot. And for another, Adie said goodbye to the girls and hurried off by herself, pretending she didn't hear Una shout after her to meet at the carnival after dinner.

Once out of sight of the others, Adie's pace slowed to a stroll. She didn't feel like going home yet. This was usually time she would spend with the girls, practising spells or chatting about what had happened in school that day. She circled the long way back to school and sat on the grass at the edge of the football pitch, watching the sun go down. At the far end of the field she could see a scrap of cloth caught on the wiry hedge, fluttering in the breeze. It reminded her of the red scarf Mrs Quinlan had used to signal them when they had their very first adventure and found the demon well.

The demon well. It seemed so long ago now. The girls had stumbled upon the well by accident, and spent part of their first year at school battling a mischievous demon that they had unwittingly summoned from it. The eccentric Old Cat Lady had helped them defeat it. Owing to the lack of technology in her home, she had chosen to use the red scarf to summon them rather than a phone.

Not knowing why, Adie now got to her feet and walked towards the flitting scrap of cloth, slipped through the wiry hedge, and into the cul-de-sac of Wilton Place. She ducked into the shadows as the front door of Mrs Quinlan's dilapidated house creaked open. Delilah stepped onto the porch.

'I'll be back by ten!' she yelled back inside.

'You'll be back by nine.' Mrs Quinlan's voice was low and grumpy, but somehow travelled out into the street. 'And it's your turn to feed the cats in the morning.'

'I won't forget.'

Delilah pulled the door shut and took off down the road with a skip in her step.

Adie tentatively made her way up the driveway and

knocked on the door. The woman who answered looked like she'd just stepped out of a tumbledryer; a tumbledryer full of cat hair, mothballs and tweed patches. Nothing she wore matched, and her grey hair fell in unruly waves down her neck.

'Well, what are *you* doing here? Is something wrong?' Her pale eyes narrowed. 'Where's Delilah? How can you lot have caused a disaster already, the girl just left the house.'

'Nothing's wrong, Mrs Quinlan, Delilah's fine. I was just passing and I...' Turning to the street as if it offered some explanation for her visit, Adie tried desperately to think of something. 'I, em, I had a witchcraft question.'

The eyes narrowed so tightly, Adie wasn't sure the woman could still see out of them.

'Lessons with me aren't 'til tomorrow.'

'I know, I got the timetable.'

'Then why are you bothering me on my day off?'

'It's a very important question.'

The woman harrumphed, then turned and marched back into the house. Closing the front door gently, Adie followed her into the kitchen. The room was usually filled with cats, and smelled like it, but only one was curling around Adie's ankles as she sat at the table.

'They're gone to the carnival, the others. You didn't go,' Mrs Quinlan said, pouring some tea that smelled like it had been steeping for hours.

'No.'

'Thought you were all dying to go live in the park now it's covered in tents.'

'No. The others are, but... You and Ms Lemon have known each other forever, right?'

'Since school.'

'Right.'

'That's not forever.'

'But it's a really, really long time.' Adie winced. 'I don't mean you're ancient or anything–'

'You're a sweetheart.'

'– I just mean, you've known each other for quite a few years.'

'Is this drivel going somewhere?'

'Do you ever feel like you don't understand her? Ms Lemon, I mean. Do you sometimes wonder why she likes certain things, or doesn't get why you're mad or–'

'All the time. The woman's a complete mystery to me.'

'Oh.'

Mrs Quinlan slurped her tea, her pale eyes curious. 'Was that the question?'

'Sorry?'

'Was that the it's-so-urgent-it-can't-wait-til-tomorrow-or-my-eyeballs-will-explode witchcraft question?'

'Oh. No.'

'Then what is it?'

Adie turned her cup on the worm-eaten wood, racking her brains for something to ask. Her gaze shifted around the grubby kitchen, finally resting on a pile of books on a crooked shelf above the window.

HyBreasal and Other Phantom Islands
The Hy Brasil Myth: A Wiccan Home Lost
In the Mists of the Atlantic: The Secret Portal

'Are you researching Hy-Breasal? Why?' said Adie.

'Cos a bunch of squirmy creatures snatched you lot from right under my nose and took you there, that's why. You forgotten already?'

'No, but we're home now. Why bother with all the reading?'

'To make sure you don't get swallowed into that hellhole again should the giant worms make a comeback. I take it you haven't got the group brain cell today.'

'It wasn't *all* horrible. We made some really good friends there – other witch apprentices. That was really nice, not being the only ones. I kind of miss that now.' Adie brightened. 'Hey, is there any way of getting in touch with the island from here?'

'Don't go messing with that now. Leave it be.'

'But Mrs Quinlan–'

'I said leave it be!' The woman held her with a frosty stare, though Adie thought she saw the shadow of worry in her eyes. 'You girls and my Delilah only just made it off that island in one piece. You don't think about it, you don't talk about it, and you sure as hell don't try and make contact with it. You hear me?'

'Yes, Mrs Quinlan.'

Adie finished her tea in silence. Picking up her school bag, she could see Mephistopheles blocking her way to the front door, growling at her and cleaning his face with elegant sweeps of his paw. In the corner next to him was a cat bowl, filled with water.

Adie had a brainwave. She whispered under her breath and, in a split second, the water curled out of the bowl in a long spiral above the large cat's head. She held her concentration until a sleek tabby ventured into the hall, then let the liquid go in one devastating splash that sent Mephistopheles tearing after the tabby in a cacophony of screeching and snarling.

'Mephis!' Mrs Quinlan yelled, dropping the teapot into the sink and chasing after the noise. 'What the bloody hell are you up to?'

The Old Cat Lady's screaming was louder than all the animals put together, and it wasn't long before she came stomping down the stairs with the scruff of a cat in each hand.

'You'll stay out all bloody night for that, and like it.'

She opened the back door with one elbow and threw the unfortunate beasts outside.

'I'd better go, Mrs Quinlan,' Adie called. 'Thanks for the tea.'

She hurried down the driveway, holding her schoolbag to her front, zipping it closed over the tattered cover of *In the Mists of the Atlantic*.

The ringmaster slammed the small wooden box down on the table inside a run-down trailer. The man sitting opposite couldn't see it; his pearly white eyes couldn't see anything. He reached his hand towards it.

'Something changed?' he asked.

'It's empty, Grigori,' the ringmaster snarled.

The blind man started. 'Is not possible.'

Felix knocked gently on the lid – his face red as if he fought the urge to punch his fist right through it – and it opened.

'Empty. See, blind man?'

The white-eyed fortune-teller pulled a set of tarot cards from his pocket.

'Then maybe is all over.'

'It ain't over, you damn fool, don't you get it? *He* took it.'

'Is not possible.'

'He took it. He thinks he can play with fire on my turf, thinks he can keep us in chains. But I'll burn this place to the ground before I let him win!'

All water is connected…

Adie lay on her front in bed, the duvet pulled up over her head shielding the large, hardback book on the mattress. Her pencil torch swept over the words of the fifth chapter as she read and re-read them. It was nearly two o'clock in the morning and she'd already read through a good chunk of *In the Mists of the Atlantic,* and learned more about the mysterious island of Hy-Breasal than when she'd been trapped on it.

A powerful spell, cast by dozens of witches born and raised on the island, had sent squirmy worms to suck Adie and her friends to that distant place, somewhere in the Atlantic. It had been terrifying – they had only just escaped with their lives – but being amongst other trainee witches had felt good for a time. Adie missed the friends they had made – sweet and understanding Gaukroger, brave young Aura who had saved their lives. She wished she could reach out to them. She was tired of feeling alone.

All water is connected, the book said. Adie was good with water spells – she was better than good. All she had to do was figure it out.

She sighed and snapped the book shut. Her brain was too tired to work now, so she might as well sleep on it. She turned onto her back, closed her eyes and thought of her Hy-Breasal friends. With school getting so serious, and the girls seemingly drifting away from her, Adie longed for some understanding.

·7

On the Waterways

'Has everyone filled a vial? Good, now give it a shake and take a quick sniff.'

Ms Lemon's classroom looked more like one of the science labs, with jars and bottles of weird-looking ingredients and flames dancing on three camping stoves.

'Ooh!' Grace gasped. 'That's rotten.'

'It smells like a bottle of vinegar ate dog poo and threw up.'

'Thanks Una. I didn't really need the visual aid.'

'It may not be a bunch of roses,' Ms Lemon said, shaking another vial, 'but that's a good, healthy smell.'

'Miss,' said Una, 'I'm sorry, but my dad says the same thing when we're driving through the countryside and there's a stink of silage. I don't believe him then, and I don't believe you now.'

'Trust me, Una, Choki balm is your new best friend.'

'Choki?'

'Short for *cho ku rei*. It's what Vera and I call it anyway. In terms of healing, this is magical First Aid. It's a universal balm and, from now on, I want you girls to carry a vial of it on you at all times. It doesn't last forever, mind, so you'll need to make a fresh batch every six months or so. You can pickle it in miso to make it last longer, but it reduces the effectiveness a bit.'

'Do you use it on cuts, Miss?' asked Rachel.

'Cuts, bruises, scrapes, gashes, rashes, you name it.'

'If you sliced off your finger, Miss,' said Una, 'would you put this on it?'

'Choki balm would slow the bleeding and keep off infection until someone could perform a reattachment spell.'

'You mean you can reattach a finger with magic?'

'Possibly.'

'Seriously? So if I cut off my leg–'

'Don't cut off your leg.'

'No, I know. But if I *did*–'

'Anybody got a bruise,' Ms Lemon said loudly, 'or a cut? Anything we can heal?'

'I've got a bruise, Miss. It's a whopper.'

Jenny pulled off her boot and wrenched down her sock to reveal a mean-looking bruise, deep purple with an angry red centre.

'Ow, Jenny,' said Grace. 'How'd you get that?'

Jenny's face coloured all the way to her auburn hair.

'Dropped a weight,' she said. 'I was lifting one of the bigger ones, just to try it out, and it slipped out of my hand. It's really sore.'

'That'll do perfectly,' the teacher said. 'Now, everyone watch. You just apply a small amount in a circular motion, like this.'

The pale brown substance went hard and flaky as soon as it touched Jenny's skin but, as Ms Lemon gently rubbed at the bruise, it turned to goo once more and was absorbed in just a few seconds.

'Oh.' Jenny sat up straight and blinked. 'It's gone all fizzy, like pins and needles.'

'Give it a minute.'

The girls watched in awe as the various shades of purple began to move around Jenny's shin. They swirled and sank, slipping back to her calf and zipping forward again, before curling into a spiral with a line through it. It looked a bit like an upside-down treble clef.

'*Cho ku rei*,' Ms Lemon said. 'The symbol enhances your body's natural healing powers.'

'How long will it stay like that?' asked Grace.

'For a few days. But try pressing on it now, Jenny. See how it feels.'

pushed a finger into the centre of what had

e, and grinned.

hurt at all,' she said. 'And it looks *awesome*. It's

!'

'And for that reason, young lady, you're going to keep it covered until the symbol fades.'

'Aw, but Miss, it's so cool!'

'It's a Wiccan badge,' said the teacher, 'and you'll keep it hidden.'

The tall girl looked sullen as she pulled up her sock.

'Okay.'

✷ ✷ ✷

Adie stood in front of a shop window. *The Penny Farthing* was a decrepit-looking newsagents on the far side of town. The sign above the door featured the old-fashioned bicycle with one huge wheel and one small, which was its namesake. Through the window Adie could see rows and rows of dusty jars, filled with boiled sweets in a hundred different flavours. The shop was always open; and always empty.

She didn't go in. Instead she slipped down the alleyway next to it, scanning the ground for a little clump of wildflowers. Smiling, she plucked a daisy from a crack in the pavement, tore it between her fingers and scattered the remains against the red-brick wall of the shop. There was a *whoosh* of perfumed air and the red bricks pulled apart, dropping to the ground which folded under their weight, revealing stone steps leading downwards. Glancing left and right to make sure no-one had seen, Adie hurried down the steps, hearing the entrance crunch shut behind her.

The air cooled at the bottom of the stairs, and Adie followed the faint light that led her to an underground cavern. The high walls were stained with damp and lit with numerous fiery torches. The cave was filled with tables and trunks, half-rolled rugs, lamps and pots of every size, shape and colour. Every flat surface was strewn with trinkets, books and wooden ornaments, and the musky scent of incense was overpowering.

Adie's fingers slid over an ancient text, bound in deerskin, with a title she couldn't read.

'Good evening, young wiccan,' said a voice behind her.

'Hello, Mr Pamuk.'

The shopkeeper's smile was welcoming as ever.

'A delight to see you, as always. Are you shopping for something special today? If so, let me tell you what treasures are new in this week. I have a range of pink amulets – perfect specimens of anthill garnet – mined by fire ants in the deserts of Arizona. I have also a stunning flute of pithed alder shoots that produces the most beautiful sound you've ever–'

'I'm looking for something in particular. A propellant.'

'My dear witchlet, that could be anything.'

'I need a propellant to help me send a message through

_rways. That's possible, isn't it? I can send a message
_ere through water, I just need ignition? Like a spark
plug in a car.'

'Indeed, it is a generous element, but water-messaging is not without risk. The telephone is infinitely better.' He picked up a bronze trinket, polishing it to a high shine, and held it out. 'When have you ever seen a more beautiful bindrune? The workmanship is spectacular, don't you think?'

Adie took the ornament and set it firmly back on the table.

'I need a spark plug, Mr Pamuk. Can you help me or not?'

✳ ✳ ✳

It was near dusk when Adie took the long, curving road that led from the back of the school, around the woods and down to the river. She walked the bank for some distance to make sure she wouldn't be seen by any passersby, then kneeling by the water with her shoes sinking into the mud, she untied the tweed bag in her hands and clutched the blackened leaves inside.

'Twice-burned mugwort,' Mr Pamuk had said, 'will ignite your message. But please, little witchlet, take care. A message sent is like a bird released; you cannot take it back. And who knows who may be listening.'

Adie took a deep breath and closed her eyes.

'_Incende._'

The leaves began to smoke and hiss, their ends glowing embers as they burned afresh. She tried not to cough as the smoke reached her lungs, then set the leaves down in the water and watched them fizzle and sink. It was now or never.

Holding back her hair with one hand, Adie plunged her face into the water. The shock of the cold made her desperate to gasp, but she fought the urge and kept her head down. Even in the water she could feel the gentle heat of the quenched mugwort and it made her a little dizzy. She opened her eyes, shuddering once more against the freezing water, and watched the muddied leaves below.

Within seconds they spat, broken bits of mugwort hopping up like frogs on a hotplate, suspended in the murky water. They were moving then, like little sea horses with minds of their own, and she followed them. Her body stayed where it was, but she could feel her mind pulling away from it. It was like she was being stretched, thinner and thinner, so thin she felt sure that she would snap. But she didn't. Leaving the discomfort of her body behind, her mind soared after the blackened mugwort leaves.

She rushed past fish and squiggling larvae, swooping through the estuary and out into the sea. The leaves picked up speed, and the crabs and lobsters and sharks and awful strings of discarded plastic went by faster and faster until she couldn't see them anymore. It was just a spinning wall of water now, varying shades of green and blue, until the leaves slowed and she began to see real things again. Creatures, weird ones, creeping, crawling and swimming above and below. A merrow, with the muscular torso of a human and the sharp-toothed mouth of a moray eel, snapped at her as she passed. She was in a river now, she could sense the banks either side, then she was in the air, carried like a feather on the millions of tiny droplets in the atmosphere.

Ahead of her was the barren, cracked land of Hy-Breasal. The stone towers and battlements of Tithon Castle brought back more bad memories than good. She saw the black turret, where she and the girls had been imprisoned. There was the outdoor arena where Una's dragon had battled the horrible beasts originated by other trainee witches. There were the narrow, arched windows, through which the vengeful faeries had crawled, some of them desperate to taste human flesh. Inside the castle, the faeries had clashed with specially trained witches – the Hunters. Adie hadn't seen the fight, but Rachel had described it in grisly detail.

She glided through one of the skinny windows, swinging through stone halls and corridors. It had been a while, but she could still remember everything. It was so quiet though, and completely deserted.

Of course it was. The Witch Trials were over and the students had gone home. Adie stopped suddenly. What had she been thinking? She could never have reached her friends here. There was no-one left in Tithon Castle.

The burnt leaf fragments hung in the air as if waiting for further instructions, and Adie's mind drifted aimlessly. She would never see the witch apprentices again. They were long gone, they would all be back where they had come from, getting on with their lives. She had never even asked Gaukroger or Aura where they were from, she didn't know why. Her heart sank in disappointment, and she cursed herself for being so stupid. She had done all this for nothing.

I want to go home now, she thought to the mugwort.

That seemed instruction enough and the fragments darted back into the hallway. Making little effort, she let the leaves drag her along like the end of an elastic band that had been stretched and let go. The stone walls shot past, the steps flew below her in less than a second, and she was through the entrance hall and out before she knew it.

She skimmed along the barren, cracked ground surrounding the castle, through the woods and into the rushing stream. She felt cold as the weird river creatures of Hy-Breasal swirled and blended until she could no longer make them out. The wall of water continued until she could finally see the seals and fish she knew filled the seas on the Irish coast.

THWACK.

It wasn't just the sound – which was loud – she felt it like a punch in the face. The mugwort let go and she rocked back on her heels, gasping for breath and spluttering water. She fell to one side, her elbow sinking into the muddy bank, and waited for her vision to clear and the coughing to ease. Her limbs felt gooey inside, like she was a deflated balloon, all wrinkly and stretched out of shape.

'Ugh.'

That and the not-so-pleasant taste of the not-so-clean river water was nauseating. Unable to get to her feet, Adie crawled up the bank, feeling the damp and dirt seep into her clothes. Her uniform was filthy, she would get in trouble at home.

A shadow flitted through the trees ahead. She stopped and ducked low, the scruffy weeds scraping her chin. It was small and quick, too quick to be a person. A fox, maybe?

There it was again. And it was no fox.

Adie pressed herself into the ground but she knew the creature had seen her. It danced between the trunks but always ended up behind the sycamore she was facing. It wasn't an animal, but it wasn't human either. Finally, skinny fingers crept around the bark and it showed its face.

The creature's face was oval, with very round and very large eyes. The skin was pasty, almost grey, and stalks of hair stood out from the head like scrawny twigs. Its mouth widened into a grin and it tipped onto all fours. Adie couldn't see it then, hidden beyond the bank above, and her heart raced. The round eyes appeared at the top of the bank and the creature wagged a finger at her. She noticed, with alarm, that its mouth was filled with sharp, triangular teeth. It grinned again and, with a swish of its skinny limbs, it was gone.

A faery, her mind screamed with panic. *I've brought back a faery from Hy-Breasal.*

She shook her head. It wasn't possible. How could it follow her? Water-messaging was just that – messaging. Her body didn't travel to Hy-Breasal on water. How could a faery's body have travelled back on it?

It wasn't possible, she knew it wasn't. But some awful knot of dread began growing in her stomach, and she lay there, in the mud, not moving, not caring about the cold damp that soaked to her skin.

There was a faery loose in her world, and she had no idea how to send it back.

CHASING FAERIES

The girls sat squashed on one side of Mrs Quinlan's kitchen table, while the woman sketched in chalk on the homemade blackboard perched on the counter.

'Who can tell me what this is?' she said, pointing to the oblong outline on the board.

'And do you know what else there is, Miss?' Una said as she traced invisible shapes on the table. 'An alligator. It's not even stuffed or anything. A real-life alligator that goes wandering round the park. It's deadly.'

'Oi!' Mrs Quinlan shouted, tapping furiously with her chalk.

'Oh,' Una said, looking up. 'No, that's nothing like an alligator.'

The Cat Lady fired the duster so fast Una barely had time

to duck. It struck an antique carriage clock on a shelf on the wall, which toppled to the floor and smashed.

'That's dangerous!' said Una. 'You could've hit my head.'

'I was aiming for your head.'

'You know, Mrs Q, you couldn't be a teacher at school. You'd never get past the Garda vetting.'

'Keep talking. I've got plenty of stuff to throw.'

Adie's hand went up.

'*Finally*,' the woman sighed. 'Yes, you.'

'Mrs Quinlan, are there Hunters here?'

Mrs Quinlan took a deep breath as the end of her chalk slid off the board with a horrible squeak.

'What?'

'Are there Hunters here, like there are on Hy-Breasal? Hunter witches, I mean.'

'What has that got to do with the diagram on the board?'

'Um, nothing. But *are* there Hunters though?' Adie persisted. Grace looked up. It was the first time Adie had spoken all day, and the first time she'd looked interested in anything in ages.

'From the garbled nonsense you were all spouting when you got back from that bloody island,' Mrs Quinlan snapped, 'I understand that Hunters hunt *faeries*.'

'Couldn't we learn to do that?'

'We could use B-brr for practice,' said Jenny, pointing to the little nymph as he scraped congealed butter from the table and licked his fingers. 'Give him a ten second head-start and then we all go after him.'

'Hunters mostly used glamour,' Rachel said, 'to entice the faeries to them. They didn't do much chasing.'

'You're not doing that!' Delilah snatched B-brr to her chest and cradled him like a baby. 'That was done to him before and... I don't know how long they had him locked in that birdcage.'

There were tears in her eyes, and Grace felt sorry she hadn't stopped the conversation when it turned to B-brr.

During the Witch Trials, trainee witches had used glamour to take on the appearance of faeries to lure B-brr from his cage. Even Rachel, excellent as she was at glamouring, had done it. Disguised as another wood nymph, she had got him to step through the open door and dance with her on a table top. After that, Rachel had been celebrated and whisked off to the Hunters' Mansion. B-brr had been locked back inside his birdcage and dumped in the black turret.

'Sorry, Delilah,' said Grace. 'We weren't thinking. Of course we wouldn't do anything like that to the little fella.'

'Wouldn't we?'

Jenny looked genuinely surprised. Grace felt like slapping her.

'No. We wouldn't.'

She gave the tall girl a stern look that eventually got a shrug in reply.

A sudden crack made them all jump. Mrs Quinlan held a pointer to the left of the blackboard. On it she had drawn a crude map, with the uppermost building labelled 'school'.

'What am I pointing at?' Her face was red and her hair more frazzled than usual.

Grace tentatively raised her hand.

'The demon well, Miss?'

'Yes, the demon well. And would someone please explain to me what a demon well is?'

Grace looked around, annoyed that all the others kept their eyes on the table. She raised her hand again.

'It's a soft spot between planes... like between worlds, where things can get through. Beings can get through. From one world to the next. Like demons. They can get through to our world from their world, through this soft spot.'

'That was very inarticulate, but you're essentially right. Demons – *demons* – have a door to our world. They could emerge at any moment, hundreds of them, thousands. All they need is for one evildoer – or gormless twit in your case – to open that door.' The woman jabbed her pointer into the spot again. 'That's why it must be watched, it must be guarded. Why do you think Beth and I are training you lot, huh? Do you think we're slaving for free so you can muck about, changing your hair colour, playing with alligators, chasing faeries? *Huh?*'

She dropped the pointer and leaned over the table, her

pale eyes as threatening as Grace had ever seen them.

'We're training you to be keepers of the well. That's your job. That's what you'll be good for when we're done. Beth and I won't live forever. We've guarded the well until now and soon it will be your turn. *That's* what we're doing here. Ensuring the safety of the next generation.'

'Dropped the ball though, didn't you?' Jenny was looking the woman right in the eye.

Grace felt a cold rush down her limbs and silently begged her friend to be quiet. Mrs Quinlan leaned further over the table.

'I beg your pardon?'

'We summoned a demon from the well, right under your nose. Have you forgotten about that? A bunch of schoolgirls, who barely knew anything about witchcraft, pulled a demon out of the well by accident, and you didn't have any idea. You would never have found out either, if we hadn't come to you for help. What kind of 'keeper of the well' does that make you?'

The silence was agonising as Jenny and Mrs Quinlan glared at each other. Finally the woman spoke, her voice low.

'Get out. All of you.'

* * *

The group, minus Delilah, walked down Mrs Quinlan's drive and into the cul-de-sac of Wilton Place. Una marked off something at the back of her notebook and squashed it back into her bag.

'What are you doing, Una?' Grace asked.

'I keep track of all the times Jenny's got us kicked out of class. You're on a roll this year, Jen.'

Jenny didn't reply. She was still seething. Grace could tell because she was having trouble keeping up with her furious stride.

'What if we don't want to stay here?' the girl finally said through gritted teeth.

'Sorry?' said Grace.

'What if we don't want to spend the rest of our lives in Dunbridge?' Jenny stopped and addressed them all. 'Aren't they taking a lot on faith here? Just 'cos Ms Lemon and that Cat Hag have deigned to teach us some magic, they think we're going to owe them the rest of our lives. I don't particularly want to park my bum on that demon well for the next sixty years. I've got plans. I wanna go places, I wanna do stuff. So what the hell are they expecting from us?'

Grace hadn't really thought about it before. She meant to learn as much as possible from Ms Lemon and Mrs Quinlan, she meant to become a great witch. But she didn't consider that that meant spending forever in one spot, watching one little patch of carpet in the school until the end of her days. Is that what their teachers really wanted them to do for the rest of their lives?

'It is a lot to ask. Maybe we should talk to Ms Lemon about it.'

'Stuff that,' huffed Jenny. 'They're both in it together. It's not worth their while teaching us if we don't grow up and let them retire.'

'Jenny's right,' said Rachel. 'If we tell them we don't want to be keepers of the well, they won't teach us anymore. And I want to keep learning.'

'Me too. So everyone keep schtum and don't bring it up in front of them. You listening, Una?'

'Don't bring up the demon-well-life-sentence thing in front of the teachers,' said Una, 'I got it. I'm not a moron.'

'No, but you do tend to talk when you shouldn't, so don't–'

'I got it! Jeez.'

Jenny nodded like it was all sorted, then took off again with her too-fast walk. Adie fell to the back of the group and Grace followed her.

'Are you okay? You seem quiet. Is it alright with you if we don't bring up the future too much with the teachers?'

'I'm fine. It's alright with me.'

'You look a bit tired.'

'Didn't get much sleep last night.'

'Is there something bothering you?'

Adie smiled, but it looked forced.

'No, I'm fine. Nothing to worry about.'

Grace was about to push further, but her friend hurried

into a jog to catch up with the others.

It was getting dark. The moon was rising beyond the river causing the shadows of the trees to stretch all the way to the bank. Adie tried to ignore the black shadowy fingers that seemed to reach for her as she stood by the water.

She wasn't the most skilled witch amongst her friends, but she had one undeniable talent – controlling water. She didn't know why, but ever since her first lesson with liquid it had seemed eager to bend to her will. She played with it absent-mindedly now, warming up her magic muscles, making small spikes dance across the surface of the river. If she was to catch the faery before anyone found out about it, this was how she would do it.

Mr Pamuk had been curious when she returned for another batch of twice-burned mugwort.

'Your water-messaging went well, little witchlet?'

She had smiled and nodded. It hadn't gone well. It had been a complete disaster. But if this supernatural creature had invaded her world via the mugwort, then surely she could send it back the same way. All she had to do was trap it, and hopefully her mind could drag it back to Hy-Breasal on another water-message. It all hung on whether or not the faery would return to the river.

She had been waiting for nearly an hour, patrolling the

trees on either side of the river for that familiar, quick shadow.

There! A shape flickered in the dark.

Adie held her breath and waited, watching. There it was again. Too fast to be a human, too skinny to be an animal.

Quiet as a mouse, she crept up the bank, never taking her eyes from the figure in the woods. It danced around tree trunks like a moth around a flame, flitting back and forth, making no noise at all. Adie was aware of how loud her steps were, no matter how carefully she moved. The *crunch* of dry leaves and the *shush* of weeds stepped on. She was moving in slow motion when she saw the figure stop suddenly. It swayed gently in the mottled light of the moon through the leaves. It was watching her. But it didn't run. Maybe it wanted the company.

'Hey there,' Adie kept her voice low and soft. 'How're you doing?'

The creature continued to sway in time with Adie's footsteps.

She could see its twig-like hair now, and the outline of its oval face. A step closer and its big, round eyes glinted like saucers.

'Remember me?' Adie asked. 'You came with me to the river. Not sure how you did that, you little rascal.' The faery didn't respond, and she wasn't sure it could understand her. 'But you've gotta go back now. You can't stay here, okay? I'm going to help you get back. Alright?'

The creature hunched its shoulders. Adie dropped to one knee, flinging an arm behind her to summon the water she had already been shaping beneath the surface of the river. Thick liquid strands erupted near the bank, clashing in the air to form a lattice. The creature grinned and turned, but Adie lashed the woven water after it, snapping her hand into a fist as the lattice closed around the faery in a ball-shaped cage.

'Gotchya!'

She laughed in relief and guided the ball towards her.

'See?' Adie said. 'That wasn't so bad.'

The faery didn't seem distressed, in fact it seemed amused. It smiled down at her with its horrible triangular teeth, then wagged its finger.

The water hit her so fast, Adie wasn't sure what had happened. She tumbled backwards, rolling to a stop at the top of the bank. Her hair and clothes were soaked, and her face stung from the force of the blow. She blinked against the drops that streamed down her forehead and saw the faery standing at the edge of the trees, free of its watery cage. It was grinning.

'How did you...?' Adie gasped.

The creature sprang into the shade of the leaves and disappeared into the woods.

'No,' Adie cried. 'You can't... Wait!'

She was weak with shock and it took a few strides before her legs would work properly. When she was sure on her feet she raced into the woods as fast as she could go. It had gone to the left, she thought... or maybe straight ahead. She stopped and listened. There wasn't a sound.

'Where are you?' she yelled into the gloom.

Desperate, she took off again, running through what seemed the most open path between the trees. She had to find it. If that thing was seen in town, if it hurt somebody, it would be all her fault. And the girls would know, and Ms Lemon and Mrs Quinlan would know, and she'd never be allowed to study witchcraft again. The girls would go to lessons without her, and she'd be alone, and she'd lose all her friends and...

The tears were streaming down her face now as she realised she was running in no particular direction. She was zigzagging through the woods and she couldn't see a thing. The faery could be anywhere; it could be up a tree, in a hole, under a rock, in the *town*.

Bump.

She hit something tall and solid, and fell back. It wasn't a tree. It was something else.

Squinting in the dim light, she gazed up at a pallid face, old and wrinkled, under the shadow of a black slicker. His eyes sent the same shiver down her spine as they had less than two years before. One of them was blue, the other pearly white. She opened her mouth, but her voice stuck in her throat.

The Mirrorman.

9

RABBIT STEW

The crackling of the fire soothed her nerves a little, as did the heat of the bowl of stew in her hands. It smelled good but Adie couldn't bring herself to eat it. She was pretty sure the meat was rabbit. What else would the Mirrorman have to hunt in these woods?

Bob, she corrected herself. *His name is Bob.*

Bob had first appeared to Grace through an enchanted mirror in Mr Pamuk's shop, hence the nickname. He had scared the group out of their wits, but it had been an attempt to reach the girls from the depths of the demon well, and save them from a terrible fate. For Bob had been thrown down the well by Delilah's wicked mother, Meredith Gold, many years before, and it was his strength and courage that saved Adie and her friends from becoming demon-possessed slaves. Grace had eventually pulled Bob free of that hell, but Adie could see the horror and torment of his time down there, written in the lines and shadows of his face.

He was even older than he looked, she knew, his life artificially extended by many years as another witch's enchanted slave. Adie sighed. Bob had really had a rough time of it. She should try to be nicer to him.

'Thanks for the stew. It smells lovely.'

She flinched, realising she would now have to eat some of it. Smiling widely, she spooned what she hoped were just vegetables into her mouth. It was delicious.

'It's lovely out here,' she continued. 'Outside, under the trees and the moon... and stuff.'

He glanced at her but didn't reply. Bob was famously quiet, and rarely spoke if he could help it. Adie gazed around at his humble stone hut, the wrought-iron pot hanging over the open fire, the fishing rod leaning against a tree. She hadn't meant it when she said it, but though it was a very simple life, it was lovely. The sweet sound of the wind through the leaves, and the distant rush of water from the river made her momentarily forget what trouble she was in. She glanced up and the mismatched eyes were staring at her. Waiting for her to speak again.

'You're probably wondering what I'm doing out here... all alone, soaking wet, running around like I've lost my mind.'

The eyes watched but there was no reply. The silence made

Adie desperate to talk.

'I'm looking for something. Something I've lost. Well, someone really. I need help, but I can't tell the others what I've done.' She gave him a pleading look. 'If I tell you a secret, would you keep it?'

Bob plunged a spoonful of stew into his mouth and chewed. After a few seconds he nodded.

'Okay,' Adie said, taking a deep breath. 'I think I've brought a faery from Hy-Breasal here. I was trying to... I'm not sure how I did it, but it's here. You know about Hy-Breasal?' The man just chewed on his rabbit stew. 'Of course you know about Hy-Breasal. You're all in with the magic stuff. Anyway, I brought a faery back from there and I don't know how to send it home. Did anyone tell you me and the others got dragged to Hy-Breasal one time? Do you ever talk to our teachers? Ms Lemon and Mrs Quinlan, I mean. Do you ever...?'

Babbling isn't the word, she thought. *Get a hold of yourself, for heaven's sake.*

'Anyway, I tried to trap the faery with a water cage and it just smashed right out of it. I mean, I'm pretty good with water and I didn't even feel it coming. It just blew the cage away like it was nothing.' Adie set her bowl down near the fire. 'I'm really worried. If the teachers find out they might kick me out of our witchcraft lessons, and the others... I'm afraid everyone will be really mad when they find out. And what if the faery is bad? What if it hurts someone? I have to send it back before it can do any harm.'

The peaceful sound of the woods was somewhat marred by Bob's squelchy chewing. It was slow and purposeful, and went on forever. Adie didn't interrupt, trying to remain patient while her leg bobbed up and down with such ferocity she was in danger of kneeing herself in the chin.

'It's been here how long?' Bob's voice was rough and gravelly and rusty – as if he didn't like to use it at all.

'Since yesterday.'

'And it's kept to the woods?'

'I guess so. I don't know where it's been the whole time, but I looked for it here first. You see, in its own world it had to stick to the woods. The witches and faeries had this kind of war, and the faeries lost, and the witches made sure they stayed in the woods.'

'It's not a water sprite?'

'I don't think so. Rachel saw a couple of those – they had blue or green skin and big fins that looked like wings.'

'Yet it controls water. So what is it?'

'Um.' Adie swivelled her toe, making a messy dent in the mud. 'I don't know.'

Bob stood, his tall figure blocking the light from the moon. Sniffing, he wiped a hand under his nose and mumbled as if talking to himself.

'No water sprite, but it can move water.' He pulled his

hood up, hiding his pallid face in its shadow. 'What else can it do?'

Crossing to the fishing rod, he picked up the lure at the end of the line – it was a fishing fly unlike any other, delicate feathers of purple and silver, and a single tiny jewel for the eye. Adie knew it was a magical object, and that it magnified Bob's power somehow.

He snapped the fly from the line and put it in his pocket.

'Coming?' he said, not waiting for an answer.

Adie jogged after him, warm with relief. If anyone could help her trap the creature, surely Bob could. The night didn't seem so dark now, and the challenge ahead didn't seem so difficult. She could do this. She wasn't alone anymore.

Keeping up with Bob was not easy. The man moved like a cat through the undergrowth. Adie tripped over roots and her own feet as she followed, trying not to fall behind. Then she gasped as he leapt up a tree, climbing like a monkey to the very top. She watched in wonder. He was old – spritely, obviously – but still *old*. To look at his face you'd think he was positively ancient. How did he move so quickly and quietly?

The black slicker slid swiftly back down the bark, and Bob landed with a thump.

'What's that?' Adie said, looking at the browny orange

scrapings in his hands.

'The beginnings of *Chalara fraxinea*. Dieback.'

'Oh.'

He took off again, grabbing a leaf here, a shoot there, as if the woods were just an extension of himself. He didn't have to stop to identify anything, and he didn't have to go looking. It was like he knew where every tree and every bit of fungus grew. After he had jammed nearly a dozen ingredients into a small cloth bag, he spat into it and gave the bag a good shake.

'Did the faery touch you?'

'No,' Adie replied. 'Just smacked me with the water from the cage I made.'

'That'll do.'

His hand shot forward and rubbed the bag vigorously on her face.

'Ugh,' she complained, putting a hand to her raw cheek. 'That had your spit in it.'

Bob ignored her, holding his fishing fly in one hand, and grinding the bag between the fingers of the other. The fly fluttered suddenly and Bob pointed.

'That way.'

Jumping over falling logs and swishing through the grabbing twigs of unruly bushes, Adie felt close to fainting with fatigue. She got only a moment's rest here and there, when Bob would stop and wait for the fly's feather to shiver.

'This way,' he'd say, and they'd be running again.

She wanted to tell him to slow down, that she needed a break, but this was her mess he was helping clean up, so she kept her mouth shut.

Just when she thought she could take no more, the black slicker skidded to a halt and she was dragged to the woodland floor.

'Shh.'

Bob held his finger to his lips, and nodded ahead.

There was the faery. Its head of twiggy hair cast eerie shadows as it twirled and spun, leaping into trees and somersaulting down.

It's like a kid that just got out of school for summer, Adie thought.

It looked so joyful she wondered for a second if it really was dangerous. Then she remembered the smack of water that left her bruised and reeling.

The fly was fluttering madly now, as Bob ran his thumb over the jewelled eye. It sparkled as he recited something under his breath, and Adie felt a sudden gust of wind. It grew and grew, coming from all directions, swiping the browning leaves from the trees and twisting them into a tornado of vegetation. Too late, the faery's head turned in their direction, before it was sucked into the swirling column, vanishing behind a wall of leaves.

'You got it!' Adie cried. 'We can send it back now.'

Bob's expression was close to a smile, until a dried leaf bounced off his cheek. He looked perplexed. Another leaf hit, then another, and another. Soon Adie and Bob were being pelted with leaves, fired like bullets from the churning twister. It went on and on, Adie barely able to glance up through the deluge. At last, the leaves ran out. Bob and Adie sat up, taking their arms from their faces.

The faery sat hunkered on a branch, staring down at them, smiling. It didn't look angry. Like before, it looked amused.

It thinks we're playing with it, Adie thought.

Then, blowing them a kiss, the creature turned and darted into the darkness.

All athletic grace was gone from Bob's movements as he staggered painfully to his feet. He looked in shock.

'That's no faery,' he said.

'What?' said Adie. 'What do you mean? What is it, then?'

He shook his head.

'It's something else. Something worse.'

The classroom was freezing. Mr McQuaid announced that the radiator was broken and that was too bad. He ignored the groans and moans that followed, turning to the whiteboard to begin the history lesson that was bound to bore the pants off everyone. Grace pulled her jacket closed against the vicious shaft of cold air from the window, and began taking notes. She glanced to her left and spotted the *cho ku rei* symbol on Jenny's leg. She flipped her scarf out to slap the other girl on the arm.

'Cover that symbol,' she hissed.

'Alright, alright,' Jenny whispered, pulling up her sock. 'Don't know what you're worried about, no-one saw.'

But at least three people *had* seen, earlier in the A block, when Jenny had marched to her locker with the symbol on display.

'Here, Jenny,' Lena Domanski had called out, 'did you get a tattoo?'

Lena and two others had trotted over to take a closer look, while Jenny had smiled mysteriously. It made Grace angry. The secret wasn't just Jenny's, it was all of theirs, and she had no right to risk the whole group.

The sky outside was filled with dark clouds. Grace felt they were invading the room. Jenny was pushing her luck with Mrs Quinlan and Ms Lemon, Adie seemed to have withdrawn completely inside herself, and the sheen had begun to wear off on the carnival just a little bit. The girls had visited again with Justine in her tent, and again been invited to dinner, but Grace had avoided seeing Drake. She felt weird about the meeting she had seen between him and the doctor. She had no idea what it meant, but she was sure it wasn't good.

Trying not to ignore Mr McQuaid's droning voice, her

gaze drifted towards the window and the grounds outside. She glanced away, then snapped back for another look. She hadn't imagined it. One of the Melancholy Clowns stood on the grass beyond the dismal, grey carpark.

He looked so out of place that Grace gave a small, nervous laugh, but she found it more frightening than funny. He stood so still he could have been a statue, his silk suit covered in faded swirls of brown and red. She couldn't tell if he could see her, though he was facing her direction.

For the whole class, he didn't move. She forced herself to look down at her copybook and write the notes from the whiteboard, but every so often, she stole glances out of the window, waiting for the clown to leave. But he didn't. Was he smiling? She thought so, but it was impossible to be sure from that distance.

With her heart pounding in her ears, she began to sweat even in the bitter cold. Finally the school bell went and, when she looked up again, the clown was gone.

'Did you see him?' she said to Jenny and Adie in the corridor as students filed past.

'Who?' said Jenny.

'The clown. There was a clown on the grass by the carpark.'

She saw the blood drain from Adie's face.

'Did you see him, Adie?' said Grace.

'No,' Adie said, turning quickly. 'I have to get to my locker.'

'Wait, hang on...'

But Adie's dark curls had already disappeared into the crowd.

'I think you're losing it, Brennan,' Jenny said.

'It was one of the Melancholy Clowns, from the carnival. He just stood there. It was so strange.'

'You're totally losing it.'

'Shut up and pull up your socks.'

10

THE STRAW dOLL

'That is seriously creepy, Grace,' Una said, on the way to Mrs Quinlan's. 'Honestly, I think I would have peed myself.'

'Luckily, it didn't get to that point,' Grace said, giving Jenny a pointed look.

'But what would a clown be doing in school?' Jenny said. 'Seriously, in make-up and everything?'

'I don't know, Jenny. Being creepy and weird, and trying to scare people into peeing themselves?'

'I'm not saying I don't believe you–'

'Yes, you are.'

'–I'm just saying that maybe you *thought* you saw a clown, but it was actually, like, a traffic cone or something.'

Grace stared at her. 'I'm ending this conversation.'

Rachel's face was buried in her phone, but she quickly

changed the subject.

'Where's Adie? Isn't she coming to class?'

'Said something strange, like she had to go to her cousin's clarinet recital,' replied Una.

'Really?' Rachel finally slid the phone into her back pocket. 'Clarinet recital instead of magic lessons?'

'I know. Weird. We hardly see her anymore, I'm starting to forget she exists. Her name's Amy, right?'

Rachel turned to Grace.

'Do you think something's wrong? I know we're at the carnival a lot these days, and it's not her favourite place, but you think she'd come the odd time, just to hang out.'

'I'm not sure. I don't know what's going on with her.'

'Maybe she's seeing a therapist,' Una said.

'Why would she be seeing a therapist?' said Jenny.

'People have their reasons.'

'If she is seeing a therapist, shouldn't she be getting better, not worse?'

'Maybe she's seeing a bad therapist.'

'Stop it, you two,' said Grace. 'We shouldn't speculate when we don't know what's going on.'

'We shouldn't use words like speculate,' Una said, 'when some of us don't know what it means.'

'It means guess.'

'Oh. Right. Well, I speculate that if we're late for Old Cat Lady, she'll have our heads.'

When they reached Mrs Quinlan's door, Rachel rapped on the frosted glass. The door opened and everyone trooped in, but Mrs Quinlan stepped in Jenny's way and blocked her.

'Not you.'

'What?' said Jenny. 'What are you talking about?'

'You're expelled.'

'What? You can't do that!'

'I just did.'

'Mrs Quinlan,' Grace said from the hall, 'we're very sorry about what happened in the last–'

'I'm not talking to you, missy!' the woman growled. There was real anger in her pale eyes. 'Mind your own bloody business.'

'You can't kick me out,' Jenny protested. 'It's not up to you.'

'Take it up with the school board, sweetie,' Mrs Quinlan said, swinging the door shut.

Jenny banged on the door with both fists.

'Keep that up,' the woman yelled, 'and I'll make you my new favourite cat!'

The banging stopped. Grace stood with Rachel and Una in the hall, shocked and unsure what to do. Inside the kitchen, Delilah slumped by the counter, a pained look on her face.

'What are you all doing standing around?' Mrs Quinlan said. 'Get inside and take out your notebooks. And where's that little, curly headed one?'

'She had to go to her cousin's recital,' Grace replied, not moving.

'Another waster.' Mrs Quinlan glared at them. 'I told you to get inside and take out your books.'

Grace could feel Una trembling beside her as the woman stalked towards them.

'You can't kick Jenny out of class,' said Grace. 'We're in this together.'

She could feel Mrs Quinlan's breath on her face as the pale eyes came close.

'Listen to this, Miss Grace, and listen well. This is not school. I don't have to pander to the thugs and the weaklings. I'll teach who I think is worthy. And she's not worthy.' She wiped a bit of spittle from the corner of her mouth. 'And if you don't cut the crap, I might just find that *you're* not worthy either!'

'You won't keep her out,' Grace whispered.

'Oh, I will, missy.'

Grace stared at the bouncing straggles of grey hair as Mrs Quinlan turned and strode into the kitchen. *No, you won't,* she thought. *Not Jenny.*

Grace shivered as the alligator slid past her. The yaw of his long frame through the grass gave her a moment's panic every time she saw him. The lesson with Mrs Quinlan had not lasted long. The girls had refused to do anything they were told, and the woman had eventually kicked them all out. Poor Delilah was left behind to bear the brunt of her guardian's bad mood.

'Hey there.' Justine came towards them, a long woollen dressing gown over her costume. 'How you girls been?'

'Okay, thanks,' replied Grace. 'Is Agata on yet, do you know? We're looking for Jenny, and she'll probably be around Agata's trailer.'

The ballerina walked with them towards Agata's spot in the park. They could see Drake curled up on the nearby tree stump, as usual, but when they saw the doctor waiting by the trailer steps with his back to them, Justine stopped short. Agata popped her head out the door, and the doctor handed her something wrapped in grey cloth. The woman took it and ducked back inside.

Justine gasped and pulled Grace behind a grimy, yellow tent. Una dramatically threw Rachel against the tarpaulin.

'Ow!'

'Sorry,' shrugged Una. 'I'm not sure why I did that.'

'Oh, my lord, girls,' the ballerina breathed, 'it's true.'

'What's true?' asked Grace.

Justine leaned her face against the tent pole and watched the trailer with a mournful look.

'I thought everyone had it wrong. I thought it was just nonsense, but it's true. They took it.'

'Took what?'

'The straw doll.'

'A toy?' asked Una.

'No, no, you don't understand.' Justine paced, running her hands roughly through her hair. 'It's precious, we need it. We can't survive without it. It's the end... If *he's* got it, it's the end.' Tears glistened in her eyes and she seemed almost out of her mind. She buried her face in her hands. 'We're lost. The doctor will burn it and we'll all die with it. We'll all die with it...'

She mumbled incoherently until Grace gently prised her hands from her head.

'It's okay, Justine, it'll be okay. We'll help you if we can. He stole something you need?'

'We all need it, all the carnival folk. He and the other two have stolen the doll.'

'You think the doctor and Agata and Drake took a doll?' asked Rachel, puzzled.

'Agata's a good soul,' Justine replied, 'but Drake... she cares for him more than he deserves, I reckon. She'd do anything for him. And then there's the doctor... '

Grace watched a spiral of smoke drift up from the doctor's cigar, as he loitered around outside the trailer, whispering to Drake.

'Who *is* he?'

Justine shook her head again and her voice dropped to a

frightened whisper.

'There are rumours about his past, and he scares me.' She rubbed a tear from her cheek. 'And if he's taken the straw doll, then we're all lost.'

'Maybe we can help,' said Rachel. 'We're... Well, we're good at solving problems sometimes.'

'Our own, mostly,' Una piped up. 'But there's more to us than meets the eye.'

Grace nudged her roughly, but Una waved away her concerns.

'You're so sweet to offer,' said Justine. 'But please, for my sake, just stay away from the doctor. If Felix can't stop him, no-one can. And...' She seemed apologetic. 'Please be careful around Drake.'

She wandered away, as if already lost, and the girls remained hidden behind the yellow tent.

'Maybe that's why the clown was at school,' said Grace. 'Maybe they missed it and he thought *we'd* taken it.'

'The doll?' said Una. 'Do you think it's an antique? Or valuable?'

'I don't know.'

'It's gotta be something really expensive, if she's so worried about it.'

'I think it's more than that. It sounded like she meant it when she said they need it to survive.'

'You think there's some kind magic involved?' asked

Rachel, looking excited.

'Yeah, I do.'

'Then we're up,' Una said. 'This is our specialty.'

'Una's got a point,' said Rachel. 'If we can do something to help, we should.'

'Justine told us to stay away from the doctor,' replied Grace.

'And my mum told me not to eat any more candy floss,' said Una, 'but what do you think I'll be munching on later? Besides, Jenny's pally with Agata, and you know there's nothing we could do would keep her away from here. We're involved already. And we take care of our own.'

She thumped her fist over her heart and Grace rolled her eyes.

'You just want to get into trouble.'

'Trouble's my middle name, Grace.'

'Your middle name's Attracta.'

'Mention that again and I'll feed you to the alligator.'

✷ ✷ ✷

It was dim inside Agata's trailer in the evening light, but Grace couldn't find a light switch.

'They use oil lamps in some of the tents.' Rachel was somewhere behind her. 'Have a look for one of those.'

'I don't think we should try lighting an oil lamp in the dark,' said Grace. 'We don't know how, and we could end up setting fire to the place.'

'Hold on, I've got a torch!' cried Una.

There was jingling and then a thin stream of light stretched through the gloom.

'Yeah, sorry,' she said. 'It's a pen torch on my keyring, so it's not brilliant.'

The girls had waited until they saw Agata and Drake leave for their evening performances; Jenny had gone with them. Grace felt bad about that. Jenny was going to think the girls didn't even try to find her after she got kicked out of Mrs Quinlan's class, but it was a risk they had to take; if Jenny knew they were planning to search Agata's home, she might try to stop them.

There were a lot of postcards and memorabilia on the walls of the trailer, some in scrappy wooden frames. There was a counter top at one end, covered in delicate teacups, saucers and a large teapot, and a kettle sat on an old camping stove.

Apart from that there was just a single cot bed, a small wardrobe and a bedside table with one drawer. Grace examined some figurines on the table, but decided none of them could be the straw doll. She rifled through the drawer and found nothing but letters and a gold locket. Inside was a picture of a couple on their wedding day. It was very old.

'I feel kind of rotten about this,' Rachel said, opening the wardrobe.

'Yeah, I know what you mean,' said Grace.

Una crawled out from underneath the bed.

'Nothing under there but old newspapers. But like, *old*. There's one there from the 1930s. It's American, I think. Maybe she got it from her grandmother.'

'Maybe she bought it,' Grace said, closing the drawer.

'Bought it?'

'Everything's so old. The pictures, the trailers, the cos-tumes. I think the carnival has been around that long. I think that's what the doll is for. It keeps them alive.'

'Since the 1930s?'

'Why not? We've seen weirder things.'

'Can't argue with you there.'

'Got something!' Rachel said, half-buried at the bottom of the wardrobe.

She pulled out a bundle of grey cloth, carefully tied with string. Grace held her breath as Rachel pulled open the bow and unwrapped the cloth. Inside was an ornament of deep red wood, carved with such intricate figures Grace barely thought it was possible. It was about the size of her fist, but had ten or more delicate engravings – people cooking fish over an open fire, hiking up a mountain trail, sitting on an outcrop by the sea.

'That's gorgeous,' she breathed.

'But you couldn't call it a doll,' said Rachel.

'No. Maybe he didn't give the doll to Agata after all.'

Grace caught the sudden scent of cigar smoke and sprang

upright. The trailer door stood a few inches ajar, but she couldn't see outside. She silently urged Rachel to re-wrap the ornament and tuck it back into the wardrobe, then crept to the door with her finger on her lips.

'Good evening, little witches.'

Grace froze. The voice came from right outside. In the silence that followed she could see dust settling in the shaft of evening light that filled the narrow gap in the doorway. The voice sounded again.

'Let's not pretend we're not aware of each other, shall we?'

There was a slow creak and the door swung outwards.

His eyes were shaded by the large brim of his hat and his dark trench coat made him seem taller up close. One hand brought a skinny cigar to his mouth. He exhaled slowly, smiling with immaculate, white teeth.

'Poor Agata,' he said. 'Little does she know, as she works so hard in the ring, that her belongings are being picked over and scrutinised.'

In spite of her fear, Grace blushed in shame.

'Steel your nerves, witch,' the man said. 'I'll keep your dirty, little secret.'

He took one more puff of his cigar, smiled, and walked away.

'How did he know we're witches?' Una gasped.

'I don't know,' replied Grace. 'But I think Justine was right. We shouldn't have crossed the doctor.'

✳ ✳ ✳

Grace, shoulders hunched, strode down Brooke Road. She was on the way to see Ms Lemon, and she hoped she was doing the right thing.

The teacher lived in a small, quiet apartment. Grace held the door for an old woman shuffling through with a little grocery cart, then bounded up the stairs. Ms Lemon did not look surprised to see Grace on her doorstep.

'Come in,' she said, and went off to boil the kettle.

Grace had been in the apartment once before; it was very small, but prettily decorated, and had a lovely view of the river from the sitting room. Now she stood against the arm of the sofa; she was too anxious to sit. She declined the offered cup of tea but, before she could speak, Ms Lemon did.

'I know what this is about. Vera called me. Poor Jenny must be very upset.'

'She is,' replied Grace. 'We all are. We're a group, we stick together. So how could she expel one of us from the class? Mrs Quinlan's being totally unreasonable.'

'Not totally,' Ms Lemon sighed. 'Jenny can be very disruptive.'

'She speaks her mind, Miss.'

'It's more than that. She's disobedient.'

Grace looked at the teacher in surprise.

'You agree with Mrs Quinlan. About keeping Jenny out.'

'Not entirely, no. But... it is Vera's class. It's her decision.'

'Okay, but Jenny can still come to *your* lessons.'

Ms Lemon put down her teacup and clasped her hands.

'Grace, the lessons complement each other. You need both lots of instruction or it could lead to dangerous gaps in your skill and knowledge.'

'So *we'll* teach Jenny what we learn in Mrs Quinlan's class. And she can still come to yours.'

'That's not good enough, you haven't the experience–'

'Then how can Jenny stay in the group?'

The teacher avoided her gaze.

'Are you expelling her?' said Grace.

'It's not up to me–'

'It *is* up to you. You're our teacher too! Are you going to let Jenny into your class, or not?'

Ms Lemon looked up, her hazel eyes pleading.

'Vera won't. So I can't.'

Grace felt a lump in her throat and a disappointment like she had never felt before. Bethany Lemon was the person Grace most looked up to in the world. She was always fair, always just; like a sensible knight in shining armour. But now Grace could see a blemish on that armour. Ms Lemon could be bullied – was being bullied – by Mrs Quinlan. Grace looked down at Ms Lemon on the sofa, with her hands clasped and her expression worried, and she suddenly saw the little girl inside the woman. All at once, Grace felt a crushing pressure. *She* was going to have to be the adult.

'That is not fair, Ms Lemon. And you know it. I'll see myself out.'

As she walked from Brooke Road, tears stinging her eyes, Grace realised she hadn't told Ms Lemon about the doctor and the missing straw doll. But, she thought, what was the point? Telling an adult didn't seem to be the cure-all anymore. She didn't feel she could depend on Ms Lemon now.

It was a truth she felt she had always known, but didn't want to admit; adults are human too. And now that she was just months away from turning fifteen, Grace realised she would become one soon, and others would depend on *her* to be sensible and fair and to know everything.

She stopped on the bridge to watch the river flow beneath her, and just let herself cry. She wasn't ready.

She wasn't ready to be the grown-up.

11

all aboard
the Caterpillar

The next day after school, Grace waited for Jenny at the school gates. They hadn't had a moment alone during the day, and she didn't wanted to embarrass her friend by announcing her permanent expulsion in front of the rest of the group.

Finally the tall girl appeared, sauntering towards her like she hadn't a care in the world.

'Jenny, I need to talk to you. It's about the witchcraft lessons.'

'I'm out of both, I know. Ms Lemon called me.'

'Oh. I didn't think she'd... I'm really sorry.'

'Don't worry about it.'

'We can all go on strike. Refuse to do our lessons, tell

them we won't guard the well. We ignored Mrs Quinlan last night, it drove her bonkers and she kicked us all out.'

'Don't do that. What's the point? That old hag would expel you all, you know she would. Don't let her ruin it for the rest of you.'

They walked on in silence until they reached the playground at the bottom of the hill. Without saying anything they both sat down on the swings and swayed absentmindedly. Grace was a little unnerved. Jenny had a glint in her eye that she couldn't ignore.

'What is it?'

'What's what?' Jenny said, turning away too late to hide a smile.

'You were miserable yesterday. What's changed?'

'Things are looking up.'

'What things?'

Jenny shook her head, but she was jiggling one leg and Grace got the impression she couldn't hold it in any longer.

'I've made a decision,' the tall girl said. She leaned in and lowered her voice to a whisper. 'When the carnival leaves, I'm going with them.'

'What?'

'Just that. I'm going with them. I'm going to be a strongwoman, like Agata.'

Jenny was smiling like it was excellent news; and like it was definite.

'No, you're not,' said Grace. 'Don't be ridiculous.'

'I am. And it doesn't matter what you say, Grace, you won't talk me out of it.'

'I won't even try, but you're not going.'

'Yes, I am.'

Jenny wasn't jiggling her leg anymore. She looked calm. She looked sure of herself.

'This isn't happening, Jenny, so get it out of your head.'

'Get it *into* your head, Brennan. I'm going. If that Cat Hag won't let me learn magic anymore I'm not sticking around to watch you lot become witches. I wouldn't miss school, I wouldn't even miss home, do you know that? If I'm not washing dishes, I'm babysitting Sarah. It's boring as hell, and I need a change.'

'Stop talking rubbish. You know you'd never leave home.'

'I would, and I am. And don't talk to me like I'm a child!'

Grace tried to keep her voice level, like this was just a silly notion that wasn't worth getting upset about, but something in her friend's face made her worry. It was as if Jenny was forcing Grace to play a part she didn't want to play. When Grace finally spoke, she was almost shouting.

'Listen to me, you're not running away to join the circus, and that's the end of it. It's ridiculous!'

'It's not a circus, it's a carnival.'

'I was being *ironic*.'

'I don't know what that *means*.'

'It means I didn't actually mean what I said, I... Look, it doesn't matter. The point is you're not running away.'

Jenny stuck out her chin.

'And how are you gonna stop me?'

'I'll tell your mum. You wouldn't get a mile out of town.'

The sudden drop in Jenny's expression told Grace that she hadn't thought that part through.

'You'd snitch?'

'Gladly.'

There was a moment's pause, then Jenny stamped her foot hard enough to throw up a cloud of sand.

'Why do you always have to be such a goody two-shoes?!'

'Because a hothead like you needs a goody two-shoes like me to stop you doing stupid things like running away from home. That's why.'

'Yeah? Well goody two-shoes like you need hotheads like me to make you do fun stuff, or you'd spend your whole life safe in your room doing homework and you'd never do anything interesting ever, ever, *ever*.'

'Yeah?'

'Yeah.'

'Fine, then.'

'Fine.'

'*Fine*.'

They both stood in awkward silence, Jenny kicking at the small mound of dirt her stamping foot had caused. Finally, she gave an awkward nod in Grace's direction but didn't look at her.

'See you tomorrow, then.'

'See you tomorrow.'

✳ ✳ ✳

Adie was ditching her second magic lesson in two days. It irked her that the girls would be learning something new without her (if they managed to get through an entire class without being kicked out, that is), but this was important. When the final bell rang, she had gone straight out the back entrance of the school and into the woods. Finding Bob's hut took longer than she'd expected — she had run into him by accident last time — and she made several wrong turns before she finally saw the pale line of smoke from a campfire.

'Hi, Bob.'

He was cooking fish this time, and the smell made her tummy rumble. She sat on the stool opposite him and tried not to stare at the spit over the fire. When it was ready, Bob scraped chunks of charred fish into a bowl and handed it to her.

'What are we going to try today?' she asked, tucking in.

He gave her a quizzical look.

'How are we going to catch the faery?' she said. 'Or the not-faery. Whatever it is.'

'We're not catching that any time soon,' Bob replied.

'But we have to. We have to send it back quickly, before anybody finds out. What if it starts messing with people in town?'

'It probably will.'

'Then we have to stop it!'

'Do you know how?'

Adie gripped the bowl in her hands.

'No.'

'Me neither.'

'So you're just giving up?' Adie didn't want to be on her own again. It was too much.

'No. But it'll take time to work this thing out. And then, I'm sure, it'll take time to catch it. There's no rushing this.'

'We have to rush it!'

'That's not possible.'

'Then I'll do it without you!'

Adie dumped her bowl on the ground, stood up and stormed off. She stamped her feet as she went, getting slower and slower, waiting for Bob to call her back. But he called her bluff instead. She looked behind and saw him hunched over the spit, scraping more meat from the fish. She could go back, apologise, and humbly ask how she could help discover what the creature was. But her chest was tight with worry now. Ms Lemon and Mrs Quinlan were going to find out. If the creature started playing games in plain sight, she would have to tell them where it had come from, that the whole thing was all her fault.

Unable to bear the feeling, Adie decided Bob had to be wrong – and she would prove it. She'd get help elsewhere, and catch this thing before anyone saw so much as a hair on its twiggy head.

'Right, girls.' Ms Lemon seemed a little unsettled. 'Mind-hopping. That's what we're in the woods for today.'

She was clearly waiting for some reaction – an exclamation of delight, or a question from Una – but she got none. The lesson had been strangely formal ever since the girls had met their teacher. Delilah kept her gaze low, as if being Mrs Quinlan's charge somehow made her complicit in Jenny's expulsion; Rachel was polite, but distant; Una kept one eyebrow raised, her mouth pursed, so Ms Lemon would know she was not impressed with what had gone on; and Grace, still a little heartbroken, maintained a chilly silence.

'Can anyone tell me what mind-hopping is?' When no-one responded, Ms Lemon picked the small girl. 'Delilah, you know, surely. I think you've read more about witchcraft than I have.'

The teacher's forced chuckle was painfully out of place, and earned her no warm response from the girls.

'It is piggybacking on the mind of someone or something else,' Delilah said quickly.

'Excellent! Very concise. Yes, it means hopping aboard the mind of another creature, so that you can see and hear and smell what it sees and hears and smells. You cannot direct the animal's behaviour in any way, however, you become an observer only. Delilah was absolutely right in saying it's merely a piggyback ride. Are there any questions before we start?'

Grace had about twenty, but she kept her mouth shut.

'Right,' the teacher said, shaking out her arms, 'let's begin, then. The first thing you have to do is find an animal. Something small and slow is easiest. Nothing worse than trying to mind-hop a little rabbit that sprints away before you've even started!'

The attempts at humour were starting to make Grace feel a little pity, but she squished the feeling and reminded herself that Jenny was not learning to mind-hop with the rest of them.

Grace spotted a bright green caterpillar on a leaf and chose it. While focussing on the tiny, hairy thing, she felt delight in the way it moved in a wave, as if a bubble of energy had erupted at its tail and was zooming along the body, shunting the whole animal forward.

'*Mens mea, mens tua, mens nostra,*' said Ms Lemon. 'That's the phrase you say. Now, when you're ready, I want you to shrug your shoulders a few times – it might take quite a few your first time round – until you feel the tiniest tingle in your neck. Hold on to that by keeping the shoulders up, then I want you to say the phrase as you exhale and relax your shoulders at the same time. Never lose concentration on your animal. Remember, that's where you're going.'

The rhyme came out as little more than a breath when Grace finally let go, dropping her shoulders and feeling her head swoon. The sounds around her boomed and shrank and then, for a few seconds, she felt like she was underwater, suspended by something she couldn't feel.

'It didn't work, Miss,' she could hear Una complaining. 'It just gave me a headache.'

'Try again, Una. It takes time—'

There was a piercing pain, right through the middle of Grace's skull. Everything went quiet and then... she was there, on the leaf.

She couldn't see it – she couldn't really see anything – but she knew she was now in the mind of the caterpillar. There was no sound, but an onslaught of other sensations. There were changes in light as leaves swayed above her, she could differentiate parts of the leaf by smell, but the most extraordinary thing was the vibration. She could *feel* the world around her. She could feel the breeze and the minuscule hairs on the leaf, but it wasn't like anything she had felt before. There were minute differences in the direction and strength of the wind, the shape and movement of the leaf, and she could sense it all. It was too much information at once, and she had an almost unbearable tickling sensation all over.

I shouldn't have picked a caterpillar, she thought, suddenly remembering her biology lessons.

Caterpillars rely on smell, taste and touch. They can barely see, and cannot hear, but the hairs that cover their bodies allow them to sense tiny vibrations all around them. That must be what was tickling. It was nearly too much.

Grace squirmed against it, trying not to laugh but unable to make the caterpillar's body do anything. It crawled along the leaf, oblivious to her, as she jerked and squirmed and tried to get away from the wriggly feeling that was driving her crazy.

How do I get out? she thought. *Ms Lemon didn't say.*

A bit of panic set in now, until a dark shape moved in front. It was big, and it was alive.

Jump, she thought and, within a few seconds she had repeated the mind-hopping spell and was moving through the woods at a swift pace.

She was low down, running on four legs. Her sense of smell was still excellent but, suddenly, she could see very well. She could hear well too. No scurrying feet or chewing teeth in the undergrowth escaped her notice. She caught a fleeting glance of a paw below her. From the size, she realised she had to be piggybacking on the mind of a fox.

It was exciting. It moved so quickly. It was stealthy and many animals around it had no idea it was there. She heard

137

a twig snap in the distance and the fox made for it. There was something coming, something big, a person, so loud and cumbersome that the fox made only the barest attempt at hiding.

It was a girl. Grace could see dark, curly hair. She had been stomping ahead, then she slowed and turned. Standing for a few moments, she walked forward again, quieter this time.

It was Adie.

She had told Una her grandmother wasn't well. It was a feeble excuse. Her grandmother lived in Carrick and, if she had really been poorly, enough for Adie's parents to drive her all the way over there, Grace's mother would have heard about it. Adie's granny was clearly fine.

And Adie was in the woods.

Grace willed the fox in the direction her friend had come from, forgetting she had no control.

Fudge! Please go that way, Mr Fox. Please.

Luckily, the fox smelled something delicious coming from a campfire up ahead. It crept forward. And that's when Grace got her second surprise. Bob the Mirrorman sat by the fire. There was a fish on a spit, and the man was scooping spoon-fuls of the meat into a bowl.

He looked up. Grace felt exposed, even though there was no way he could see her.

'Away with you,' the man said.

But the smell of the food was too good and the fox stayed

where he was.

'Away with you, I said.' Then Bob leaned forward. He stared at the fox as if he knew there was something strange about it.

Peeling a piece of flesh from the fish, he threw it near the fire. The fox hesitated, suspicious. Bob threw another piece, about a metre further out, and the fox took a few steps. It watched him, its ears and eyes alert. Then darting in, it grabbed the piece nearest and ran back.

No, Grace thought. *Stay where you are.*

But the fox felt safer now. Slowly this time, it moved in to gobble up the piece of fish by the fire.

Bob extended one arm, his expression curious, and with a flick of his fingers Grace felt like she'd been smacked in the forehead, hard. She tumbled off the fox's mind, hurtling backwards, not able to make out the trees around her. She landed back in herself with a thud – and the feeling that she might throw up any minute.

'You're back!' Una cried.

Grace blinked, her vision clearing, still feeling sick.

'You were stuck like this,' Una imitated a zombie with its mouth hanging open, 'for ages. Where did you go?'

'Caterpillar,' Grace groaned. 'Then fox.'

'You mind-hopped from one animal to another?' Ms Lemon sounded halfway between concerned and impressed. 'That was a little more advanced than I had intended for this class, Grace.'

'It tickled,' Grace mumbled in explanation, as saliva filled her mouth and she begged herself not to vomit.

'I mind-hopped a bird,' Rachel said, a little too loud for Grace's delicate state. 'It was brilliant!'

'I was in a beetle for a little bit,' said Una. 'Then I fell out.'

'Adie,' Grace whispered.

'She's not here, remember? Her granny's sick.' Una turned to Ms Lemon. 'Did the mind-hopping break Grace, Miss? She's all skewy.'

'She'll be fine, Una.'

Ms Lemon smiled at Grace, like everything was back to normal. Grace wanted to indicate that it was not, but the queasy feeling in her stomach would only let her walk slowly from the woods, slightly bent over, and groaning in discomfort.

12

Girls in Glass Houses...

Tink.

Tink, tink.

Adie fired pebbles at Delilah's bedroom window. She was more than nervous standing in Mrs Quinlan's back garden, knowing one of those dreadful cats could announce her presence at any moment. There was one weaving through weeds on the far side, eyeing her suspiciously.

Finally, Delilah's small frame appeared at the window. She gave Adie a confused wave and disappeared. A minute later she was at the back door.

'Adie, what's going on? Are you alright?'

Adie nodded at first, then shook her head.

'I need help.'

✳ ✳ ✳

Adie admired Delilah's brazenness. The girl, having dressed and collected B-brr from her room, deftly crept outside and shut the back door without even a hint of concern. Adie had been so terrified sneaking out of her own house at night that she had turned back twice.

'Are you sure Mrs Quinlan won't notice you're gone?' she asked.

'She sleeps like a log. It's fine.'

Delilah had been the perfect person to tell, Adie realised. She didn't balk when told about the water-messaging and Adie's attempt to make contact with her friends on Hy-Breasal, in fact, she had nodded as if it had been a perfectly reasonable thing to do. But she had seemed confused by the creature that followed the message back.

'What do you mean, it came back with you? How?'

'I don't know, it just did. I sensed something the second I got out of the water and then the faery thing appeared.'

'Nothing corporeal could travel on a water-message. It's spiritual. It's only your mind that moves.'

'I know that,' Adie said, thinking she should have asked Delilah about messaging when it first occurred to her. Some-times she forgot how much the small girl knew. 'But it must have done. Somehow.'

'Can't be corporeal then.'

'Bob said it's not a faery anyway. He tried to trap it in this leaf tornado thing, and it escaped.'

'Slipped through it, you mean?'

'No, it burst out. Sent the leaves flying everywhere, like they were missiles. It really stung when they hit.'

'It has power then.'

'Yes, but... it's almost like our stuff is nothing to it. It brushes off our magic, like it's immune or something. And...'

'What?' Delilah pushed as they walked past the school, approaching the woods.

'It's like a little kid too, let out for the first time. When Bob and I found it, it was dancing around in the trees. And both times we trapped it, it looked at us as if we were playing games.' Adie hesitated before they entered the shadow of the trees. 'Like hide-and-seek or something.'

Delilah was quiet for a while and, as they approached the river on the right edge of the woods, she pulled something from her pocket. It was a bronze-coloured stone, with a shallow curve like a small bowl. It was smooth and polished to a high shine.

'What's that?' said Adie.

'I found it in a chest my mother left behind after... after she left. It's called a magnesia stone. It has to be carved under a waning moon, and then infused with sesame oil – not sure how they do that – and then you can use it to discover secrets. At least, I know you can use it to see a creature's true self. Sort of.'

'We could have used one of those when your mother... well...' Adie broke off and looked apologetic.

'Yeah, maybe. It's not very subtle, is the only thing. Was it near here that you found the creature before?'

'Yes,' Adie replied. 'Bob tracked it using a bag of his spit and other ingredients. Haven't a clue what was in it, sorry. Wait, something called dieback! That was one of them. Can't remember the rest, though.'

'Doesn't matter,' Delilah said, tapping her shoulder. B-brr emerged from beneath her collar, yawning and smacking his lips. 'We've got a mini-bloodhound.'

The girl gave the little wood nymph a few minutes to stretch himself out, swing from her hair a few times, before he somersaulted back onto her shoulder, ready and waiting.

'It's not one like you,' Delilah said to him gently, 'but it doesn't belong here. Can you sniff it out?'

B-brr didn't react at first. Adie wondered if he understood English. Delilah talked to him often and, though he seemed to understand eventually, Adie suspected it wasn't the actual words that he followed.

Gazing out into the woods, the nymph finally sniffed. Then sniffed again. He climbed to the top of Delilah's head, grabbed handfuls of her hair like they were reins, and stuck his nose in the air.

'Ow!' Delilah scratched at her head where the hair was pulled. 'This way.'

The wood nymph was every bit the bloodhound Delilah declared him to be. Far quicker than Bob had done, he led them to a spot near one edge of the woods where, in a shallow dip in the ground, the creature sat pulling at twigs and strands of vegetation and examining them, as if they were fascinating puzzles. The girls ducked down, out of sight.

'You ready?' Delilah whispered.

'Ready,' Adie replied.

'Okay. Then be prepared to run.'

Adie didn't know what she had expected, but she was startled when Delilah leapt to her feet and fired the stone at the creature's head. It struck it with some force, and the huge, round eyes widened. The magnesia stone flew back to Delilah's hand, like a boomerang, and the woods erupted in noise and fury.

'Run!' shouted Delilah.

A massive wave of nothing, like the aftermath of an atomic bomb, ploughed into the girls as they ran, sending them flying and spinning through the air, bouncing along the woodland floor, rolling beyond the trees to the riverbank. Adie's head was ringing when she felt Delilah grasp her hand and pull her down the bank where they couldn't be seen.

'Stay down.' The small girl was breathless, clutching the stone between thumb and forefinger.

'You weren't kidding.' Adie was gasping for breath. 'That was not subtle, Delilah.'

'Nope.'

But Delilah didn't seem bothered. She watched the stone as wisps of colour curled from the shallow bowl.

'That faery thing? That's not its true form.'

'Okay,' Adie replied, 'so what is its true form?'

'I can't tell,' Delilah watched the moving wisps, perplexed. 'It's complicated. See all these strands? There shouldn't be so many. And they're all intertwining, they shouldn't be doing that either. A person should have just one. Or at least one main one, maybe a few others if they depend on other living creatures in some way...' She turned the stone, looking at it from all directions. 'It's looks like it's *made up* of many other lives, or dependents, or... I don't know. And this clear line keeping them all tied together? I'm not sure what that could be.'

'Has is got some cosmic Multiple Personality Disorder?'

Delilah gave her a look, and Adie shrugged.

'You're the one describing it!' She lowered her voice, remembering they were hiding. 'I didn't know you were going to whack that creature in the head. No wonder it got mad. What if you've given it brain damage or something?'

'It doesn't have a brain. Not a brain in the way we think of it, anyway. Besides, the stone's lighter than it looks.'

She bounced the magnesia off her hand and Adie caught

it. It was much lighter than she expected.

'I take it we're not catching this thing tonight?'

'No, we're not,' said Delilah. 'Bob was right. We can't catch it until we know what it is. I'll have to do some reading.'

'Read quickly, please,' said Adie. 'I don't want anyone else to find out.'

Delilah gave her a comforting look.

'I know you don't.'

Justine's pointed feet dangled ten metres off the ground. She hung with her waist wrapped in thick, white rope and her hands reached for the tarpaulin ceiling. Arching back into a mid-air crab, she spied the girls waiting for her in the bleachers.

'Well, hey there,' she said, flipping herself right side up and rolling out of the wrap.

Her right hand was all that kept her fixed to the rope until she wound one leg around it and slid gracefully to the ground.

'One of the stall operators told us you'd be here,' said Grace. 'Are you working on a new routine? It looks great.'

'Thank you. Yeah, it's new.' The ballerina took a seat in between Rachel and Una, and stroked her beard softly. 'I'm glad you came around. I was worried about what happened the other day outside Agata's trailer. I came across a little strange, I know. You can just ignore all of that, it didn't mean nothing.'

'It did,' replied Una. ''Cos when we ransacked Agata's trailer later on, that weird doctor appeared out of nowhere and creeped us all out.'

Grace stared at Una open-mouthed. After much discussion, they had agreed that they would tell Justine about the incident, but very carefully.

'You did what?' The ballerina's eyes were wide with shock.

Taking a deep breath, Grace told her exactly what had happened, leaving out their own little secret at the end, though Una seemed keen to spill that one as well.

'It was like he looked right into our souls,' the girl said theatrically. 'Because he *knew* things. He knew things about us.'

'Knew what?' asked Justine.

'Things. He knew *who we were.*'

Grace gave Una a dig in the ribs that was too obvious to be ignored by Justine.

'That's okay,' she said. 'You got your own stuff, I get it. We all need secrets.'

Grace smiled gratefully.

'Why don't we forget about serious stuff for a while?' said Justine. 'Let's go have some fun.'

'Could we have a go on the rope?' asked Rachel.

'Sure, I can show you a few things. And if you wanna be all

proper, it's a *corde lisse*.' Justine winked. 'Fancy word for rope.'

It wasn't like regular rope – all rough and scratchy – it was made of strands of cotton, and much softer. First, Justine showed them how to stand up on the rope by wrapping one leg around and flexing the foot, using it as a platform to step onto. They all got that bit fairly quickly. Then she showed them how to climb, and that was much harder. Grace stood on her foot, then released her legs, bending her knees, and tried to repeat the stand a little further up the rope. But the *corde lisse* wouldn't behave. It swung away from her feet, leaving her dangling and kicking to get it back around her leg.

'You'll get it,' Justine laughed. 'Keep trying.'

Of course, Rachel, who was graceful to the point of annoying, picked it up quicker than the other two. Her toes pointed, her legs never flailed, and she got halfway up the rope before Grace and Una could manage a single climbing step.

'Aw, Rach,' Una moaned. 'How are you doing that? You're like a big, elegant... thing in the air.'

'Thanks, Una, but it's not so hard once you get the hang of it.'

'Yeah,' Grace muttered, 'for you.'

While Una had another go, Justine unhooked a large hoop from the wall. It hung on a vertical rope on the opposite side of the tent from the *corde lisse*, and was just within reach of someone standing on tiptoes on the floor.

'This hoop bruises a bit,' she warned.

'I think the rope bruises a bit,' Grace said, rubbing her foot.

'Yeah,' Justine said, smiling, 'but that wears off when you get used to it. The hoop, though? For some reason it's always mean to me. I never finish a set on it without fresh bruises.'

She leapt up, threading her feet through the centre, and hung from her knees.

'Cool,' said Rachel.

'There's loads of great stuff you can do on this. You wanna have a go? Just make sure—'

'Look at me!' Una squealed suddenly.

Grace spun around to see Una's black bob swinging upside down at the top of the *corde lisse*.

'Una, be careful!'

'Oh, honey,' Justine said urgently. 'Come down a little bit. That's too high.'

'I can nearly touch the ceiling!'

Una reached up with one hand and, at that second, her other hand slipped. There was a moment when Grace thought the girl's legs would tangle in the rope and prevent a fall but, as Una scrabbled with her hands, her feet came loose and she plummeted to the ground.

Grace screamed and slapped her hands over her eyes, waiting for the heart-stopping *SMACK*.

But it never came.

Slowly opening her eyes, she saw Una face down, hovering half a metre off the ground beside the *corde lisse*. The girl was gasping in huge breaths and glanced up at the others with great effort.

'Oh,' she said, looking to Justine. 'Oh, whoopsie.'

Then she dropped face-first into the dirt with a loud 'Oomph!'

Grace was first at her side.

'Una! You gave us such a fright,' she exclaimed, helping Una to her feet.

'*You* got a fright?' Una said. 'I nearly had kittens.'

'Are you hurt at all?' Rachel said, dusting off Una's jumper and jeans.

'Nah, I'm good, but...'

She looked to Justine, who still stood by the hoop, her bearded jaw hanging open.

'Oh,' Una said, still shaky on her feet. 'Yeah, see, Justine... I, um... I can fly. But it's just me. And I'm not a witch. So... so, we can just forget that happened and move on. Hey, show me another trick on the hoop.'

Grace winced at Una's lousy attempt at distraction. There was nothing for it but to come clean.

'Justine, we practise witchcraft,' she said firmly. 'We're witches. Sorry we didn't tell you before, but it really is a secret.'

Justine was glassy eyed. She pointed a wavering finger.

'You were hanging in the air. You should have been killed but, but... that was *amazing*.'

'Yeah, well.' Una cracked her knuckles in a blasé manner. 'I don't like to brag, but I'm pretty good.'

The ballerina seemed rattled. Grace was afraid Justine might scream or run away, but the girl suddenly cried, 'Do something else!'

Grace, Rachel and Una stood awkwardly. Grace wasn't sure of the ethics of showing off spells to a non-witch. Wasn't there some sort of code, that you should only use your powers for good? That doing tricks to impress other people wasn't very dignified. It belittled the huge importance of their power, didn't it?

But her heart swelled. She was dying to show off. So she didn't stop Una when the girl stepped forward and instantly disappeared.

'Ah!' Justine squealed in delight. 'You're invisible!'

'Cloaked,' Una said, reappearing. 'But I'm still there. You can still bump into me and see my footprints and stuff.'

It was odd, but even Una seemed a little abashed at revealing their spells.

Rachel went next. Sweeping her hands over her face, she glamoured herself into another Justine.

The ballerina stepped back, but was still grinning.

'Nooooo. That's scary! Take it off.'

Rachel shook off the glamour and grinned back as herself.

'You guys are incredible,' Justine gushed. 'I mean, you look like regular schoolgirls, but you're... And you?'

Grace was happy not to miss out on showing off her own skills. Using the *corde lisse* as a life template – something that is or has been alive – she originated a stunning baby panther. Its sleek black fur shone like marble as it crept around her feet, looking up at her expectantly.

Justine was shaking her head.

'I feel like crying. I really do.' She looked at them earnestly. 'I'm so honoured you've shown me this. And so happy, because,' she wiped her watering eyes, 'I think you can help us. We need saving, and you can save us. I *know* you can.'

She approached them, taking a hand each of Grace's and Una's.

'Will you? Will you save us?'

13

don't go killing each other

Delilah's bedroom door flew open, banging against her desk, on which she had been having a nice little nap. Mrs Quinlan's formidable frame darkened the doorway.

'Told you she might be doing her homework,' the woman said to Adie, just behind her.

'Yes, I think she's just finished, Mrs Quinlan, thanks,' Adie replied as Delilah smacked her lips and rubbed her eyes sleepily.

'Beth said you missed her one of her classes,' the Cat Lady said. 'Slacking off, are you?'

'No, Mrs Quinlan. I had to go to my... uncle's... funeral and then I had, em, another funeral. My, em, granduncle was–'

'I'll stop you there,' said Mrs Quinlan. 'There's nothing worse than listening to a bad liar. You miss another class of mine, you'd better have a *real* excuse. Is that clear?'

'Yes, Mrs Quinlan.'

'And what are *you* up to?' the woman said suddenly to Delilah, approaching the desk. Delilah slammed her hands down on the piles of books in front of her.

'Homework.'

'Homework? On foreign entities and mystical combinations?' Mrs Quinlan said, tilting her head to read the spines.

Delilah didn't answer but watched her guardian defiantly. Adie was impressed again. Delilah could stand her ground when she wanted to, and hardly anyone stood their ground against the Old Cat Lady.

'Well,' the woman said, a smile playing on her lips, 'you've got five minutes before we head off for the football field, so time to wrap up your *homework*.'

'Wow,' Adie breathed when the door slammed shut. 'You just gave her the evil eye. I wouldn't dare.'

Delilah shrugged.

'Sometimes she likes it when I defy her, I think it impresses her.'

'Only sometimes?'

'Other times she threatens to lock me in the basement.'

'You don't have a basement.'

'She says she'll find a basement somewhere.'

155

✳ ✳ ✳

Adie and Delilah were already with Mrs Quinlan on the school football pitch when Grace arrived. Una and Rachel followed soon afterwards and, as the woman began the lesson, Grace almost shouted out to stop because Jenny wasn't there yet. But, of course, Jenny wasn't coming. She wasn't invited.

Mrs Quinlan began with a long and accusatory lecture on self-control. Grace found her thoughts drifting to a red-and-white striped tent, and a boy with strange, green skin smiling from the doorway...

'Oi, are you listening?' said Mrs Quinlan. 'Bookwormy one. What's her name again?'

'Grace,' said Adie.

'Grace!' Mrs Quinlan yelled, snapping Grace out of her daydream. 'Are you paying attention?'

'Yes, Mrs Quinlan.'

'Then tell me where you start the build-up for the push spell.'

The pale eyes glared. In her peripheral vision, Grace saw Rachel pointing surreptitiously to her lower back.

'Eh, in the bum?'

'Perhaps for you that is the greatest source of all magical power. For the rest of us, we prefer to start this one in the lower spine. Like so.'

The woman pushed up her baggy sleeves, letting her arms fall to her sides where they curved a little with palms upwards. She flexed her fingers suddenly and Grace stumbled backwards like someone had grasped her shoulders and given them a shove.

'Ow!'

'"Ow", she says,' Mrs Quinlan sneered. 'I barely touched you.'

Grace blushed. It hadn't really hurt, she'd just exclaimed out of shock.

'I wasn't expecting it.'

'Then wake up and life won't be full of so many surprises.' Mrs Quinlan gave Adie a nudge over to Rachel. 'Pair up, and start pushing each other. Delilah, you can practice with me. Remember, visualise the energy like a weight pulled tight in a slingshot and, when it's ready, let it go. And take it easy, don't go killing each other.'

By the end of the lesson Grace had twice managed to push Una back a step or two. Una's pushes had somehow become pointed, so that it felt more like being jabbed with a snooker cue than being shoved by the shoulders.

'Ow, *hsssss*,' Grace sucked in a breath and clutched her ribs.

'Aw, sorry,' said Una. 'Was that another sharp one?'

'Yeah. I think they're getting bigger though, that one was less needly.'

Grace overheard Delilah tell Mrs Quinlan that she would stay out a little longer to practise more with Adie. But when Grace asked Adie if she'd like to stay on the pitch and work on the spell, her friend declined.

'My dad's coming to pick me up in a few minutes, sorry. I'd better go meet him at the gates.'

'Okay,' said Grace, disappointed. 'No problem. We can practise tomorrow.'

As Grace walked down the hill, she glanced back at the school in the dark. She saw two figures, one very petite, one with curly hair, hurrying from the school gates towards the woods. It felt like another snooker cue in the ribs.

She found herself veering off towards Dunbridge Park, even though the carnival would be winding down for the night. Bristling at the thought of Adie and Delilah sharing some secret together, she realised she had her own. With a confidence that followed every successful magic lesson, she decided she would begin the girls' mission to help Justine.

Slipping through the tents, she cloaked. Invisible to everyone else and herself, she made her way to the trailer parked farthest from all the others. Justine had pointed it out as the doctor's. There was a dim light inside. The doctor was home.

The door was creaking on its hinges, swaying open, shut, open, shut. Grace realised she could step right into the trailer and the doctor would be none the wiser. Her heart fluttered in her chest; it was nervousness, but also excitement. The doctor scared her, but knowing she could sneak into his home, right under his nose, made her feel powerful. When the door swung wide again, she smoothly took the three steps up and over the threshold. She was in.

He sat at the far end, in a tattered grey armchair with a skinny cigar between his lips. His hat and coat lay on a table to one side, but he still wore his fingerless gloves. The top of his head was bald and scarred, with one red mark running all the way from the top down to his left cheek. He wore small round spectacles and the glass was tinted a dark pink that hid his eyes. He held a cloth-covered volume in his lap, and smoked as he read.

The sight of him shook Grace's confidence and she took a deep, silent breath. Moving her feet daintily, she began to have a look around the trailer, keeping clear of the doctor's corner. If he didn't give the doll to Agata, then he must have hidden it somewhere himself.

There were books everywhere, on shelves, on the table, on the bedside locker, but little else in terms of personal items. Two strange mobiles hung either side of the door, dream-catchers of broken yellow glass that turned with the slightest breeze and sent flashes of mottled light around the trailer. Grace knelt down and looked under the bed. There were a couple of boxes under there – the doll could be have been in either of them – but they weren't well taken care of, and she felt nothing precious lay within. The door of a narrow ward-robe stood ajar. She could see some folded clothing inside, but didn't dare open the door further.

'Polished sanidine may look pretty,' whispered the doctor,

'but it is no friend to the witch.'

Grace's hand shot to her heart. He hadn't raised his head, he couldn't be talking to her. She held her breath and waited. The silence was broken only by the papery scrape of the doctor turning the pages of his book... until he spoke again.

'The yellow light burns through a cloak. Look down, witch.'

Grace glanced down and nearly choked on her own breath. Shards of her were visible. Everywhere the yellow light touched, a piece of her was revealed; part of her thumb, the dark weave of her jumper, a triangle of her hair, a chunk of her leg. Tiny pieces that, put together, made a visible human shape.

Horrified, she threw herself through the door of the trailer and stumbled down the steps. She broke into a run across the park and didn't slow down until she was halfway home. Leaning against a tree for support, she tried to calm the panic racing through her.

He's not chasing you, she told herself, *and he couldn't have made out your face.*

Still, the doctor knew more about witches and witch-craft than she would have liked. To find the doll, she and her friends would have to be much more careful.

✳ ✳ ✳

Old Cat Lady refused to have B-brr around while she was

teaching, so the clever little nymph had remained hidden beneath the folds of Delilah's jumper for the entire lesson, enduring any number of Mrs Quinlan's magical jolts. Now, set free, he perched atop the small girl's head, stretched his tiny limbs, and giggled into the night air. He had caught the creature's scent once more and was guiding the girls with firm tugs on two strands of Delilah's hair that served as reins.

'This way,' Delilah said, 'towards the river.'

'When you said you had a spell...' said Adie.

'I'm sure it'll work, if I can get all the ingredients. It's a really old book too, so the spell will definitely be strong enough.'

'So why are we chasing the non-faery again?'

'We need a hair.'

'A hair. From its head?'

'That would work.'

Adie stopped abruptly.

'Delilah, are you mad? This thing could squash us, and you want to pluck a hair from its head. How are we going to do that?'

Delilah grinned.

'That's the clever part. We play a game.'

'Come again?'

'You said it yourself, this creature thinks we're playing games with it. It enjoys it. So let's play a game.'

'I don't like this.'

'We need a hair in order to do the spell, Adie. There's no way around it.'

✳ ✳ ✳

When they found the creature it was at the water's edge, up to its knees in mud, plucking its feet up one after the other, delighting in the sucking noise as its toes were pulled clear.

'Hello,' Delilah said, her brazenness evident again, 'I've come to play a game.'

Delilah was the decoy, Adie was the striker. She would hold her position, hidden in the shadows, as Delilah played a game of catch that would lead the non-faery closer and closer to the mark. When the moment was right, Adie would snatch a hair and then run like her life depended on it. Which it probably would.

The creature showed no sign of understanding, until Delilah rose into the air and veered back and forth, smiling all the while. It mirrored her at first, hovering above the bank, then grinned widely when Delilah zipped away as it got too close. It began to follow her, clenching its fingers in excitement when Delilah slowed down, letting it nearly catch her. She zipped away again, and the thing somersaulted and clapped in glee. Now it was in the game for real. It could move like nothing Adie had ever seen before and, she suspected, was well able to catch Delilah any time it wanted. But it was enjoying the game, so it followed, grasped at the small girl's heels as she sped away, twirled and chased after her again.

Adie rose into the air in the shade of a large oak, staying hidden behind the trunk. Twice, Delilah had led the creature in that direction, and Adie had even reached out once, but missed by inches. Across the river, Delilah was going for a third attempt. She skimmed over the water, heading straight for the big oak tree, glancing back to ensure the creature remained in the game. She looped around the trunk, a little higher than Adie, and the creature was finally within reach.

Holding onto a branch Adie lurched forward... and missed. She didn't know how, the creature had been right there. But it had vanished, spun away like a feather in a hurricane. Feeling suddenly uneasy, Adie turned and nearly dropped out of the air in fright.

She and the creature were nose to nose. Its huge, round eyes were watery in the starlight, and its skin was too smooth – no pores, no freckles, no blemishes, just smooth grey skin, like paint poured over glass. It bared its teeth and held her gaze, as if trying to determine what role she played in the game. This was it, there wouldn't be another chance.

Bracing herself for the blow that would follow, Adie reached up and plucked a twig-like hair from its head. It came out slowly, then suddenly, like a weed pulled from soil. Flinching, the creature snatched her by the front of her jumper and soared into the air. The speed was unbearable.

Adie's teeth clenched and pain groaned in her chest. She couldn't see; the wind was like a million needles jabbing at her eyes. When they finally slowed, she realised they were higher than she'd ever been before. She couldn't make out the town below, there were just specs of light and dark bits and darker bits and, worst of all, she couldn't breathe. There was no air, at least not enough to fill her lungs. She gasped and gasped while the creature held fast to her jumper and stared with its saucer-like eyes.

Then they were plummeting. Adie wanted to be sick but she wasn't able. It was as if the entire atmosphere was pressing on her from all sides, squashing her into a bullet shape that made their descent even faster. She blacked out for a second but a sudden jerk on her top brought her round and told her she was about to be thrown. They were near the ground when she came to, over the football pitch. She knew she wouldn't survive the fall.

There is nothing like the fear of death to focus your mind and, in that fraction of a second, time slowed to a crawl. Evening dew had settled on the pitch and, in her heightened state of terror, Adie could feel every drop. She raised them all at once, every single bit of water. Her mind reached out and grabbed puddles, rainwater from windows, from leaves nearby, from the roof of the gym. Then the creature let go and Adie fell through the air like an arrow.

She pierced the first circle of water and already she could

feel the drag on her speed. The second circle was smaller, but she had more than enough room to get through. She sailed through the third, fourth and fifth; she was slowing, but the ground was still moving towards her at a horrible pace. The sixth circle she just about fit through, and the seventh was more like being hit with a bucket of water. She clasped her head in her hands, her fist still clenched around that twig-like hair, and curled up as tightly as possible.

The impact was dreadful. It started at her side and reverberated through every bone in her body. She was slammed into a star-shape, her head no longer protected, rolling awkwardly and painfully across the field. Her joints stung as they were twisted into unnatural positions and her skin smarted with deep grazes and bruises that erupted almost immediately.

When it finally stopped she lay still, thankful for the coolness of the grass that did little to ease the pain but made her feel finally safe on solid ground. It was some time before Delilah found her, and Adie remained still until her friend's voice forced her to move.

As far as they could tell, there was nothing broken, but Delilah began applying generous blobs of Choki balm from both their stashes. When Adie shakily got to her feet they searched the sodden grass, and found the little twig hair that had caused all that pain.

✻ ✻ ✻

The new plan was simple. Grace would mind-hop aboard the carnival's alligator, and try to listen in on Drake and the doctor in the hope they would reveal what they had done with the straw doll.

Grace fought to keep her nerves under control. Mind-hopping was still brand new to her, and staring intently at the alligator gave her the willies. The reptile slid comfortably over her feet and she shuddered. But the tension seemed to help the spell. When she finally released her shoulders she hopped aboard the alligator's mind with only a hint of the piercing pain she had felt with the caterpillar.

I'm getting better, she thought.

'Ooh hoo hoo,' Una chuckled, waving her hand close to the alligator's face.

He snapped at her fingers.

'Oh God,' she said, jumping back. 'I forgot you're just piggybacking. The alligator's still the alligator.'

She said the last bit very loud, as if making sure Grace could hear her through the thick skin. She needn't have bothered. Grace could hear everything.

She had seen the animal slither over the ground with some speed before, but right now it was moving slowly as if taking a stroll. It circled the group and Grace had the uneasy experience of seeing herself, expressionless and standing stock still, like a mannequin.

'Don't worry,' Rachel said, patting Grace's body on the

back as the alligator ambled off. 'We'll take good care of you.'

They weren't entirely true to their word. When Grace returned to her body after an unsuccessful piggyback ride around the carnival, she was sporting an eye-patch and a moustache, both drawn in black marker.

'Una!'

'Ah, I couldn't help it. You were standing there all lifeless, waiting to be drawn on. Besides, you were gone for so long we were bound to get bored.'

'Did you overhear anything between the doctor and Drake?' Rachel asked.

'No,' Grace snapped, licking a tissue and scrubbing her face. 'The alligator didn't go anywhere near them. It was the stalls mostly, and the main tent. We'll have to try again.'

Grace mind-hopped a few more times that night, but it wasn't until the following evening that the alligator finally moseyed its way to the doctor's trailer. The reptile scuttled after Drake when he passed in front of it, and Grace had the impression it liked the green-skinned boy. The alligator followed him for some time, around the dining tent, to Agata's trailer, to Drake's performance tent where he set up for the following day's show. After a while Grace was beginning to lose her grip on the alligator's mind, but she clung on for dear life as she watched Drake make his way furtively to the trailer that sat at the very back of the park, away from all the others. When he went inside, the alligator slipped beneath the trailer's wheels as if to wait for him.

At first Grace could hear only indistinct mumbling through the trailer floor, but when the alligator adjusted his position, resting his head against the wheel frame, the mumbling became hollow but much clearer.

'... that little brat, Justine.'

'I'll take care of Justine.'

'You haven't got it in you, lizard boy. You talk tough, but you're as soft and green as your cracked skin.'

'But not you,' Drake snarled.

'One man's heaven is another man's hell, lizard boy, and this life is my hell.' There was a sound like the doctor sucking in air through his teeth. 'If only to break this tedious existence, this endless charade, I'd gladly go out in a fiery blaze, you can count on that. I will be ruthless because I have nothing left to lose.'

'I can be ruthless, just–'

'I tire of this whimpering. The whole plan hinges on the doll, and it is–'

SNAP!

Grace couldn't believe it. She had been straining so hard to hear every word that she hadn't noticed her grasp on the alligator's mind failing. At the crucial moment the connection broke, like an overstretched elastic band, and her mind was flung back through the park, past the stalls and tents and trailers, and into her body with such terrific force that she toppled over.

'Woah,' Una said, rushing to her rescue. 'Are you alright? That was an epic return.'

Out of breath, Grace sat cross-legged on the grass for a few moments.

'Did you get near them this time?' said Rachel.

Grace nodded.

'Great!' said Una. 'So, what's the story? Where's the doll?'

'I got snapped back before I could hear where they'd hidden it,' Grace said, still getting her breath back. 'But they were talking about...'

'About what?' Rachel asked.

Grace shook her head.

'Nothing good.' She climbed to her feet. 'Come on, we should get home. It's late.'

She was crestfallen. Some part of her had held on to the notion that Drake was an innocent, that he was unaware of or had misunderstood whatever devious plan the doctor had made.

I'll take care of Justine. I can be ruthless.

Grace thought of the gentle ballerina, and the casually brutal way Drake had spoken. There was nothing innocent in those words.

14

bLack woRm

Delilah upended her rucksack and emptied the contents onto Adie's bed. She seemed excited.

'Will this work?' asked Adie.

Delilah shrugged.

'We don't know until we try.'

Adie was hoping for something more concrete. Delilah believed she had found a way to single out the clear line from the creature's coloured strands they had seen through the magnesia stone.

'It's something they all have in common, all these entities,' said Delilah as she laid out the ingredients and tools in order on Adie's bed. 'It binds them together. So, it could be a spell or a body or an object. But if we can grab that clear line, it might be like grabbing all of them. Then we might be able to banish it back where it came from.'

'But if we grab it,' Adie said, 'might we break it? If it's holding them together like string around a bunch of flowers, what if we snap it? Wouldn't all those entities be loose on their own?'

Delilah's gaze drifted to the ceiling for a moment.

'No,' she said firmly. 'I don't think so. We're not physically grabbing hold of it, remember. It's more like a spiritual movement. We're just displacing its essence for a minute.'

It all sounded a bit vague, and Adie had the impression that Delilah was enjoying their branching out on their own, researching and casting spells, and just wanted to try something new. But Adie wouldn't complain. She was desperate to try anything, and Delilah seemed sure enough for the both of them.

'Want any snacks, girls?' Adie's mum popped her head around the door. 'I've got some mini-brownies and some chilli peanuts. Very moreish.'

'Mum!' Adie said as Delilah flung the rucksack over the ingredients on the bed. 'You're supposed to knock.'

'Oh, deary me,' her mum said with that over-the-top jolliness that drove Adie mad.

Mrs McMahon shut the door, knocked rhythmically from the outside, then popped her head around once more, grinning widely.

'Just me again! Will you have some snacks? Go on, something sweet. Delilah, can I tempt you?'

'No thanks, Mrs McMahon.'

'Call me Anne, love.'

'Anne. No thanks, I'm not hungry.'

'Adie,' her mother went on, 'are you rumbly in your tumbly?'

'No! Mum, go away, we're working on something for school.'

'Ooh, secret project. Not going to blow up the house with any chemistry stuff, I hope?'

'Mum!' Adie said, exasperated.

'I'm going, I'm going.' Mrs McMahon playfully rolled her eyes. 'Snacks are in the kitchen if you get hungry.'

'Okay!'

Her mother finally left and Adie turned the key in the lock to avoid any more interruptions.

'Sorry,' she said.

'That's okay,' Delilah said. 'Your mum's lovely.'

'When she isn't driving me mental. Have we got everything?'

'Pretty much. All we need is a candle. Something thick that won't fall over easily.'

Adie crossed to the cupboard above her desk and opened the double doors. The shelves inside were packed with candles of all shapes and sizes, all unused. Some were rainbow-coloured and sparkly, some were scented and short. Adie never burned any of them, but she always asked for new ones every birthday and Christmas. The vanilla ones were her favourite.

'Pick one,' she said.

'Which one don't you mind lighting?' Delilah asked.

Adie smiled and picked a plain white church candle, unscented.

With the lamps switched off, the only light in the room was the flickering flame of the candle. Three bowls surrounded it on the carpet. Some brown, herby mush that Delilah had warmed in one bowl smelled slightly rotten. The dish nearest Adie was filled to the brim with grey powder – crushed obsidian, Delilah had said – and the final bowl had just a few crumbs of stale bread and the creature's twig-like hair. The bread was meant to be some special kind of flatbread from the Middle East, but Delilah thought a bit of pitta would work fine.

'I thought you said the spell was in Arabic,' Adie said, glancing at the English verse scribbled on the page on the floor.

'I translated it online and rewrote it a bit. It'll still work,' Delilah replied.

When the bowls were pushed into a perfect equilateral triangle, Adie felt a ripple over the bare skin of her arms. It could have been a cool gust of air, but the window was

173

closed. Delilah held both hands over the candle and recited the verse.

'*One that binds these broken pieces,*
Keeps a hold that ne'er decreases,
Silent, secret, shy and hidden,
Never more, your form is bidden.'

They waited; Adie sitting cross-legged on the floor, and Delilah with her arms held out. They looked at each other as the minutes dragged on and on.

'My arms are getting sore,' said Delilah.

'Then put them down. It didn't work.'

Delilah sat back on her heels and huffed.

'I don't know why. I spent ages picking the leaves off that tiny Little Pyramid plant. Do you know you have to add them individually? And they're minuscule. And we had the obsidian ground really fine and everything.'

'Maybe we shouldn't have used pitta bread.'

Delilah looked despondent and didn't reply.

They cleared up the remains of their spell, emptying the brown gunk and the grey powder into the wastepaper basket in the bathroom. Adie covered it with tissue and hoped no-one would notice the smell.

'I'll keep looking,' Delilah said at the front door. 'There's got be another spell, something similar. I haven't looked through Vera's South American textbooks yet. We'll find something.'

Adie nodded, but couldn't bring herself to say anything in return. She watched Delilah jog across the street in the dark.

'Your friend's not staying for dinner?'

Adie jumped. Her mother was right behind her.

'No, she had to get home.'

'Never mind, my sweet.'

My sweet? Adie turned to give her mum a sarcastic look, but her mother looked down at her with a smile, not a grin, fixed and perfect. The smile didn't reach her eyes, which were wide and round. And, as Adie watched, something black wriggled across her mother's eyeballs, and disappeared.

'Time for dinner, my sweet.'

Adie chewed on the piece of beef in her mouth. She couldn't swallow it. It just got drier and more stringy as she chomped and chomped and tried desperately not to stare at her mother. She drank a big gulp of water, hoping that would help. The meat stuck in her throat momentarily, and she nearly leapt from her seat in panic.

'And the thing is,' her father was telling another boring work story, 'you mix a third colour in there and you're bound to get brown. I tried to explain it to her, I said, "you add another colour in there, you'll always end up with brown. That's the thing with mixing paints." I mean, I'd given her the colour swatches. I said to her, "what more can I do?"'

'Mmm hmm,' his wife replied.

Adie could feel her mother's gaze on her. That fixed smile; that polite response to her dad's endless chatter.

'Of course, she could've just mixed a sample. But, oh no, she had to go dump the whole lot in a great big basin. I said to her, I said, "we can't unmix them now." Do you know what I mean? That's just gone to waste.'

'Mmm hmm.'

Adie's brothers were oblivious. They fought over a set of trump cards – some superhero or other – snapping them off each other, and lying about which cards had come from which packet. Niall had started at St John's that year. Adie had hoped he would suddenly mature now he was in secondary school, but no such luck.

'Can I go to my room?' Adie said. 'I'm finished.'

'You've barely eaten a thing, my sweet.'

Adie had to glance up at those blank eyes, that quick slither of black.

'I'm not hungry. I don't feel well.'

'You don't want some of my lovely apple crumble?' her dad said. 'Podge made the topping, you know.'

'I made the topping,' said Padraic, grinning.

'No, thanks. I'll try some later.'

'Never mind, my sweet.'

It was her dad that said it, and when she looked him in the face, he wasn't her dad. For just a moment, his eyes went wide, there was a flash of black, and then he was back to normal.

'We could take some to school, sister,' said Niall.

She couldn't stop the whimper that escaped her lips. Niall's innocent, freckled face seemed too old, too wicked.

'*Sister*,' Padraic sneered. 'You're so lame, Niall.'

Then it was Padraic, then Niall again, then her dad. Like a maggot wriggling through rotten fruit, it moved around the dinner table, through her family, always fixing its gaze on her.

'Adie, are you alright pet?' her mum asked.

Before Adie could reply, the thing slunk back to her mother once more; the whites of her eyes marred by that tell-tale flick of a black tail.

'Perhaps you should go to bed early, my sweet. Sleep well.'

Adie stumbled off her chair, her hand to her mouth.

She didn't think she'd ever sleep again.

'Una, come on. Jenny will get ticked off if we're late.'

Una took her earphones out and caught up with Grace on the road up to the school.

'Sorry,' she said, 'I was listening to some Heart. Trying to pump myself up for the crime we're about to commit.'

'We're not committing any crime, Una.'

'Are Ms Lemon and Mrs Quinlan aware that you're planning to teach Jenny everything that we learn in magic class?'

'No.'

'And Ms Lemon has expressly forbidded...ed it?'

'Forbidden. Yes, sort of.'

'It's not like you to break the rules, Grace.'

'Yeah, well, when the adults aren't playing fair I think we've a responsibility to break a few rules.'

'Ooh,' Una squealed, patting her on the back, 'get a load of Ms Rebellion.'

Grace tried to scowl, but it came out more like a smile.

They turned left before the school and took the lane that led past the gym to the football pitch. Jenny stood at the halfway point with her arms folded.

'Let's get this show on the road,' she yelled at them.

'Right,' said Grace when they finally reached her, 'what do you want to do first?'

'What have you got?' said Jenny.

'You can crawl into the brain of an animal and look around, but not control it or anything,' Una replied, 'or you can punch people without touching them.'

Jenny grinned.

'I'll take punching, please.'

'I could have guessed,' Grace sighed. 'Okay, it starts in the lower back.'

She explained the spell as best she could, trying not to leave out anything that Mrs Quinlan had said.

'And you have to start small, if we're trying it on each

other. No knocking anybody out because if we have to call an ambulance up here, Ms Lemon and Mrs Quinlan are bound to find out.'

'Don't worry, I'll take it easy on you.'

'You haven't tried it yet,' Grace said, irritated by Jenny's cockiness already, 'so maybe you should wait before you brag.'

'Take a look at these muscles.' Jenny flexed her biceps. 'This spell is made for me.'

'It's not about physical strength, it's—'

The blow was enough to knock Grace off her feet.

'Pow!' Jenny cried. 'First try and it's a knockout.'

Una helped Grace to her feet, brushing stray bits of grass from her jumper.

'I said start small,' Grace snapped. 'I'm not Mrs Quinlan, so cut it out.'

Grace was expecting an apology, but didn't get one. Instead, Jenny shrugged.

'That wasn't intentional,' she said, 'but I guess I'm just *that* good.'

Grace tilted her head.

'Really?'

It wasn't much harder than Jenny's push, but it sent the tall girl rolling. Stopping on her stomach, Jenny snarled.

'I was going easy on you, but maybe we should take this up a notch.'

'Oi, stop,' Una said, 'it's all getting a bit agro here. Anybody wanna listen to some Heart?'

Grace was knocked off her feet and hit the slope at the edge of the field. This one would leave a bruise, she could feel it. Without a moment's thought, she pushed back and Jenny sailed several metres into the air, landing with a thud. When the girl got to her feet, her face was puce.

'Stop it,' Una cried, stepping between them. 'Seriously, stop it. 'Cos one of you is going to get killed and I know I wouldn't handle that very well. I mean it, no more pushing. Shake hands.'

Grace and Jenny both looked at her like she was being ridiculous.

'I don't care if it's lame,' Una said, 'shake hands so I know you're still friends. And that you're not going to kill each other.'

It was impossible not to be amused when Una took things seriously, and Grace could see the shadow of a smile on Jenny's face. She reached out her hand...

Grace awoke several seconds later at the far end of the pitch. It felt like there was a flock of tweeting birds trying to escape from her skull. She sat up, rubbing her temple, and could hear Una shrieking in the distance. She staggered to her feet with every intention of screaming at Jenny, but she could see the tall girl lay at the opposite end of the field, motionless.

Despite the pain in her head, and her weak knees, Grace

ran to the other end of the pitch. It felt like running in slow motion.

Una was frantic. She was pacing around Jenny with her hands to her head, taking out her phone, then putting it back in her pocket.

'I can't wake her!'

Jenny lay absolutely still, her arms and legs splayed at strange angles.

'What happened?' Grace asked.

'What happened?' Una said. 'You both went mental, that's what. Why did you do it? All you had to do was shake hands.'

'That's all I did.'

'Fudgeballs!' Una said, pointing a finger accusingly at Grace. 'You pushed her, and she pushed you. You both did it and you both went flying.'

I did push her, Grace thought, playing the moment back in her mind, *but I didn't mean to.*

Jenny stirred and moaned and Una fell to her knees in relief. She gently took Jenny's head onto her lap, stroking her hair.

'I thought you were dead. Can you talk? What year is it? Count to fifty.'

'I'm alright, Una,' Jenny groaned, sitting up on the grass. 'What...' She glared at Grace. 'You pushed me.'

'I know,' said Grace, 'but I didn't mean to. You pushed me too. Was that on purpose?'

'I... no, no it wasn't. I *felt* something just before it happened.'

'Like you sucked energy out of my hand.'

'Yeah,' said Jenny, rubbing her eye as she looked up.

'I felt the same thing. I somehow took energy from you and it made the push much stronger. You must have done the same.'

'But how? Why?'

'I was really angry,' Grace replied. 'I think that must have been it.'

'Jeez,' said Jenny. 'Did Mrs Quinlan say anything about not getting angry during a push?'

'No, but she did give us a lecture on controlling our emotions in general. I guess they were linked. Sorry I left that bit out.'

'No worries. You okay?'

'I'm grand,' said Grace. 'You pack a mean punch though.'

Jenny smiled.

'You too, Brennan.'

'I love you guys,' Una said, pulling her mp3 player from her pocket. 'And I've got the perfect song for this moment.'

✵ ✵ ✵

It was pouring rain. Adie's curly hair hung in long, straight tails down her back, and she was soaked to the skin.

The downpour hid her tears, and the noise of the wind

hid her sobs. It didn't matter that much. There was nobody about in Wilton Place so late at night, the street was empty. Sneaking out of her house this time had terrified her to her very core. The hours she spent, locked in her room, waiting for her family to switch off the lights and go to bed, dragged on like an eternity. The fear that her weird-eyed mother might come into her room kept her curled up against the wall in one corner of her bed. Her legs had cramped but she hadn't moved for hours. No-one had knocked on her door.

She was overzealous throwing pebbles at Delilah's window, and cracked one of the glass panes. The small girl seemed alarmed when she appeared, waving her arms to tell Adie to stop.

'There's something in my house!' Adie cried when Delilah opened the back door.

'Shh! You'll wake Vera.' Delilah stepped outside and shut the door, pulling her coat over her head. 'What do you mean? What's in your house?'

'I don't know,' Adie sobbed. 'Whatever we conjured. It's in my house. It's in my *mum*.'

Delilah stared and then shook her head.

'Yes!' Adie said, hiccupping with the cries that wouldn't stop. 'There was a black wormy thing in her eyes. And it kept moving. It moved into my brothers, into my dad. What is it, Delilah? What did we do? You said it was an object, or a spell. This isn't a spell. It's alive. Whatever it is, it's alive and it's inside my mum.'

When it came to magic, this was the first time Adie had seen Delilah look completely lost.

'I'm sorry,' the small girl breathed.

'I don't care about sorry,' Adie wailed. 'What do we do?'

'I don't know.'

'You *have* to! We have to do something. Kill it, get rid of it. You have to think of something!'

Delilah stared at nothing and then shook her head.

'We should go to Bob.'

15

RODENTS IN
THE LUNCHROOM

The paths into the woods had all become mud in the storm. Adie and Delilah picked their way through, as if they were walking through treacle.

A thin string of smoke twisted its way from the remains of Bob's fire. He sat next to it, repairing his fishing rod in the rain.

Doesn't he ever sleep? Adie thought.

The two girls sat down awkwardly, sharing the only other stool outside the stone hut. Adie hoped Bob would invite them inside, out of the bad weather, but he spoke without looking up.

'What have you done?'

Adie's chest tightened as she figured out what to say, but Delilah beat her to it.

'I did a recovery spell–'

'*We* did the spell,' Adie interrupted.

'–to pull out an aspect of the creature. We'd seen it in a magnesia stone. It was a clear line wrapped around all these other ones. The creature is not a faery.'

'I know that,' Bob grunted.

'But it's not a single entity even.'

'I know that too.'

Delilah seemed stumped for a moment, and Adie wished she had trusted Bob from the beginning. He had figured out as much as they had, and he had done it without conjuring up any weird black worm.

'What did you recover?' he asked, still working on his fishing line.

'We don't know,' Delilah replied. 'I thought it would be an object, a talisman or something. But whatever it is, it's alive. And… and it's inside Adie's mum.'

Bob looked at the girls for a moment and then nodded his head at the trees to his left.

'And I take it *that* is your mother?'

A figure lurked in the shadows. It chuckled softly and stepped into the clearing. Adie's heart broke when she saw that perfect smile on her mother's face.

'Hello, my sweet.'

Delilah grasped Adie's arm and whispered,

'What is it?'

'That's a witch,' Bob said, finally tying off the line.

'No,' Adie said, 'it's my mum. My mum's not a witch. There's something inside her.'

'That's a witch.'

Adie saw her mother's eyes brighten at something in Bob's hand. It was the jewelled fishing fly. His fingers closed around the purple and silver feathers.

'No,' Adie gasped, lurching forward. 'Don't hurt my mum!'

But she was blown backwards by a powerful blast that singed her arms and pounded her head against the woodland floor. Crawling to her knees, untangling her limbs from Delilah's, she saw her mother hunkered down with one hand on the ground and a look of sheer delight on her face. Bob sat against the wall of the hut, panting, his clenched fist held out against her. Several stones from the hut had come loose or broken. He had hit the wall hard.

'You don't know,' the woman said in a voice that wasn't Adie's mother's, 'how long I have waited to be back in a young body. Look at these arms.' She stretched her arms out like they were spectacular. 'So strong and able. This body is a gift.' She smiled at Bob like he was an old friend. 'And this will be so enjoyable. Let's meet again soon.'

With that, she sprang into the trees with the agility of a cat and disappeared.

Adie and Delilah had to help Bob to his feet. He looked worryingly frail, but shook off their concerns.

'You know what it is,' Adie whispered.

Bob shrugged.

'If the creature is a pet,' he said, 'then that's the owner.'

Adie walked home. Where else could she go?

Delilah had tried to insist she stay at hers, but Adie's family was back in her own house. And that thing was there with them. If it wanted to kill her, there would be nothing she could do about it, no matter where she was. Better she be with her mum, dad and brothers.

The thing hadn't gone home quietly. At the entrance of the woods several trees had been ripped clean out of the ground. Two Garda cars were parked next to a hole in the tarmac off North Street. It looked like the road had buckled under some huge weight, and discoloured water spewed out like a fountain. And as Adie approached her own street she saw a lamppost bent over, like an old man, its light flickering and buzzing.

Her heart thumped as she turned the key in the front door. The hall light was off but she could see straight through to the kitchen. Her mother stood at the counter, staring out the window. For a few moments Adie dared to hope that the thing had abandoned her mother's body, that it had found

188

someone else, someone she didn't know.

'So you followed me…' it said, still staring into the night.

'Where else could I go?'

Adie wanted to switch on the kitchen light but she was too afraid. The thing chuckled.

'Not you.'

Adie looked past her mother, through the window, to the treehouse at the end of the garden. The twig-haired creature sat there, its long fingers curled around a branch. It looked serene.

'It got out,' her mother said. 'Clever thing.'

'It was me,' Adie's eyes were stinging with tears. 'I brought it here.'

'Goodness, my sweet.' The thing that was her mother turned and gently put one finger under Adie's chin and stared into her eyes. 'You do like trouble.'

It swept past her and went upstairs. In the dark, Adie continued to watch the creature in the treehouse, as tears rolled silently down her face.

Adie sat in the corner of the lunchroom, chewing on her cheese sandwich. She was so distracted she didn't even notice her brother plop down in the chair beside her.

'Tell me more,' he said, making her jump, 'of this witch in the woods.'

Pained, she turned to Niall just in time to catch the black flick over the whites of his eyes. The thing had followed her to school.

'Leave me alone. Please.'

Niall propped his chin on his thumb, in a way Niall would never do.

'I assume he lives there, in that little shack. *Quel mystère*, when he could crush you all like ants. I wonder what makes him tick.'

Niall looked to her as if expecting an answer. Adie tried to react as little as possible.

'I don't know.'

'He permits you and your friend to sit with him, share his space. He has affection for you?'

'Not really. I don't think so.'

'Then what does he care for?'

'I couldn't tell you.'

Niall's wide, flickering eyes bored into her. He was so close she felt like she was suffocating.

'No matter,' he said finally. 'I can always kill *you*. Perhaps that will provoke him.'

He said it so casually, Adie felt physically sick.

'Hey, Adie, where ya been?' Una marched into the room and flung her bag on the desk in front of them. ''Sup Niall? You don't usually eat in here. Did they kick you out of your own lunchroom?'

Niall made no answer and, luckily, Grace and Rachel showed up to break the silence.

'You weren't in Irish this morning, Adie,' Grace said, concerned. 'Are you okay?'

'I was in the toilets.' The words came out of Adie's throat with a croak. 'I wasn't feeling well.'

'Aw, you poor thing,' said Una. 'You should tell a teacher and go home. Sit on the sofa and watch bad telly.'

'I'm alright now.'

'Hey, Niall,' said Rachel. 'How's your first year going?'

'Have you got any bullies yet?' Una asked. ''Cos if you do, point them out and we'll take care of them.'

She punched her hand and grimaced like a boxer.

'Unless it's Tracy Murphy,' said Rachel. 'Then we'll just run away, and you should too.'

'I can handle the Beast,' Una growled, punching her hand again.

'She's behind you.'

Una jumped and spun around on the desk. There was no-one there.

'Oh, you're hilarious, Rach. You should be on stage.' She suddenly poked Niall in the arm. 'So come on, tell us how it's going? Have you made lots of friends?'

Niall stood up to leave.

'Are you leaving already? Ah, come on,' Una playfully punched him in the ribs, 'tell us all about it.'

Water suddenly spurted from Grace's bottle, hitting her in the face. At the same moment, a dozen mice erupted from the table and scattered in all directions, sending the girls screeching and leaping onto chairs in fright.

'Adie!' Grace cried, as Niall slunk out through the door. 'What the hell?'

Adie shook her head helplessly. She wanted to scream, *it wasn't me!* but the words wouldn't come out. She felt dizzy. Grabbing her bag, she ran for the door leaving the others staring after her.

✳ ✳ ✳

'But *why* would Adie spray water at you? That's not like her,' Una said as Grace checked through her bag for mice.

'Water's her thing. Who else could have done it? Was it you?'

'No, I'm not that good.'

'Wasn't me either,' said Rachel, 'in case you were wondering.'

'If it was Adie,' said Una, 'she's getting really good at origination. That was a whole load of mice at once. I can only do one. Could you do a whole load at once, Grace?'

Grace shrugged, still digging in her bag. She didn't know what was worse, that one of her best friends might have attacked her with water and rodents, or that she felt a stab of jealousy at the thought of Adie bettering her at origination.

'She's keeping secrets,' said Grace. 'And she's visiting Bob.'

'What? When?' said Rachel.

'The other night, when she bunked off mind-hopping class. I saw her walking away from his camp when I was mind-hopping on that fox.'

'You didn't mention it on the way home.'

'I was too busy trying not to throw up. Then I thought... well, I thought maybe it was none of my business. But why did she lie?'

'Do you think she's getting extra magic lessons from him?' asked Una.

'I don't know. But it looked like she was walking off in a huff that night.'

'Maybe she asked him to teach her magic, and he told her to get lost.'

'Maybe.'

'That doesn't make sense,' said Rachel. 'Jenny's the one who got kicked out of magic class, not Adie. Now, if it had been Jenny storming off, then I'd be ready to believe it.'

'Me too,' said Una. 'Jenny could storm off for Ireland. She's got that temper.'

'Whatever the reason,' said Grace, 'whatever she's talking to Bob about, I don't think we should tell her about helping Justine. If she tells Bob, we might get in trouble.'

'Yeah,' agreed Una. 'Adults are always overreacting. Anyway, I think I'd freak out if Bob turned up at school one day to give out to us. I mean, he's the creature from the demon lagoon.'

'It's not his fault he was thrown down the demon well, Una.'

'No, but he was down there for ages. That's gotta do things to your brain.'

Grace couldn't argue with that. Remembering Bob's face when he emerged from the well gave her shivers down her spine. How could somebody be right in the head after spending decades in hell?

'Delilah!'

Grace caught up with the small girl in the corridor after the bell rang to signal the end of lunchtime. Delilah looked as she did when she started at the school the year before. Her shoulders were hunched, her bag looked like it weighed a ton, and she glanced around warily as if the Beast could pounce on her at any moment.

'Where've you been?' said Grace, falling into step beside her. 'Haven't seen you at the carnival for a while.'

'I've had some stuff to do. Have you seen Adie today?'

'Yeah. She threw water in my face.'

'She did what?'

'Threw water in my face. Then originated a load of mice. Then she ran out of the room. I mean, I know that's not like

her, but it wasn't me or Una or Rach, so it had to be Adie.'
Grace shook her head. 'There's something big going on with
her, but I don't know what. I wish she'd talk to us. Do you
know what's going on?'

Delilah's big, brown eyes were wide.

'Was her mum there?'

'No, no, no, this was in our lunchroom, just now. Why? Is
something wrong with her mum?'

Delilah's complexion seemed to pale for a moment.

'No. I don't know what's wrong with Adie, but I'm sure
she'll be better soon.'

Grace could see Delilah knew more than she was telling
but she didn't dare push it any further.

'Okay. Well, I'll talk to her later, I guess. And listen, since
you haven't been around the carnival,' Grace lowered her
voice to a whisper, 'we found out that something's been
stolen from Justine and the others. Something really important. And we're going to help them out.'

Delilah stopped abruptly.

'Help them out, how?'

'Nothing big. It's just mind-hopping and things like that.
But we were thinking, you could help us research a spell
for–'

'No! No spells.'

'It's alright, Delilah, we're being careful.'

'It doesn't matter. You don't know what you're doing.

195

You might do something terrible and not even know it. You might...'

'What are you talking about?'

'You can't do any spells outside of class. You just can't. It's too dangerous.'

Grace was so taken aback she laughed out loud.

'What do you mean? You're the queen of doing magic outside class. You're always up for this stuff, Delilah. And we need you. You know more than any of us. And, as I said, we're being really careful–'

'No!' Delilah leaned close and Grace could swear there was fear in her eyes. 'If you start doing magic in the carnival, I'll tell Vera.'

'*What?*'

'I mean it.'

Grace stared at the small girl. It was as if she was a stranger.

'Promise me,' Delilah said, leaning even closer. 'Promise me you won't do it.'

They stared at each other, one emphatic, the other non-plussed. Finally, Grace nodded her head.

'Okay, I promise.'

'Pinky swear.'

Delilah held out her little finger, as if this would cement Grace's vow. Grace linked it with her own little finger, shaking the fingers up and down together. The small girl seemed relieved.

'Good,' she said, smiling for the first time.

Grace didn't follow her to the main hall, instead she back-tracked through the A block and up to the C block where Una and Rachel stood outside their classroom, waiting to go in. Grace was breathless by the time she got there.

'Delilah said she'd squeal to Mrs Quinlan if we do any magic outside class.'

'Are you serious?' cried Rachel. 'You can't be serious.'

Still panting, Grace nodded. Una spread her hands in disbelief.

'Has the whole world gone mad?'

It felt like it had. Grace was always the one to follow the rules and discourage any bad behaviour in the group. But since Mrs Quinlan expelled Jenny, and Ms Lemon let it happen, she didn't feel so beholden to the adults' rules anymore. In contrast, Delilah grew up with magic, and practising it for only a few hours each week never seemed natural to her – she was always up for doing more. But now Delilah was threatening to snitch on any extracurricular witchcraft, and Grace felt no guilt whatsoever in disobeying the rules. Things really were upside down.

'We're still gonna help Justine though, right?' Rachel asked.

'Yeah, we are,' replied Grace.

'Woohoo!' said Una.

'But we have to keep it quiet. From Delilah, from Adie...'

'And from Jenny,' said Rachel.

'While she's still close to Agata, yeah,' said Grace.

There was silence for a few moments.

'It feels like we're getting divorced,' said Una.

'Six people can't get married,' said Grace. 'And they can't get divorced.'

'Still, that's what it feels like.'

They followed their class sombrely into the room, and Grace knew what Una meant.

16

back in the box

Adie had loved that treehouse. It had been built for her when she was tiny, too small to climb up by herself, and it remained the place she ran to when she wanted comfort. Now the twiggy creature had invaded it. It sat in the entrance, its long fingers curled around a branch, watching the kitchen window with those huge eyes. Adie ran a hand over the ribs that still ached from her fall back to Earth.

'Mammy, what's for dinner?'

Adie turned to see Padraic in the doorway and her mother, watching her from the kitchen table. She hadn't realised the woman was there.

'Mammy?' Padraic said again.

'Leave, little boy,' the woman said, not taking her eyes from Adie. 'You're tedious.'

Padraic looked confused but didn't move. Finally the woman turned to look at him, and Adie saw an angry flash of black in her eyes.

'I said, *leave*.'

'We're getting pizza tonight, Podge,' Adie said quickly. 'You can take the money out of mum's purse. Tell dad that mum said it was okay.'

'Cool!' Padraic danced into the hallway.

'Very diplomatic, my sweet,' said the woman. 'You saved his neck. This time.'

Adie struggled to remain calm, but she couldn't stop the shaking in her voice.

'It's in the treehouse again.'

'I see it.'

'The boys play in the back garden, and dad looks after the flower beds. They'll see it eventually. It might start playing games with them, it might hurt one of them.'

Her mother smiled like the thought was a pleasant one.

'It might.'

'I know things about Bob. I know where he came from, how he learned the craft, why he's in the woods. I'll tell you stuff if you get rid of that thing in the treehouse.'

'Bargaining, my sweet?' Her mother laughed. 'I could drag the information out of you, along with your blood and entrails.'

'I'm stronger than you think, I could hold out—' More

laughter broke over Adie's declaration, but she refused to give in. 'Torture me if you want, but wouldn't it be easier this way? Just get rid of it and I'll tell you anything you want to know.'

Black worms swam over the whites of her mother's eyes. She looked amused.

'You know, I may start to like you, my sweet.' She rose and walked to the window. 'And as it happens, it is about time my little boo went home.'

Adie knew Bob's history, about his growing up in Black-wood Manor and the cursing of his home by a resentful witch. She knew he had served time as that witch's familiar, and that he had remained in the woods after her death. She also knew that, in his efforts to save others, he had been trapped down the demon well for decades. She knew he was essentially a good man, but she had no idea how powerful he was, what drove him, who he cared about. Adie decided she would tell her mother nothing about the demon well – God only knows what that thing might do if it knew there was one in Dunbridge – but she was willing to surrender every other detail she knew about Bob's life. She hoped none of it would be useful to her. She agreed to deliver the information as soon as the creature was out of the treehouse and away from her family.

So she was surprised when her mother took her by the arm, led her out of the house, across the town and towards Dunbridge Park. Out of the corner of her eye, she saw twiggy hair dancing through the trees that lined the streets. The creature was following them.

There was a familiar brash clashing of sound as they approached the park; the tumbling harpsichord notes, the *ching-ching* of coins pouring out of hands into purses, and out of purses into hands, the whoops and hollers as someone won a big prize at the coconut shy, and the enticing calls of the game operators. Adie didn't ask why they had come to the carnival, she just followed her mother obediently to a pale blue tent in the far corner. They stood outside the tent, a table and bed behind the tarpaulin silhouetted by the light inside.

'Into the box,' the woman said, almost to herself.

Within seconds Adie saw the twig-haired creature creep into the tent. She then watched its silhouette as it climbed onto the tabletop, opened the small box that lay there, and stepped inside. Even as Adie watched, she couldn't understand it. The creature's entire body had somehow disappeared into that small box. The lid snapped shut.

'There,' her mother turned to face her. 'Now, I believe you have information to give me.'

But before Adie could open her mouth, another figure entered the tent. Adie saw his silhouette take off his top hat and rub at his forehead. He picked up something from the bed and seemed ready to leave when he suddenly paused. The figure moved to the table and knocked gently on the box. The lid swung open and Adie expected the creature to spring out of it. But it didn't. Nothing happened. The man stared down at the box for a while, then quietly shut the lid and left the tent.

'I'm waiting.'

Adie looked up into the wide eyes that weren't her mum's, and began telling Bob's story.

Grace waited at the ferris wheel, checking her watch. Rachel and Una were late. The girls were making one last attempt at eavesdropping on the doctor and Drake, and Grace was tempted to mind-hop the alligator before her friends arrived. But the idea of leaving her mindless body alone was a little too daunting. She sighed and checked her watch again.

The main show must be starting up in the big tent by now, but she noticed a figure in a wide-brimmed hat slipping through the red-and-white tarpaulin across the park.

The doctor.

Without thinking, she followed. He kept to the shadows, and so did she, leaving plenty of space between them. She didn't want him catching her scent. He slunk between trailers, appearing suddenly much further ahead, and kept moving until he reached a pale blue tent. It wasn't one of the performance ones, so it had to be somebody's home, she didn't know whose. She watched him circle the tent to the back, then felt a hand on her shoulder.

'What are you doing all the way over here?'

Drake was smiling, as if amused that she was lost. She had no idea if he'd seen who she was following.

'I'm just waiting for Rach and Una.'

'Funny place to meet.'

'I got bored, I was just... having a look around.'

'I'll walk back to the stalls with you, if you want.'

'Thanks.'

He glanced at her as they walked, smiling all the time, but she couldn't bring herself to smile back.

'Listen,' he said at last, 'I wanted to say something to you. It's...'

He stared off into the carnival lights and the green skin of his cheeks flushed a little darker. She thought he must be blushing. He smiled again, shyly this time.

'I like you, and I wish I could get to know you better but... we're not gonna be here much longer.'

'You're leaving? When?'

'Can't say exactly, but it's gonna be soon.'

She looked into his blue, blue eyes and tried not to find them lovely.

'Everyone's going? Justine too?'

The smile slowly vanished.

'Yeah. Justine too.'

'I'm sorry to hear that,' Grace said. 'I really like Justine.'

He dug at the ground with the toe of his shoe. She couldn't tell if he was angry or disappointed or both.

'Yeah, well,' he said, 'see you round.'

He turned and walked away, and she let him.

The ringmaster removed the straw doll from its wooden case, turned down the flame of each oil lamp and blew them out. He sat on a stool, pulling a bookcase forward to hide his presence from the tent entrance. The doll rested on his lap.

He was puzzled. Where had it gone when it went missing, and how had it got back? Sweat from his palms seeped into the woven strands of straw. The silence dragged on until a figure snuck quietly into the tent. The ringmaster held his breath.

The sneaking shadow wore a long dark coat and wide-brimmed hat. He grabbed the box on the table. Opening the lid, he gasped.

'Looking for this?'

The ringmaster struck a match off the doll's belly, and held the light aloft.

'You knew I'd come for it,' the doctor said.

'I did. In fact, I thought you already had... But never mind that now. I've caught you red-handed. Everything is arranged, and I am going to set us free.'

The doctor took a menacing step forward, but dark shapes crawled out from beneath the bed, from under the table, from folds in the tent walls. They wore glumly coloured silk suits and painted faces, and they encircled the man before he could move another inch.

'They won't be enough.' The doctor's face was nearly obscured beneath the brim of his hat.

'Then I'll cue my secret weapon, shall I?' said the ring-master.

'Me first!'

Sparks flew from the doctor's hands and two Melancholy Clowns were sent flying over the table. Two more grappled him to the floor, but the sound of hissing from the doctor's sleeves threatened more fireworks.

'Sing, dammit, sing!' the ringmaster cried, as he leapt to his feet.

From outside, a perfect harmonious melody drifted through the air. Two voices sang a song of devastating sorrow, high and sweet and haunting. The searing notes weakened Felix's knees and he stumbled against the chair for support

'Feel that, fool?' sneered the ringmaster. 'That's your doom.'

The doctor's strength faded, but he realised the clowns were not bothered by the sound. The ringmaster grinned at him as he grabbed a walking stick from beside the bed and struggled to his feet.

'My melancholy friends have never been much affected by the boys' music.' His breath wheezed with the effort of moving. 'Indeed, they've never been much affected by anything at all.'

Outside, in the cool night air the twin boys sat on a bench, swinging their feet as they sang their sad song and watching the doctor being dragged from the tent by the Melancholy Clowns. Drake was waiting, nearly on his knees, the music like a weight on his shoulders.

'I'm sorry, doctor,' he whispered, 'I didn't know they were already in there.'

Two of the Melancholy Clowns silently pushed him to the ground, tying his hands behind his back with grey scarves.

'Get Agata, too,' the ringmaster said. 'Keep them all in the cart until the thing is done.'

Some time later, when the song had stopped, the ringmaster strolled back and forth in front of a cart enclosed with metal bars. Inside sat the doctor, smoking a skinny cigar, while Drake growled and cursed, and Agata moaned with her head in her hands.

'It's gonna happen, isn't it, Felix?' said the bearded girl who watched from a safe distance.

'It sure is, honey,' the ringmaster replied. 'It sure is.'

17

down in THE sewers

Justine seemed troubled. She paced back and forth in her tent, taking heaving breaths with one hand on her belly.

'Justine?' Grace said, ducking under the tarpaulin door. 'Are you okay?'

The ballerina nodded. She smiled shakily at Rachel and Una as they entered the tent.

'I'm okay, honey, thanks. But... I think I know where the doctor and the others have hidden the doll.'

'Where?'

Justine opened the jewellery case on her dressing table and took out a crumpled sheet of paper. Opening it up, she placed it on the bed where the girls could take a good look.

'It's a map,' she said.

'Oh yeah,' said Una, 'It's the town. Look, there's North

Street.'

'And that,' Justine said, tracing her finger from word to word, 'is Drake's handwriting.'

Grace felt a twist in her stomach. 'Are you sure?'

'Umm-hmm.'

Clunk. Another twist. 'Where did you get this?'

Justine smiled as if she couldn't believe it herself.

'I searched the doctor's trailer.'

'What? On your own? What if he'd caught you?'

'I had to do something. I was so scared, but he never came. I got in and out without anyone seeing. Honestly, sweetheart, I'm okay.'

Grace forced herself to read and re-read the scrawled handwriting.

'We don't know if this shows where the doll is, though. This could be a map to nothing.'

'Why draw a map that leads to nothing?' said Rachel. 'And, anyway, there's an X.'

Grace's disappointment swelled inside her like a rotten balloon.

'I was gonna go get it now,' Justine said shyly, 'but I've got a show. If I miss a performance, the doctor will know something's up.'

'We'll go get it,' Grace replied.

'Are you sure?'

'We know the town, and we can stay hidden.' Grace lifted

her head but couldn't bring herself to smile. 'It's better if we get it.'

'I gotta confess, I was hoping you would say that. I can't thank you guys enough.'

'No thanks required,' Una said, bouncing off the bed.

'Oh there'll be thanks,' the ballerina said. 'You bring that doll back here and you can stay on the ferris wheel as long as you like, play any of the stalls for free, watch the shows... This carnival will be your playground for as along as you want.'

'That sounds pretty good, doesn't it Rach? Grace?'

Rachel nodded enthusiastically, but Grace simply followed the others from the tent, scrunching the map into her jacket pocket.

* * *

Grace smoothed out the crinkled map as best she could, but the smudged writing made it difficult to follow.

'It's off Macken Street anyway,' she said, 'past the library towards the river. What's that little alleyway called where they used to have the flea market years ago?'

'Gallows Lane,' Rachel replied, turning up her collar against the spitting rain.

'Euch,' Una said. 'That place is grim.'

'Then it fits, doesn't it? The perfect spot for two fiendish baddies to hide their loot.'

'One fiendish baddie,' Grace corrected. 'And Drake.'

'Oh, yeah,' Rachel replied, not meeting her eye. 'I forgot he was an innocent victim.'

Grace let the comment go as the three girls traipsed down North Street in the miserable weather. There was a small part of her that hoped they wouldn't find the doll, and that Drake's involvement was still some kind of misunderstanding.

I can be ruthless.

She shook her head as if she could knock Drake's words out of it. She couldn't.

They turned down Macken Street and slowed when they approached the turn-off for Gallows Lane.

'Check the windows too,' Grace said, 'in case anyone's looking out.'

They scoped out the street and, when the coast was clear, they each turned down the lane and cloaked.

'Ow!' Una gasped.

'Sorry,' said Rachel, 'was that your foot?'

'Watch where you're going, will you?'

'I can watch where I'm going all day, Una, but I can't watch where *you're* going. You're invisible too, remember?'

'Shh,' hissed Grace. 'Keep it down. They could be here.'

They had a prearranged signal, that Grace pick up and drop a pebble when she reached the spot. Which she did, opposite an empty space in the lane. There were rundown buildings all along the alleyway, except for this one spot.

It looked like the building had been demolished, probably because it had already begun to collapse, and now there were just piles of rubble.

Grace uncloaked and held the map up to the light.

'I don't get it,' she said. 'This is it. This is the spot.'

'So we're uncloaking then,' Una said, reappearing.

'Yeah, because this is where the map points to. Except there's nothing here.'

Rachel appeared, staring up at where the building should have been.

'Maybe they crouch down behind the rubble when they meet. Are you sure it's here?'

'Yes,' Grace snapped, 'X marks the spot.'

'Maybe X just marks near the spot,' Una said, snatching the map to scrutinise it.

'Or maybe,' Rachel said, looking down at Grace's shoes, 'X does mark the spot.'

Grace looked down and saw she was standing on the grate of a sewer drain.

'Oh... oh, okay.'

'Just so you know,' said Rachel, 'I'm not going down there. This top is new.'

'And I'm not going down there,' Una said, 'because it'll be smelly and also probably scary.'

'What?' Grace exclaimed. 'You're both going down there. I'm not going on my own.'

'Do you know how much this cost?' said Rachel, pulling on the front of her shirt.

'I don't care.'

'The patches on these boots are suede. The stains will never come out.'

'Then hover and keep your feet off the ground.'

'I can't do that and cloak at the same time. If I lose my concentration I'll fall in.'

'Then walk on the bloody ground. Seriously, Rach, we came here to get the doll and that's what we're going to do.'

'But can I stay out here because I'm scared?' said Una.

'No!'

'Alright, alright, don't pop a blood vessel in your eye.'

Grace took a deep breath to calm herself, then knelt to pull up the grate. It was very heavy, but didn't stick. It had been opened recently.

'Cloak as soon as you're inside,' she said, lowering her feet into the drain.

'That won't keep my shirt clean.'

'Rach!'

'I'm getting in,' Rachel huffed. 'What more do you want?'

Grace lowered herself inside the drain and found metal footholds embedded in the concrete. About three metres down she stepped onto a stone ledge. The tunnel was big enough for her to stand up straight, but the ledge was worryingly narrow. Dark water flowed next to it; she tried to imagine it was just a little stream, but the foul odour was unmistakeable. She cloaked, hoping that would somehow shield her from the smell.

'Oh my God, that's disgusting.' Rachel was nearly to the ledge.

'Be quiet,' said Grace. 'And cloak.'

'You'll owe me a new pair of boots after this.'

The tunnel was blocked to the right by a stone wall that reached nearly to the ceiling, the foul water flowing through a gap underneath. Grace ignored Rachel's complaining and moved along the ledge to the left. There was very little light, the darkness punctuated only by daylight that came through drain grates further along the road above. A couple of times, Grace's foot slipped in something and she nearly toppled into the icky stream, saved only by throwing herself against the stone wall that was slick with damp. She didn't check the ledge to see what it was she had slipped on. Gulping, and breathing through her mouth, she crept further and further into the sewer, hearing the occasional grunt and scuffle of feet behind her.

Suddenly the tunnel veered right. Grace stopped short. It widened considerably at the corner, and the ledge on her side grew into a triangular concrete platform. She inched forward and peered into the murky light. Several stones had been knocked out of the wall at hip height, making a shallow shelf. Tucked into the shelf, was the doll.

Even from some distance she could see the frayed straw ends that served as hands and feet. It looked to have been hastily made, with bits of wire holding it together at the joints, and stray strands poking out from the face and belly. The doll was pretty, in a homemade kind of way.

'Wow,' Rachel breathed behind her, 'is that it?'

Grace took a few more steps, then halted. Rachel banged into her from behind.

'What are you doing?' she said. 'No-one's around. Go and get it.'

'Wait here.'

The others didn't need to follow, and then they wouldn't bump into each other again, but that wasn't what made Grace say it. Getting closer to the doll, she didn't find it so pretty anymore. There was something unpleasant about it. She couldn't put her finger on it, but it looked *mean*.

That makes no sense, she thought, and forced herself to go on.

The feeling got worse the closer she got. It wasn't just mean anymore. The doll was ugly. Those golden strands seemed like sandy worms up close, and even appeared to slither over each other, making slimy sounds.

She stepped onto the triangular platform and started to reach for the doll. She couldn't do it. It was revolting. It was the most hideous thing she had ever seen. She didn't want to take it.

'What are you doing?' Rachel's strained whisper came from back down the tunnel. 'Pick it up and let's go.'

Grace stared at the doll, and its face grimaced back at her from the nest of worms that knotted and unknotted, wriggling and squirming.

'I don't… something's wrong.'

'Put the pedal to the metal, Grace,' said Una, 'we're on a schedule here.'

'Grace, pick it up for God's sake,' said Rachel.

'Grace, have you gone hard of hearing? Just pick up the stupid thing. The baddies could show up any minute, and it *smells* down here!'

Silence.

'Come on, Grace,' said Una.

'Grace, pick it up!' said Rachel.

Grace grabbed the doll and felt her stomach heave. She couldn't hold on to her cloaking spell and dropped it as she worked her way along the ledge.

'Eh,' said Una, 'we're supposed to be incognito.'

'Move!' Grace replied with an aggression that surprised herself.

'Okay, okay, we're moving. What's got into you?'

Rachel and Una uncloaked and scuttled along the ledge, getting no reply from Grace. They crawled out of the drain and into the twilight descending on the town. For a moment Grace felt better, but one glance at the doll made her feel sick again.

'Let's get to the carnival and get rid of this thing.'

Rachel and Una exchanged glances, but said nothing. With Grace setting the pace, they walked, then jogged, then ran towards Dunbridge Park.

The park was empty. There were flattened circles of grass, and muddy patches, and thick tyre tracks – but that was all that remained of the carnival.

'I don't understand,' said Rachel, looking around. 'Where are they?'

Una thumped her heel into one of the postholes left by a signpost.

'Well, that's rude! We went to all that trouble to get their doll back, and they went and scarpered.'

Grace stood in mud, clutching the doll to her belly, with the inexplicable sensation that she was holding a bag full of squirming worms.

'Maybe the doctor and Drake did this,' said Rachel. 'Took over the carnival and forced them to leave.'

'No-one forced them to leave,' Grace whispered.

'What?'

Grace spoke louder this time.

'We have to get rid of the doll. Now.'

'Okay, then just leave it here.'

'No, not where someone else could find it.'

'Why not?' asked Una.

'Because it's not just a straw doll.'

'Then what is it?'

'Something bad. We need help.'

'Ms Lemon's place is that way,' said Rachel.

'No,' replied Grace, 'to Mrs Quinlan's.'

She had a feeling that whatever badness the girls had landed themselves with, the Old Cat Lady would put up a good fight.

✳ ✳ ✳

Adie and Delilah hurried through town.

'I don't think this is a good idea,' Delilah said, breathless.

'The creature is her pet,' Adie replied. 'It might be the only leverage we have.'

'But you don't know it's safe to take it, just because it's in a small box–'

'She ordered it in, like it was supposed to stay there. I don't think it can leave the box now. If we take it, hide it somewhere, we could use it against her.'

'What if she doesn't care about it? For all we know, it means nothing to her.'

'She could have killed it, but she didn't. She put it safe inside some box. Trust me, she feels something for it.'

'Adie, last time we tried to do something on our own we

summoned that thing that took over your mother.'

Adie didn't respond to this. It was getting harder and harder to think of her mother's face without feeling afraid, and the urgency she felt now was more about seeing her mum's jolly grin again and hearing her bad jokes than it was about saving the town.

Even before they reached Dunbridge Park, she saw it was empty. She had been watching for the great curve of the ferris wheel, the clashing of loud music and the lights flaring as evening fell. But it was quiet, the trees surrounding the park hid no lights behind, and the giant wheel was nowhere to be seen.

Adie sprinted ahead, leaving Delilah gasping behind her.

'No!' she said, tripping into one of the wide tracks left by the trucks. 'It can't be gone. It's all we had!'

Delilah finally caught up and grasped Adie's arm.

'I don't get it,' she said. 'Why would they leave so suddenly?'

Adie just shook her head helplessly.

They stood there, alone in the park, for the longest time; Adie too crestfallen to go, and Delilah reluctant to leave her friend. The stars were coming out when they saw a figure in the gloom. It was rushing across the grass towards them. He was very close by the time Adie spotted his green skin. His hair was damp with sweat and he was nearly keeling over with exhaustion.

'Where are your friends?' he panted.

Still rude, Adie thought.

'They're not with us,' she answered dully.

'Why?' Delilah said in a much more accommodating tone. 'What's wrong?'

'They were set up,' Drake said, still gasping for breath, 'by Justine. They were sent to take something from me and the doctor, a doll that Justine said we had stolen. But that's not it at all...'

He bent over as if about to throw up and Delilah hurried to rub his back.

'Just breathe,' she said. 'Calm down, or you'll be sick.'

He shook off her arm, determined to continue.

'We're cursed,' he said, 'all of us, the whole carnival. By this sorceress, Murdrina. Grigori upset her and she hexed us, and the only way for us to be free is if someone takes the hex, willingly.'

'How do you take a hex?' Adie wondered aloud, and then caught herself. 'I mean... What is a hex?'

Drake raised one eyebrow.

'Don't pretend. They know you're witches, Grigori saw it in your cards. And hell, that only made 'em more determined for you to take on the curse. The hex is a doll, a simple, little straw doll. All they needed – Felix, Justine, all of them – was for someone to take it willingly. But that's the kick. It looks harmless, but no-one would ever steal it. Felix tried to give it away so many times; he'd hand it over, still inside this pretty wooden box, and people would tell him to go hang. It drove him crazy.'

Adie felt the strangest sensation of fear mixed with anger mixed with just a tinge of relief. She had not dragged the creature into this world. It had been nothing to do with her all along.

'Why wouldn't anyone take it?' said Delilah.

'Get close to the thing and you'll know why. Inside a box or not, you can tell it ain't right,' Drake replied.

'That creature?' Adie exclaimed. 'It's been out, playing games, hurting people. And all this time I thought it was my fault.'

'Out?' Drake said. 'You mean you saw it?'

'We've been beaten up by it!'

'I don't get it, it's just a doll. How could it—'

'I don't care how it happened, the point is I thought this whole time that I was to blame for all of this, but it's you. It's you people.'

'*We people*?' Drake's expression hardened.

Adie looked as if she might cry.

'Everything was great until your stupid carnival came here.' She turned to leave. 'Now I have to find my friends before it's too late.'

'It's already too late, don't you get it?' Drake snapped. 'The carnival was able to leave town the second somebody else picked up that doll. The carnival is free because your friends have taken on the curse.'

'And you just let it happen?!'

'I've been locked up! They dragged me out of town with them. I had to dislocate both shoulders to escape the jailcart, and I ran the whole way back.'

There was a long pause as all of this sank in.

'You stay here,' Adie said finally, 'in case Grace and the others come to the park looking for the carnival. Delilah and I will search for them outside.'

'What are you going to do? There's nothing you can do.'

'Like you said, we're witches. We'll fix this.'

Adie marched out of the park with Delilah scurrying after her.

'Are we?' the small girl asked. 'Going to fix this? Because I don't know how, do you? And you didn't tell him about Murdrina. That's who we summoned, Adie.'

'I know that.'

'We couldn't beat her pet, and we can't beat her. If Grace and the others already have the doll, what can you do about it?'

'I can take it from them.'

18

Too many doors

'There they are,' Adie said, spotting the girls on Mrs Quinlan's porch in the distance. 'Thank God for that.'

Adie and Delilah made their way into Wilton Place with relief. They saw Mrs Quinlan open the door and appear to speak gruffly to the girls. Then Delilah pointed.

'What's that?' she said. 'Grace is holding something.'

They started jogging towards the cul-de-sac, speeding up as panic gripped Adie's heart.

'It's the doll!'

Both girls broke into a sprint, waving their hands and yelling. But Mrs Quinlan had already snatched the doll from Grace's hands, let the girls in and shut the door.

'No!' Adie screamed.

They reached the dilapidated house and hammered on the

door. There was no answer. Adie pounded her fists on the frosted glass of the porch, half hoping it would shatter. But she stopped suddenly when she realised she could see nothing through it. It looked like glass, it sounded like glass when she knocked on it, but there was nothing visible through the transparent window. She could see no colour, no light, the glass just seemed to go on and on.

'Don't you have a key?' she said, still smacking her hands on the frosted window.

'I'm trying.' Delilah already had the key and was trying to get it in the lock, but it wouldn't go in. 'There's no hole for it. It looks like there is, but I can't get the key in.'

Adie ran her nails around the door frame.

'There's no gap,' she said. 'It's not a door anymore, it's solid.'

The letterbox opened with a sudden clatter, and a violent gust of wind blew them off the porch onto the yellowed grass of the front garden. Adie rolled over and gazed at the door. The letterbox smiled, puckered itself to blow them a kiss, then flattened back against the sturdy wooden panel.

'It's too late,' Adie whispered. 'We're too late.'

'What the hell is that?' Spittle flew from Mrs Quinlan's lips as soon as she opened her door to the three girls stood on her porch.

'A doll made of straw,' replied Una.

'Not just a doll,' said Grace, nearly gagging. 'It feels squirmy in my hands.'

The woman furrowed her brow at Grace's pasty complexion.

'A couple of carnival folk stole it from the other carnival folk, and then we got it back for the other carnival folk, but when we went to return it to the other carnival folk, they'd left,' Una said.

'What?' the woman spat, still watching Grace.

'The carnival's gone. They just up and legged it. Without this doll.'

Mrs Quinlan snatched the doll and Grace felt the burden lift off her.

'Come in,' the woman said, suddenly pale in the face, and eyeing the doll with as much disgust as if it was a bag of cat poo.

The girls stepped into the hall. For a split second Grace thought she heard yelling. She turned and saw Adie and Delilah racing up the road towards the house. They looked panicked. They looked *terrified*. The door swung shut, and they were gone.

The door to the kitchen slammed shut at the same time, with Mrs Quinlan on the other side.

'Charming,' Una said. 'I take it we're not getting any tea then. That is one rude lady.'

A little worm of worry wriggled in Grace's chest. She

pulled at the latch on the front door. It wouldn't open. She tried again, putting all her weight on it, eventually putting both feet on the wall next to it, but it wouldn't budge.

'Rachel,' she said, 'try and get into the kitchen.'

Rachel hurried down the hall and pushed on the door handle.

'It's stuck,' she said.

'Hold on,' said Una. 'What's going on here?'

'Something's locked the doors,' said Grace, trying to push her nails into the door jamb. 'More than locked. It's fused the front door to the frame.'

'You mean, like, glued?'

'Shh!' Grace put her ear to the frosted glass. 'Do you hear that?'

There were voices, shouting, yelling, but a million miles away.

'This isn't going to open,' Rachel said, between bouts of slamming her shoulder against the kitchen door.

'This one's locked as well,' Una said, leaning on the door handle of the front room.

Grace sprinted up the stairs but, three steps from the top, she bashed against something invisible and went tumbling back down.

'Grace!'

Una and Rachel rushed to where she lay at the bottom the stairs. Her head was spinning and there was a trickle of blood from her nose. As Una lifted her to her feet, she couldn't feel anything broken.

'I'm alright.'

'What was that?' said Rachel.

Una tentatively walked up the steps with one hand out in front. She stopped with her hand pushing against thin air.

'It's like a wall,' she said. 'What the hell is going on?'

Seconds later and the girls were banging and shoulder-slamming the kitchen door.

'Mrs Quinlan! Mrs Quinlan!'

They went on until the heels of Grace's hands were red and sore. Then, without warning, one of Una's shoulder-slams flung the door wide open, and they fell over each other, hitting the linoleum with a *smack*.

But it wasn't Mrs Quinlan's kitchen anymore. The cooker was where the cooker normally was, the fridge and table were in place as usual, but everything was the wrong colour – the cupboard doors were fluorescent orange, the counter-tops a nasty pink – the floor and shelves and ceiling clashed in yellows, greens and blues. That, and there was a new door to the right. It was bright white and cleaner than anything in the Cat Lady's run-down house. Grace placed her hands against it, and jumped when it shook.

'Girls?' Mrs Quinlan's voice sounded from within. 'Girls, is that you? What the hell is this? Get me out of here.'

'Mrs Quinlan?' Grace cried. 'Mrs Quinlan, we're here. Just

hold on.'

Una grabbed a puce-coloured broom and jabbed it next to the door handle, over and over.

'We need something bigger,' Grace said, pulling one of the benches from under the table.

Rachel held the other end, while Una grabbed the middle.

'On three,' said Grace. 'One, two, three!'

The bench smashed into the wood, sending clumps of plaster and dust toppling to the ground. When the air cleared they could see that the door was gone. They had rammed the bench into the wall.

Grace stood back, then whirled around to see two new doors at the opposite end of the room. They were both shaking in their frames with thumps and shouts from inside. As she moved closer, Grace could also hear the scratching and mewing of cats. She put her ear to the door on the left.

'She's behind this one. I can hear her and the cats.'

'No,' said Una, with her ear to the door on the right. 'It's this one. I can hear her.'

Rachel dragged a second bench from under the table; it squeaked along the lino.

'Try again,' she said, lifting the back end.

Grace gripped the wooden bench with sweaty hands.

'One, two, three!'

Plaster again. Both doors had disappeared. The hammering and meowing now came from above and behind them.

A door had appeared in the ceiling, another on the far wall again, but Grace could also hear Mrs Quinlan's voice behind the door they had come in.

'She's in the hall,' she cried.

Flinging the door open, she was met with the dark quiet of the corridor, and nothing more. White doors had matriculated along the right-hand side where there had only been one to the front room before. She listened in trepidation as the whining of cat miaows and the distant yelling of Mrs Quinlan began to reverberate through all of them.

The stairs on the left had vanished, replaced by a smooth white travelator, which revolved from the first floor to the ground floor with absurd speed.

'I take it we're not supposed to get up there,' said Rachel.

'Then let's go up there,' said Grace.

Mumbling under her breath, she rose half a metre into the air, and sailed upwards keeping her feet above the travelator. She lowered herself gently when she reached the next floor. She looked up, expecting to see the square opening to Mrs Quinlan's attic and the rickety ladder below, but there was only a big, red X where the entrance should have been.

Rachel landed gracefully behind her, Una with a thump. She steadied herself with a hand on Grace's shoulder.

'Tell me you know what this is, and how we get out of here.'

Grace scanned the landing, shaking her head.

'Oh, fudgeballs,' Una whined.

'I saw Adie and Delilah in the street,' said Grace, 'before the door shut. And I'm sure I heard them yelling outside. They knew something we didn't.'

'About what?' said Rachel.

'About the straw doll.'

'You think the doll is doing this?'

'Yes,' said Grace. 'And I think Justine knew this would happen when she asked us to steal it. She and the ringmaster weren't forced to leave. They planned it.'

Grace felt Una's head land against her back, and heard her muffled voice,

'Why are half the people we meet pure evil? Seriously. Like, statistics-wise, that can't be right.'

'That door's open a crack,' said Grace, pointing at one of the bedrooms.

'Are we going to search each room?' asked Rachel.

'Mrs Quinlan's here somewhere.'

'Alright,' said Una, grabbing the back of Grace's jumper, 'but nobody leave me alone in here. I don't want some evil spirit pushing me down the stairs... or the travelator.'

'You can fly, Una,' Grace reminded her, 'and much more. Remember your training, and stay on your toes.'

'I don't like being on my toes.' Una followed the other two to the open door. 'I fall over.'

Grace ignored this last comment and pushed on the open

door. It swung out to reveal a huge, well-lit room. The polished wood floor was bathed in light from three large skylights, and the ceiling was impossibly high. Stone statues were dotted all around the place, elegant and beautifully carved. There were men, women and children, and they all reached for the sky with joyful expressions.

The girls strolled between them, looking for anything that stood out, any kind of clue. When Grace reached the back of the large room, she sighed. Nothing. Then one of the statues caught her eye. It was a boy, stood on a small platform of stone, and he wasn't looking up. He was looking right at her. Had he been that way before?

'This one's different,' she called to the others as they roamed throughout the room. 'He's...'

She trailed off as she gazed into his blue glassy eyes. They seemed to be marble, rather than grey stone. She didn't like his expression. Backing away she felt a tug on her hair.

She whipped around and saw a woman of stone with her hand out. Grace's hair had caught on the outstretched fingers. The statue's eyes were blue glass too.

'She wasn't like that before,' Grace said to herself. 'I'm sure of it.'

When she turned again the boy's arms were splayed out in front of him, still frozen, but as if he had tried to catch her while her back was turned.

'Rachel,' she cried, 'Una, be careful. I think these statues are moving.'

'Really?' she heard Rachel reply. 'I hadn't... Ow!'

'What was that? Are you okay?'

'Yeah, but... I think I'm stuck.'

'Hang on, I'm coming.'

But Grace tripped and went sprawling to the ground. Getting to her feet, she was suddenly in a forest of outstretched, stone limbs. She wove between them and felt a clamp above her elbow. One of the men had fastened his stone hand around her arm. She didn't see him move; it was like he had always been there. Then, *clamp*. She felt the same on her ankle. A little girl, her glassy eyes fixed, gazed up from the ground, her hands clasped around Grace's leg. Grace never saw any of them move; everything in her sightline was fixed, motionless, and then she felt another grab. Her waist this time. A woman's stone arm was closed around her belly like it had been carved there.

'Rachel, Una!'

'One of them's got me, Grace,' Una yelled from somewhere amongst the stone bodies. 'I can't get out. Ah! There's one on my arm as well!'

'I can't move either,' screamed Rachel. 'Three of them have got me. Grace, help!'

Grace thought she'd soon be crushed by grasping hands of granite. She writhed against them, but she was only hurting herself.

Remember your training, that's what she had told Una. *Relax. Just think.*

She couldn't fly, glamouring and cloaking would do no good, mind-hopping was useless and...

It was a little nuts, but it was the only idea she had. She focussed on a section of the wooden floor that she could see through the throngs of stone shapes. It was wood, she could use it as a life template. She concentrated and pulled a creature out of thin air.

It was massive, with thick square lips and two formidable horns on its snout, one longer than the other. The hunch above its neck and tough grey skin made it look armoured, and its sheer bulk was terrifying. Grace had seen a real-life rhinoceros only once at the zoo, but many times in books and online. She was impressed by how authentic her originated animal looked.

It snorted, blowing blasts of air from its large nostrils, and stepped back and forth, restless on its thick legs. She sent the animal encouraging thoughts before losing sight of it behind a maze of stone bodies. She felt the impact of its charge before she heard it.

Suddenly statue fragments were flying in all directions, and smashing to the ground. She directed her animal's behaviour as best she could without being able to see it. She needed it to break through the stone wall, without crushing her or her friends in the process.

Over and over the rhino charged. She could see it now, the grey head ploughing towards her. The statue holding her arm shattered, jerking Grace backwards and leaving just a stone hand in place. The jolt dragged at the woman's arm still secured around her waist, and Grace cried out in pain; her ribs and hips would be terribly bruised. The arm was broken by the next blow though, and the statue fractured in several places, allowing her to escape from its grip.

She could now work herself free of the remaining hands, giving her rhino a rest while she clambered over the remains of her captors and searched for her friends. Breaking Rachel and Una free was easier; she could see exactly what she was doing. Again and again, the rhino's horn slammed against the granite figures, demolishing the stone crowd. Her friends emerged from the rubble.

'Just a few bruises,' Rachel assured her. 'We'll be grand.'

'Fair play, Grace,' said Una. 'That is one awesome rhino.'

'Thanks,' Grace said, giving the exhausted animal a grateful smile before dismissing it with a wave. It popped into nothing, and the girls were left alone with sad statue remains in piles of rubble.

They crept into the hallway. A second door was open just a crack.

'I vote we don't open the door offered,' said Rachel.

'I second that emotion,' said Una, rubbing a bruised leg.

Grace moved quickly along the hall, trying to get into

any other room.

'They're all locked,' she said. 'Fused like the front door.'

'Girls?'

The voice came from behind the door that was ajar. It opened by itself and there stood Mrs Quinlan. But she was backing away from the doorway, like there was something dangerous between her and them.

'Girls, get out!'

The door slammed shut. Grace rammed it with her shoulder, and it opened again without trouble. She nearly fell into the room, which wasn't a room anymore. It was a garden, at night, with stars twinkling in a clear sky.

'Mrs Quinlan!' Una yelled out, wandering across the grass. 'Mrs Quinlan!'

'She's not here,' Grace said, turning with a knot of apprehension in her stomach. 'And the door we came through? It's gone.'

19

in THE night garden

It was cold. The grass was ankle-deep and nighttime dew was seeping into their socks. There were trees everywhere; tall ones, short ones, ones with prickly leaves, ones with big star-shaped leaves, horse-chestnuts with hanging conkers in spiky green cases, oak trees with little acorns waiting to fall. Rachel rose into the air, turning slowly.

'Greenery in every direction. It doesn't seem to end. Want to fly for as long as we can and see if it runs out?'

'I can't stay in the air as long as you guys,' Una said, pouting.

Rachel dropped back to the grass.

'That's okay, we can walk it.'

They trudged on and on, searching for a way out, but couldn't seem to make any headway.

'That's what's odd,' Grace said, after some time. 'The trees are all different.'

'*That's* what's odd?' Una replied. 'We're in a giant garden at night, that's actually inside a house during the day, we got here via a door that's disappeared, we appear to be going round in circles even though we never change direction... oh, and our magic teacher was here but she's not really. Or maybe she is. But do you know what's *really* odd? The trees are all different.'

'Thanks for the sarcasm, Una. I get your point.'

'Good.'

'What I meant was that there's a sycamore tree there, a conifer right next to it, then a big willow. Trees don't grow like that. Look at that horse-chestnut tree, with the conkers about to fall off.'

'So?'

'So you would expect some new ones to be growing near the old one. But all these trees are completely different. How did they all get clumped together?'

Una stared at her in the moonlight.

'Do I have to tell you the facts again? See, this whole thing is mental. This garden, all of this,' she gestured with her hands, 'is inside a house–'

'Alright, alright, I'm sorry I mentioned it.'

'You should be. We've more important things to worry about than ornithology.'

'That's the study of birds, not trees.'

'This is what I'm talking about, Grace; context. In the context of our impending death – probably – trees and birds and study-related things are not what's important.'

'Shh!' Rachel said. 'Do you hear that?'

In the silence of the night there was faint whistling in the distance. It wasn't the wind through the trees, but a cheerful melody that seemed out of place. It came closer and closer, until Grace could make out a figure in the dark, pushing a wheelbarrow.

'Should we run?' Rachel said, grabbing Grace's arm.

'If we do, I think we'll just keep on walking in circles until we can't walk anymore. Let's just wait here. But everyone be on guard, okay?'

Rachel and Una nodded. They could hear the squeak of the barrow's wheels now, and make out the tall man pushing it. He wore a loose-fitting shirt tucked into brown trousers, muddied boots and a small scarf wrapped around his neck. He whistled the same few bars over and over again, and his approach felt ominous.

'Evening, ladies. Enjoying my garden?'

He didn't seem surprised to see them, but greeted them with a bow.

'We're looking for a friend,' said Grace, watching his every move. 'She was here before, but now we can't find her.'

'Oh, my place is full of friends,' the man said. 'Just look

around. Any shape, any size, whatever you fancy.'

'Who are you?' said Una.

'I'm the gardener.' He leaned close to her and grinned. 'Aren't you a lovely little thing?'

Una's lip curled.

'And haven't you a lovely little wheelbarrow? How about you tell us where our friend is. She's old and cranky and got grey hair.'

The man stood straight and reached into his barrow, pulling out a spray bottle.

'Oh, you'll fit in lovely here.'

In one sudden movement, he squirted the bottle in Una's face, and then turned it on the others. Grace's hands flew up. The droplets stopped and hovered in the air for a moment before disappearing.

'Huh,' the man said, shaking the bottle as if it were at fault. 'Not to worry. We've all the time in the world here. Enjoy the garden, ladies.'

Grace was ready to fly into him with as much power as she could muster, but one look at Una told her the girl wasn't hurt. She spat and wiped her face, but she was more annoyed than injured.

'Forget him,' Grace said as the gardener wandered off, whistling his tune. 'Was it just water, Una?'

'No,' Una said, spitting again. 'But I don't think it was weed-killer or anything. What a git.'

'Was that you, Grace?' said Rachel. 'Stopping the drops in mid-air?'

'I think so.'

'That was worthy of Adie. You'll have to tell her when we get out of here.'

'*If* we get out.'

It was getting colder and colder in the night garden. The girls trudged on, shivering, until Rachel stopped and pointed.

'We've passed that tree before,' she said. 'It's got that crooked long branch, look.'

'We're still going round in circles,' Una huffed. 'My feet hurt.'

'You've got something on your cheek,' Grace said, reaching out to scratch at a brown patch on Una's face.

'Ow!' the girl cried.

'Oh, sorry. It's... it's attached.'

Grace fingered the little bump while Una winced. It was dark brown and hard, with a darker bump in the middle.

'Oh God, Una,' Rachel gasped. 'I think it's a giant wart.'

'On my face?'

'It can't be a wart,' Grace said. 'It wasn't there a minute ago.'

'What if it's a magic wart,' said Rachel, 'from that spray bottle?'

'I've got magic warts?' Una looked panicked.

'Stop it, Rach,' said Grace. 'I don't know what it is, Una.

240

Don't start worrying yet.'

'When would you like me to start worrying?' Una's voice rose. 'When I'm covered in warts? When an army of toads arrive and make me their queen? Get it off me.'

She scratched mercilessly at the brown bump until the skin around it turned raw and bled a little.

'Stop it!' Grace forced Una's hands down, then stared at her friend's fingernails in shock.

Several of them had turned brown, a lighter shade than the bump, but rough and grainy, like bark. As she watched, the bark spread slowly down Una's fingers.

'It's a knot,' Grace said, gently touching Una's cheek again, 'like in the bark of a tree.'

Grace ran to the nearest tree — a young sycamore with bright green leaves — and examined the trunk. She tugged at the lowest branch and thought she felt a tremor that came from beneath the bark.

'I'm sorry,' she whispered, and pulled on the branch as hard as she could, almost enough to crack the wood.

Seeeeeeeeeeee! The sound was high-pitched and strange, and the tree definitely trembled.

'What are you doing?' Una called. 'Can we please get back to the fact that I'm turning into a warty toad?' She held her hands up at eye level, gazing at her brown fingernails. 'I don't want to be a warty toad.'

'You're not turning into a toad, Una,' said Grace, taking a

deep breath. 'You're turning into a tree.'

Una's grey eyes registered nothing.

'I'm sorry, can you say that again, please?'

'These trees,' Grace said, 'they're all different because they're *not* trees. They didn't really grow here. They're... I think they're people. That gardener is collecting people. And you're next.'

Rachel and Una stood in silence, staring at Grace like she'd just given them a complex equation to be solved. Eventually, Rachel spoke.

'How long will it take? How do we stop it?'

'Why are you asking me?' said Grace.

'Because you seem to know all about it.'

'I don't know anything, but I can see her skin's turning to bark.'

'You must have some idea how long it will take.'

'Rachel, I don't know. What do you expect me to–'

'Owwwwww!'

Una hopped back on one heel.

'What's wrong?' said Grace.

'My shoe, my shoe, my shoe, my shoe. My shoe's too tight. Get it off!'

Grace and Rachel scrambled to pull off Una's shoe as she howled in pain. What they saw made them recoil.

Una's toes had lengthened into woody roots, and the skin of her foot had taken on the same roughened, barky quality as her fingers.

'Aaaaaah!' Una screamed when she caught sight of it. 'My toes! Oh my God, my toes are gross. They're so gross. Please cut them off!' She poked at the roots with her fingers.

'Una, we're not cutting off your toes,' said Grace.

'Pleeeease!'

'No. Look, you're going to be alright. We'll find a way to fix it.'

'I want my mum.'

'Your mum can't help.'

'I don't care. I want my mum.'

'If we ever get out of here, I'll give her a ring. In the meantime, you better take off your other shoe.'

'I don't want to see it,' Una sobbed.

'That foot's going to start hurting soon, and if you don't get the shoe off quick it might get stuck on. And that'll really hurt.'

Una woefully removed her other shoe, a little whine escaping her lips when she saw the toes curling into more pale brown roots.

'We have to find the gardener,' Grace said.

'Then what?' said Rachel.

'We kill him,' Una said, sniffling.

'I'm not in the mood for murder, Una,' replied Grace. 'Let's try reasoning with him first.'

'He didn't strike me as the reasonable type,' said Rachel.

'Yeah, he seemed like an evil-madman-scientist-ornithologist to me,' said Una, following the others with some difficulty on her woody, clown-sized feet.

'That's still birds, Una,' said Grace.

'Really?' Una said, sticking one foot in the air to point with her rooty toes. 'Is this the time, Grace?'

'Shhhh! Listen.'

At the distant sound of whistling, they all froze. That same awful, cheery tune.

'He's not going to turn Una back just 'cos we ask nicely, Grace,' said Rachel. 'This creep collects people. We'll be next, you know.'

Grace stared through the moonlit garden, her mind whirring.

'How good is your glamour, Rach?'

Rachel smiled.

'It's good.'

'Can you be a tree?'

Rachel's brow furrowed, but she was still smiling.

'Haven't tried that before.' She shook out her arms. 'But there's no time like the present.'

The night sky seemed to echo the gardener's tune as he pushed his wheelbarrow slowly through the grass. The trees shuddered as he passed, the *shushing* sound of their leaves following him along the garden. He stopped short of a weeping willow, its long, slender leaves hanging over a crooked black trunk like golden hair. He set the barrow down and approached with his hands on his hips.

'Well now, aren't you beautiful?' he said. 'I told you you'd fit in lovely here. Where did your little friends get to?'

He had his back to the barrow. Now was Grace's chance. She hovered about twenty metres in the air, the muscles in her sides aching from holding the position.

I'll have to start taking more exercise, she thought to herself, ignoring the pain.

Silently swinging upside down, she dove. The gardener noticed a second too late, as she snatched the spray bottle from the barrow. Wrenching the spray top off completely, she threw the bottle's entire contents in his face. He snarled and fell backwards, spluttering and rubbing his eyes.

It started almost immediately. His head was pulled back as bark crept swiftly up his neck and knots appeared on his face.

'No!' he cried, scratching at his skin. 'No.'

But his fingers were already turning. He clawed at his arms, but quickly stopped, his gaze turning to the barrow. Like a cat pouncing, he shot forward, but two of the willow's branches melted into human arms and grabbed him as he ran. Rachel's porcelain face appeared in the bark.

'It's in the barrow, Grace,' she hissed, her glamour continuing to melt away as the gardener struggled in her grip.

Grace raced back to the wheelbarrow, sifting through the tools and junk inside.

'It could be anything,' she cried.

The gardener snorted a laugh, firing one branch-like arm and striking Rachel in the head. He crawled forward on woody limbs, but something large came ambling from the dark and landed on him with a thump.

'Ugh,' he grunted as Una, her jeans torn on both sides by thick trunk-like legs, pushed his face into the ground.

'Now, you,' she said, 'tell us what's in the barrow that'll turn me back to normal, and maybe we'll let you use it.'

'The tin box,' the gardener croaked. 'Powder, in the face, like the spray.'

Grace rummaged in the barrow and pulled out a small, tin box. It was filled with white powder. She took a pinch in her palm, and blew it in Una's face.

Una sneezed and hiccuped, rolling off the gardener's back. Grace moved to sit on him, but she didn't need to. His feet had pushed their roots firmly into the ground, and his face had nearly disappeared behind a wall of bark.

'Ah, ow, ow, ow!' cried Una. 'It hurts!'

Una's root toes and twig fingers where shortening and pulling back into her limbs. Her head lolled about as her skin smoothed out and faded in colour, leaving her cheeks their usual pleasant pink. She sank to her knees, her torn jeans spreading out like huge 1970s-style flares.

'Seriously,' she said, rubbing her head. 'That was really sore.'

There was groaning from the gardener tree, which lay at a strange angle. Its roots were lodged in the soil, and the trunk lay across the ground with branches stretching awkwardly skywards.

'If there's any left after we've rescued these others,' Una snapped at him as she grabbed the tin box from Grace, 'we'll think about *maybe* letting you go.'

Marching to the next tree, a sturdy oak, she took a pinch of the powder and blew.

The garden vanished.

'Jenny, Jenny!'

Adie waved frantically, even though Jenny was clearly headed straight for Mrs Quinlan's house. Under the street-lights of Wilton Place, Adie could see the change in Jenny's shape since she had taken up weight-lifting. She was definitely bigger. She looked sturdy; she looked *strong*.

'Where's Delilah?' Jenny wasn't the least bit out of breath, though she had sprinted the length of the street.

'She's gone to find Bob.'

'Have you heard anything from inside?' Jenny said, immediately heading for the porch and putting her ear to the door.

'Nothing. We saw them go inside and that was it. We banged on the door and shouted for ages, but we didn't hear them at all.'

Jenny moved around the porch like a seasoned investigator, running her nails down the door jamb, peering through the frosted glass that showed nothing, and examining the outer wall as if for a weak spot. At the window to the front room, she wiped the glass clean to look inside.

'You can't see anything,' Adie said. 'It's misty, like the glass on the porch. It doesn't let you see inside.'

Jenny stepped back and sighed. Taking a quick glance back at the street to make sure nobody was around, she rose into the air to face one of the first-floor windows.

'Someone's in there,' she said.

Adie gasped, but as Jenny flew in to to grab the sill, the window moved to the right, like a tile in a sliding puzzle game. The front-room window moved up, the far window down, and on they moved. Jenny backed away, then shot forward again, missing a window by inches and hitting the wall.

'Oh, Jenny,' Adie cried. 'Be careful. If you knock yourself out, you'll fall.'

Jenny took a deep breath and tried again, this time missing a window by some distance and scraping her jaw and arm. She lowered to the ground, pressing one hand to her face.

'Are you alright?' said Adie.

'Yeah, but I definitely saw movement in there.'

'The windows keep changing speed when they move, that's why you're missing them. Let's wait for Bob.'

'They're locked in there, Adie, and we don't know what's happening to them. They could be dying for all we know!'

Adie bit back tears. 'But we can't get in!'

Apparently not caring who saw her this time, Jenny went back onto the street and rose several metres into the air. She watched the sliding windows with a look of brutal determination, her eyes flicking from side to side as the house continued its game. After some time, she moved slowly forward in a zigzag motion. The house seemed to have a moment's apprehension and the windows picked up speed.

'Jenny?' Adie called, as her friend snaked through the air above her.

Jenny tightened her turns, moved a little faster. Again, the house seemed to hiccup at her change of pace and the windows sped up once more. This meandering went on and on until Adie thought the anticipation would kill her. All at once, Jenny hurled herself towards the house, her hands out in front, her head low and focussed on one spot. It was wall. She was firing herself right at the wall.

'No, Jenny!' Adie shrieked, but it was too late.

Jenny soared through the air, the windows moved faster and faster and faster until...

SMASH!

A window had slid into place just as Jenny hit. She speared through the glass like a bullet and disappeared inside the house. Adie hugged her chest and let out the breath she'd been holding.

'Thank goodness for that!' she whispered to herself.

For what, though? She stared up at the windows that had slowed to a crawl, and realised that *four* of her friends, and Mrs Quinlan, were now trapped inside the dilapidated house. She looked helplessly around for support, but saw only the empty lawn. Frustrated beyond belief, she yelled at the top of her voice.

'What bloody good did that do?!'

20

THE MONSTER in THE HOUSE

Grace, Rachel and Una stood in a clean, white room. At one end, there was a door. The tin box with the powder in it had disappeared from Una's hand.

'This isn't funny anymore,' she grunted.

They could hear Mrs Quinlan's voice again and the scratching and mewing of many cats. There was no other way out of the room. Grace had no choice but to open the only door. There was Mrs Quinlan, in all her moth-eaten glory. Several cats clawed at her skirts and her grey hair hung in waves to her shoulders.

'Mrs Quinlan!' Una rushed forward and smacked straight into a large mirror.

Grace glanced behind them, but the woman wasn't there. There was only her reflection in the glass.

'Mrs Quinlan?' Grace said. 'Can you hear us?'

The woman didn't respond, just stood there with her hands on her hips, letting the cats whimper at her feet. Grace edged past the mirror to the room beyond.

It was filled with mirrors. Big rectangles of glass, with no frames, that stood without any support – and Mrs Quinlan inhabited all of them. In one, she pounded her fists on the glass, screaming to be let out. In another, she held Mephistopheles fondly in her arms, stroking his head and smiling when he purred. In yet another, she sat at a small desk, scribbling notes from a pile of magic books. She stood at the cooker, stirring the foul contents of a pot that Grace could smell; she yelled at someone unseen, pointing a threatening finger; she clutched Delilah's schoolbag like a lifeline, her forehead creased with worry.

Then the mirrors moved, closed in around Grace until she was stuck in a corridor of mirrors, a corridor of Mrs Quinlans.

'Rachel?' she called.

'We're back here,' was the reply. 'Keep walking, I think it's a maze.'

'Which way?'

'I don't know.'

'Can you get back in through the door?'

'It's gone.'

Grace walked to the end of the corridor and took a right. She walked to the end of the next and took a left, but on the following turn, she saw mirrors shifting into the place. She ran to the next one and again saw the mirrored walls shift as she turned the corner.

'Oh fudge, they're moving,' she yelled out. 'The walls are moving.'

'I know, Una and I have got separated,' Rachel shouted back. 'How can we find each other if the maze keeps shifting?'

'I think that's the point. Una, are you alright?' There was no reply. 'Una?'

Again, silence. Grace ignored a Mrs Quinlan throwing her trusty glowing boomerang and catching it as it zipped back to her.

'Una? Una, please answer me. Are you okay? Una? *Are you there?*'

'Yep.'

'Then why the hell didn't you answer me?'

'I was checking something.'

'Checking what?'

'Yeah, it's moving now,' Una replied. 'See, I was cloaked for a while.'

'Why did you cloak?' asked Rachel.

''Cos one of the Mrs Quinlans threw a cat at me and I panicked. But, when I was cloaked, I noticed the walls stopped moving. They couldn't see me. They're moving again now though, so they can hear me.'

'So all we have to do,' Grace began.

'Is shut up and cloak,' Una finished.

'Right. I can do that. Everybody aim for the side we came in on, and we'll try to meet up there.'

'Is this you shutting up?'

'Shush, Una.'

'Yes, sir.'

Grace sighed and then cloaked. She'd never said it to the girls, but she found cloaking difficult. The initial spell was okay, but maintaining it for any length of time got increasingly hard. It didn't physically hurt, like hovering for ages or flame-running, it was more that the thought of being invisible made her anxious. The longer she appeared to be nothing, the more afraid she was that she'd stay that way. She knew it wasn't rational – she could drop the spell any time she liked – but that didn't stop the feeling.

She looked down now and saw nothing, not her hands or legs or feet. The little knot of panic was already growing in her belly and a voice chimed in her head, *drop the cloak, drop the cloak, drop the cloak*. She pushed the anxiety away and saw that the mirrored maze was no longer shifting, that she could amble quietly through and find the best way to reach Rachel and Una. Lucky Una, thought Grace, she could stay cloaked all day and not be bothered at all.

She was getting closer. It was still a maze but, with the corridors fixed, Grace could backtrack and try different routes. It was tempting to call out to the others and see how they were doing, but she kept quiet. Until she saw a wall shift to her left. It was down the far end of the corridor, but it definitely moved. She stopped dead. She'd been careful not to make noise, she was still cloaked, but the maze had shifted. Tiptoeing to the end of the corridor, she was startled when it moved again. But the wall was shifting right in front of her, and she was able to slip through. She couldn't understand what the maze was up to until Jenny appeared. She was scowling and swearing under her breath.

'Jenny!' Grace couldn't help it.

Jenny nearly leapt out of her boots, and slammed against a sneering Mrs Quinlan reflection.

'Who's there?' she said.

'Sorry,' said Grace, uncloaking. 'It's me.'

'Finally,' Jenny gasped, grabbing Grace in a bear hug that knocked the wind out of her. 'I've been looking for you for ages. I'm trying to work out this bloody maze, but it's impossible. The walls keep moving.'

'Cloak,' Grace said, grabbing Jenny's hand, 'and don't speak. I'm on my way to Rachel and Una over there at the far end.'

The tall girl looked perplexed, but disappeared as commanded. Grace kept a firm grip on her hand as, together, they moved silently through the maze.

✳ ✳ ✳

They seemed to be walking for hours, but eventually they collided with Una. She was standing next to the first Mrs Quinlan – the one that stood with hands on hips like a superhero – and waiting impatiently for Rachel to arrive. After some time, they heard a small voice in the empty corridor.

'Please tell me you guys are here.'

'Rachel?' said Grace.

'You *are* there! Fudge, I've been standing here for ten minutes. I was afraid to talk in case some wall moved on you guys and got you lost. Is Una with you?'

'And Jenny,' Grace said, uncloaking. 'Here, grab my hand, before we get separated again.'

They all held hands with relief, and Jenny gave a riveting report of her daredevil entrance through an upstairs window.

'And Adie and Delilah?' asked Grace.

'Adie's outside, Delilah went to get Bob. What's the deal with all the fake Mrs Quinlans? Where's the real one?'

'We don't know. We kept hearing her behind doors but...'

'Do you think she's dead?' said Jenny.

'You'd better not smile.'

'I'm not smiling! For fudge sake! I mean, she's a bitter twisted old hag with no soul and I hate her with the fire of a thousand suns but, you know... doesn't mean I want her *dead*.'

'I hope she's not.'

The floor trembled, breaking their conversation, and another door appeared in the wall.

'Hey,' said Jenny, turning, 'a way out.'

Rachel stopped her.

'Don't bother,' she said.

'You see, you start playing the game,' said Una, 'and it doesn't end. Plus, you get turned into trees and attacked by statues and stuff.'

'Better to stay where we are for now,' said Grace.

All four girls huddled together, but when they ignored the open door, the house seemed to lose its temper. There was a rumble, then another, then the first mirror crashed to the ground, smashing into smithereens. The row of mirrors behind them did the same, then the next, and the next. Soon there was shattered glass everywhere. The ceiling pushed up while the walls moved out, and the room became a great cavernous space, with boulders next to rock walls that were filled with jagged nooks and crannies.

The girls watched in astonishment as the mirror pieces melted and moved like liquid metal, gathering together into a great pool. A shape rose out of the centre, growing taller and taller. The head and shoulders reached almost the height of the cavern, and the figure solidified and towered over the friends.

It was a very strange figure indeed. Its limbs were long and thin, the arms a little too long for its body. The giant eyes were very round and set in an oval-shaped face. Hair stood straight out from its head like twigs or great, thick strands of straw and its mouth... its mouth held a tempestuous frown, like a toddler that's had its favourite toy taken away, and in the darkness behind the lips were the points of huge, triangular teeth.

'We should have taken that door,' Una groaned.

The creature's movement was a little on the slow side, perhaps because of its great size, and yet the first spear missed Grace by mere centimetres. The giant had pulled out a single strand of its twig-like hair and fired it. The hair was about half the width of a wrist, rigid, and razor-sharp at the root end. It embedded itself in the rock face and stayed there, wobbling slightly with the impact.

'Run!' Grace said. 'Everybody run!'

'But we should stay together!' Una cried, running awkwardly backwards.

'Just run!'

The second spear hit between Una's feet. She skirted the creature's great leg and ducked behind the nearest boulder.

The spears came thick and fast, splitting rock, revealing hiding places. Rachel took off into the air and was nearly skewered.

'Keep to the rocks,' Grace yelled. 'Stay out of sight!'

As she squeezed into a crack in the wall, Grace saw the creature's expression. Its frown had turned upside down, and when she was half buried in falling debris she heard it clap with delight. The whole cavern shook with the creature's glee.

'It's a game.' Jenny was hurriedly unburying Grace. 'It's playing with us, having fun. It won't end.'

'What are you doing?' Grace said. 'Go and hide, it can see you.'

The next spear grazed Jenny's cheek, and blood trickled down her face.

'Get out of here!' Grace shouted.

'No, we have to fight it.'

'Has your brain gone to mush? It's a spear-throwing *giant*.'

'And beating it is the only way out of here. That, or we end up playing its games forever.'

Grace grabbed Jenny's collar and rolled her clear of an incoming spear. Grabbing the back of her jumper this time, she pulled them both behind a boulder.

'I'm assuming you've got a plan.'

Jenny nodded.

'But we need the others.'

Evidently the creature had taken a fancy to Una. Grace and Jenny joined Rachel easily enough, but Una was getting more than her fair share of spears. She ducked repeatedly behind a chunk of rock that had broken free of the wall, but couldn't get a break between attacks to hide somewhere else.

'Una, we need you!' Grace shouted from her own sheltered spot. 'Jenny's got a plan to beat this thing.'

'Don't yell that you've got a plan to beat this thing *in front* of the thing,' Una shouted back.

Grace looked up at the oval face and its expression of playful glee.

'I don't think it speaks English,' called Grace.

'*Cómo estás?*' Una yelled up at the creature.

It didn't reply.

'*Conas atá tú?*'

There was no response but another spear, and Una shrugged.

'Doesn't speak Spanish or Irish either.'

Grace rolled her eyes.

'Excellent. Now that we've established it doesn't speak English or Spanish *or* Irish, can you get over here? Jenny needs all of us for this to work.'

But Una got only a few metres before being pushed back by two near misses.

'We need a distraction,' said Jenny.

Something to distract a big baby, Grace thought.

Without a word, she grabbed Jenny's wrist and focussed on her leather bracelets. She was using them as a life template to originate the most complicated thing she had ever attempted. Minutes later Grace's creations filled the air. The others were awestruck.

'Holy crap,' said Jenny. 'I'd no idea you could do that.'

'Neither did I,' Grace replied, sweat dripping down her freckled cheeks.

There were tiny creatures hovering in the air in front of her, each with a needle-like body and delicate wings like the finest silk. They were white, but glimmered with a sparkling sheen, and they fluttered upwards like gravity-defying confetti.

One hundred dragonflies. She had originated one hundred dragonflies. Grace, exhausted but elated, was positively glowing with pride.

It had the desired effect. The creature seemed intoxicated, its round eyes widening even further as it grasped at the teeny insects. But Grace couldn't hold them for long. Within seconds, they began popping into nothing like bubbles in the wind, and the more the creature grabbed at them, the quicker they vanished.

Una had wasted no time though. She picked her way around the creature's feet to join the girls on the other side. As the last dragonfly popped, together they ran, hunched and silent, to a new hiding place in a large crevice in the wall.

'What do we have to do?' asked Rachel, huddling into a corner.

'Nothing,' Jenny whispered, 'just hold on to me.'

'You're the boss,' Una said, gripping her elbow firmly.

When all three girls had hold of her arms, Jenny stood up in full view of the creature, and got angry. Grace could see it in her neck, the tendons that stood out and the skin that flushed red.

There was plenty to get angry about. Grace thought about Rachel nearly being impaled by a spear, about Una's feet twisting into roots, about Jenny getting lost in a shifting maze of mirrors. She thought about Justine letting the girls believe she was their friend. She imagined the ballerina, or one of those awful clowns, hiding the straw doll in the sewer. She thought about the fake map, how Justine had told her it was Drake's handwriting, how Drake had been maligned and made to look like a monster. Looking up at the creature that towered above her, she thought of the danger into which her friends had been led, and she got angry too. Very angry. So angry she felt she could explode. Energy rushed out of her arms into Jenny's, and that's when the push happened.

It shot through the tall girl like an enormous shudder of relief, like a wave bursting onto the shore. It widened as it left her body, engulfed the entire cavern, splitting boulders and making pebbles on the ground dance. The creature reached for its head, but it never got the chance to pluck out a deadly hair spear. The wave hit the giant like a massive blunt object, smashing it into the rock face. It slid, unconscious, to its knees and fell face-first to the ground. There was silence.

'Holy crap,' said Una.

The cavern shook, creaking like a great rusty machine. The creature's body began to shrink. And as it shrank, it pulled the cavern with it. The rocks and boulders and pebbles were pulled towards the shrivelling creature, revealing carpet underneath. The walls slunk away to reveal grubby wallpaper and a broken window. The mirage disappeared inside the body that was now a fraction of its original size, still lying face down on the floor.

'Now,' Grace said, 'before it wakes.'

She didn't wait for an answer, but grabbed Jenny by one of her weakened limbs and took flight. Jenny was woozy and limp, it was like flying with a dead weight, and Grace needed help to lift her through the broken window. They sailed over patchy, yellow grass, a poorly maintained front wall, the pavement beyond it, and landed on black tarmac.

Jenny slumped on the road, surrounded by her friends, her head lolling about. Grace held her face and lifted her eyes to the light of a streetlamp.

'She's okay,' she said. 'She'll be okay.'

Everyone hugged the girl sitting on the tarmac, squeezing and patting her back.

'Mrs Quinlan.' Jenny slurred. 'Mrs Quinlan's still inside.'

Grace swept the auburn hair back off her friend's face.

'I know.'

21

no more secrets

Almost as soon as Grace had touched down on the tarmac, clutching Jenny's arms with Rachel and Una holding her legs behind, the house had shut itself up. If it looked dilapidated before, now it looked condemned. Planks of wood were nailed across the doors and windows, the yellowing grass of the front lawn had withered to brown, and a grey gloom had set in all over the grounds, as if the house had its own stormclouds permanently poised above the roof.

By the time Jenny was standing on her own feet, Adie and Delilah were jogging back towards the group on the street, and Bob had materialised nearby.

'We can't even get into the driveway,' Adie panted, rubbing knuckles that Grace noticed were skinned and raw. 'It's like bulletproof glass blocking any way into the garden.'

'Jenny hurt it,' said Grace. 'Maybe it doesn't want to play for a while.'

'So Mrs Quinlan kept hold of the doll then, after she took it from you?'

Adie looked enquiringly at Grace. But Grace still felt an inkling of distrust.

'Yeah,' she replied. 'Why?'

'I think she's the focus of the hex now. Drake said that someone has to take the doll willingly, in order to bring the curse on themselves.'

'So how do we get her out?' asked Una.

'I don't think we can,' Delilah replied.

'That's rubbish.' Grace was surprised by her own outburst. 'What's going on with you two? Adie, you've been lying to us and ditching classes, and Delilah? You never worried about casting spells outside of class before, and you never believed there were limits to magic. Now it's as if you're afraid to cast a basic spell. Something's happened with the two of you, and I want to know what.'

The two girls seemed reluctant to talk, and Adie turned to Bob.

'Don't look at him.' Grace was aware she was speaking as the adult she wasn't ready to be. 'I asked you a question, and I want you to answer. And tell us everything. No more secrets.'

And so Adie and Delilah told their story. They told about Adie's water-messaging spell and the creature she believed she had pulled back from Hy-Breasal; they told of how she had asked for help to catch it, first from Bob and then from Delilah. They told about their disastrous attempt to identify the creature, and their summoning of the witch Murdrina. Adie held it together when she spoke of her mother, of the black worm in her eyes and how it could jump from person to person, and of Niall's odd behaviour in school.

'So it wasn't you,' Grace said when they had finished, 'who sprayed the water, and originated the mice.'

Adie shook her head.

'I'm sorry. I couldn't explain that without having to explain everything.'

'I knew that couldn't have been you,' Una said. 'You're too nice to throw rodents at people. Hey,' she turned abruptly to Bob, 'where are *you* going?'

Bob was nearly to the hedge that led to the football pitch by the school. He turned and glared at Una with his mis-matched eyes.

'What I mean is,' Una gulped, 'it's very nice to see you again, Mr Bob. It's a shame we haven't kept in touch all this time, but I was just wondering,' she gestured to the house, 'can you get Mrs Quinlan back?'

'In time,' the man grunted, 'perhaps.'

He pushed his way through the hedge.

'Well, that sounds fair,' Una called after him. 'Any time you're ready. We'll keep an eye on the house in the meantime and, eh, nice to see you again! Have a good night. Bye, Bob.'

'Una, he's gone,' said Jenny.

'I know.' Una wriggled her shoulders. 'He makes me nervous.'

'Can he stop Murdrina?' said Grace.

'I don't think so,' replied Adie. 'She talks about him like he could be her nemesis or something, but she's looking forward to the fight. She doesn't seem scared at all.'

'And he does?'

'He doesn't seem sure, anyway.' Then Adie snapped to attention as if she had just realised something. 'Hey, you lot lied to us as well. We didn't know anything about the straw doll before Drake told us. You kept secrets too.'

'Oh,' said Grace, 'yeah, I suppose we did... sorry about that.'

'How come I wasn't in on any of the secrets?' Jenny asked.

'You were fraternising with the enemy,' replied Una.

'Oh right, so I make friends with Agata and I'm out of the group. I'm out of all the groups?'

'There were just two groups – after Adie and Delilah broke off.'

'Three if you count me.'

'You can't be a group on your own. There were two groups, and you on your own.'

'I don't know what either of you are talking about,' said Rachel, looking from Jenny to Una.

'What has happened to us?' Grace said it to herself, but

everyone heard and was silent for a few moments.

'As relationships go,' said Una, 'ours for the last couple of weeks have been very unhealthy. But music is a great healer. I've got some brilliant stuff here—'

'Oh God, Una, please, no...' said Rachel.

✷ ✷ ✷

As they made their way home Grace pulled away from the others to avoid the tinny noise emanating from Una's mp3 player.

'She's not dropping that any time soon, is she?'

Adie caught up with her and they smiled shyly at each other.

'No, I'm afraid the power ballads album might be a keeper.'

'Could be worse. She could have discovered death metal.'

Grace laughed, then felt suddenly sad.

'I've missed you.'

'I've missed you too.'

'You know, you left out a bit of your story.'

'Did I?'

'Yeah,' said Grace. 'You started at the point when you tried to send Gaukroger and Aura a water-message.'

'Yeah?'

'But you had stopped hanging out with us before that. Why?'

Adie shrugged, but Grace could tell she'd touched a nerve.

'I didn't like the carnival,' Adie finally replied.

'What was so bad about it?'

'Nothing, I just didn't like it.'

Grace was interested now.

'Could you somehow tell that some of them were wicked?'

'No,' said Adie, 'because I didn't like having tea with Agata either. And she's lovely.'

'So what was it?'

Tears started rolling down Adie's cheeks.

'I'm a bad person.'

'What?' Grace snorted. 'Of course you're not. What are you talking about?'

'I didn't like the carnival people because...' Adie choked out the last few words, 'I thought they were weird.'

Grace was perplexed.

'They *are* weird.'

'No, I mean the way they looked, they way lived, the food they ate, everything. I found it weird, and I felt bad about it but I couldn't help finding it weird. So I stayed away from them.'

'So, you mean...'

'I'm a racist!' Adie snuffled.

This time Grace laughed out loud.

'Don't laugh,' Adie snapped. 'I didn't like them because they didn't look and talk like me. I am a racist... or a xeno-phobe or something, I'm not sure which.'

Grace had the urge to laugh again, but Adie was too distressed, so she patted her friend's shoulder and let the silence drag out instead. As the sky darkened further, they could hear distant arguments from the other girls. Finally, Grace spoke.

'Jenny puts chocolate in her ham sandwiches.'

Adie gave her a queer look.

'I know.'

'I find that weird.'

There was no answer, and Grace went on.

'Rachel spends half an hour on her make-up and picking out clothes every morning. I find that *really* weird.'

There was only a stubborn sniffle from Adie, so Grace continued.

'You collect candles, but never light them. I find that weird.'

Adie retaliated.

'You love homework. I find that weird.'

'I don't love it, I just don't mind–'

'You love it.'

Grace grinned.

'Una could dance and wiggle her bum in front of the whole school and not get embarrassed. I find that weird.'

'That *is* weird.'

Grace looked at Adie's tearful face in the moonlight.

'It freaked me out when I met her first,' she said. 'But now I like it.'

'Me too.'

'So I guess we shouldn't worry about thinking new people are a bit weird. 'Cos we're all weird.'

Adie smiled reluctantly and gave Grace a firm nudge in the ribs. After a minute she said, 'I'll never like power ballads, though.'

'Oh God, neither will I.'

Ms Lemon's pretty little sitting room didn't easily seat seven people. The girls were perched on the arms of the sofa, the coffee table, the windowsill, with only Una sharing the couch with their teacher. They all instinctively felt that Ms Lemon should be given plenty of room while they filled her in on the bizarre series of events that had led them to their current predicament and, also, to the imprisonment of Mrs Quinlan in her own house.

Their teacher sat with her hands clasped in her lap, her gaze focussed on the floor as they spoke. As soon as the extent of their rule-breaking became apparent, she stopped interrupting them for further details. Her hazel eyes grew wider as she listened, her face almost expressionless except for a deep crease in her brow. Grace thought she saw a flicker of recognition at the name Murdrina but, other than that, Ms Lemon didn't react at all. When everyone had finished telling their part of the story, the room settled into an uncomfortable silence, broken by the occasional cough or someone fidgeting in their seat. In the distance, Grace heard the faint wail of a siren and the beeping of traffic on the road outside.

'Delilah,' Ms Lemon said suddenly, 'you will stay with me. It'll be a bit of squeeze with the two of us, but we'll manage.'

'Um, yes, Miss,' the small girl replied.

Ms Lemon returned her focus to the floor and fell silent again.

'Miss?' Grace said. 'What should we do?'

'Nothing. You do nothing. Bob will battle this witch and, if we're lucky, that will be the end of it.'

'But we don't know if Bob is a match for Murdrina. What if he loses?'

'It's our fault she's here at all,' Adie said. 'We can't let Bob fight her alone. What if she kills him?'

'Then you will have to live with that,' Ms Lemon replied.

Grace was taken aback. The teacher looked drawn, her face pale and her voice filled with resignation. It seemed like she had given up before even trying.

'You've heard of her, haven't you?' said Grace. 'You know who she is.'

'I've heard a legend,' the teacher said, 'a fable about some sorceress, that's all. Murdrina is a name thrown about by some witches like a bedtime story made to scare children. She doesn't exist.'

'She does exist,' Adie said. 'She's in my house.'

Ms Lemon sighed with one hand over her eyes.

'If what you've told me is true, if she's stronger than Bob, then I haven't a hope of beating her.'

'Mrs Quinlan would try,' said Grace.

Ms Lemon looked up with red eyes.

'She would. But you handed her a hex that made sure she never could.' The teacher got to her feet. 'I'll get you some blankets and pillows for the sofa, Delilah.'

'You can't just give up, Miss,' Jenny interjected. 'There has to be something we can do.'

'*I* will research Murdrina and give Bob whatever help I can. You lot are staying out of it.'

'But, Miss—'

'No buts! This is not up for discussion. Don't you realise what you've …'

The teacher rubbed her head hard, and seemed oblivious to them for a moment. When she spoke again she was mumbling to herself.

'If Mr Pamuk still has those Creole volumes, then maybe there's something in there. Maybe …' She tutted. 'Enough, I need to think. Out you go.'

Grace slipped her mobile into Delilah's hands as the girls got up to leave.

'We'll text you,' she whispered.

Despondent, everyone said their goodbyes on the street. Slowly they started to make their separate ways homewards.

Grace stopped on the bridge and rested her chin on her arms, watching the water flow solemnly underneath.

'Not going home yet?'

Adie stood beside her and copied her pose.

'Not yet. You?'

It was a silly question. Adie's watery eyes were the only reply.

'Sorry,' said Grace. 'I can't imagine what it's been like for you, with that thing in your house.'

'Do you think it would be ridiculous for me to stay out all night? I could wander around town, sit by the river.'

'What about your brothers? And your dad?'

'Yeah, they might worry, I guess,' said Adie. 'I envy them. They haven't a clue. I'm not sure how, she's nothing like mum. She's a great big stranger sitting at the dinner table.'

'If you knew nothing about magic and hadn't seen all the stuff we've seen, you probably wouldn't suspect for a while either.'

'Yeah, s'pose.'

Grace sighed.

'We can't stay out all night, but we could go talk to Bob before we go home. What do you think?'

'Anything to pass the time.'

✳ ✳ ✳

Bob's campfire wasn't lit. In fact, Bob's campfire wasn't

there. There was a scorched scratch in the earth suggesting there had once been a fire, and that was all. No wrought-iron pot, no stools, no fishing rod, no hut. Worse still, Bob's camp looked like a blast site, as if something had exploded in the small clearing leaving the surrounding woodland scarred. Large stones were embedded in the trees circling the camp, some of them had hit so hard they had burst right through the bark, splitting the trunks in two.

The girls stared around in shock. Grace bent down and picked up one of the rocks – a remnant of Bob's stone hut.

'What happened?' she said.

She was answered by a groan that came from deeper in the woods. She and Adie followed the noise, finally stumbling upon Bob tangled in a web of brambles. They tore at the stringy branches and rolled him out onto the flat ground. There he lay, taking big gasping breaths. His face was battered and bruised, tiny cuts covered his skin with some of the bramble thorns still buried in his jaw. Grace was horrified.

'Murdrina,' said Adie.

Almost apologetic, she pulled a small pot of Choki balm from her pocket and began rubbing it into the wounds on his face. He pushed her away but she persisted. Eventually, the dried blood and bruised purple swirled over his skin in unnerving patterns. When they settled his face was clear, except for a *cho ku rei* symbol on his right cheek.

'That's a little better,' Adie said, 'but we should cover any bigger cuts, in case they get infected.'

She tried to pull up his sleeve, but he swatted her hand away.

'That'll do,' he growled.

Grace noticed the telltale glint of a jewel clenched between his fingers. Her heart sank. The jewelled fishing fly added to Bob's powers; he was holding it when he was attacked, and yet he still couldn't prevent the destruction of his camp.

'It *was* Murdrina, then,' Grace said.

He didn't reply and she took that as an affirmative.

'Ms Lemon says you're the only one who can beat her,' Adie said. 'That you're the only one who can save us.'

'Can you?' Grace asked. 'Save us?'

He got up off the ground and pushed past them. He paced around the remains of his home. He picked up stones here and there, depositing them in a pile on one side of the clearing. His dented iron pot was dragged from a cluster of nettles and thrown on top of the stones.

Grace watched Bob clear the wreckage of his hut and despaired.

'Anything we can do?' she said. 'Do you need help?'

'No,' was the gruff reply.

She signalled to Adie and they left the clearing.

'Yes, you do,' Grace whispered as she pushed her way through the woods in the dark. 'You *do* need help.'

22

THE PLAN

Grace and Adie stood at the back at of the school holding their jackets closed against the fierce wind. It was bitterly cold. Grace hadn't once mentioned Murdrina, knowing that Adie must be worried sick about her family after witnessing the state of Bob's camp. But her friend hadn't questioned her for a moment when Grace asked for her help in gathering a few things for a spell, and texting the others about an urgent meeting. Adie was no use to her family all by herself, and she knew it.

One by one, the girls arrived. Grace thanked her lucky stars that she had given Delilah her mobile phone. Being the only one of the girls without one, calling Delilah would have meant calling Ms Lemon's landline.

'FYI,' Una said, trotting towards them from the back gate,

'if my parents notice I've snuck out in the middle of the night, I'll be on dishes 'til I turn eighteen.'

'Your sacrifice is noted,' Jenny said. 'Grace, what's up?'

'We're going inside,' Grace said.

She took a damp ribbon from her jacket pocket and wrapped it around the lock of the school emergency exit that led straight into the P block.

'Open sesame,' she said.

There was a click and the door drifted ajar.

'You're gonna have to show me how to do that one,' Una said, enthralled.

Grace didn't say anything more until everyone was safely inside a lab in the P block, surrounding one of the heavy wooden desks in the centre of the room.

'So,' Jenny said, 'you gonna spill, or what?'

Grace took a deep breath and let it out slowly.

'We're starting a coven.'

'We have a coven,' Rachel replied.

'No, our own coven. Not one organised by our teachers, where they make the rules and tell us what to do. We're starting our *own* coven. We make the rules. We decide what to do. It's our coven, no-one else's.'

'I'm liking the sound of this,' said Jenny.

'Wait,' said Rachel,' is this about stopping Murdrina?'

'She attacked Bob,' Adie cut in. 'His hut was blown to bits, and he was all cut up and bruised.'

'Bob can't beat Murdrina,' Grace said.

'And you think we can?' Rachel exclaimed.

'I don't see why not.'

'*I* see why not,' Una said. 'She's an all-powerful sorceress witch-type thing, that could turn our insides out and smash the entire town to the ground. And we're a bunch of school-girls.'

'That's it,' Grace said. 'That's the problem right there.'

'That we're a bunch of schoolgirls?'

'That we don't admit that we're so much more. I *know* we are, you know we are, but we still turn to Ms Lemon, to Mrs Quinlan, to Bob, when we need help.'

'Because they have more experience, Grace,' Rachel said. 'They're grown-ups.'

'They've been doing it longer than we have,' Grace conceded, 'but who's to say that's what really matters?'

'Em, I'll say it,' said Una.

Grace ignored her.

'We've beaten demons, we've tricked and fought our way off a magical island, we've battled faeries and Hunters and evil witches, and who always comes out on top?'

'We've had help with that,' said Rachel.

'Not all of it, Rach. It's come down to us, too, what we can do. Your glamouring is out of this world. Jenny can outfly anything in the sky. Adie owns the rivers, Delilah's practically an encyclopaedia of witchcraft, my origination's just taken a giant leap forward, and Una–'

Una raised one eyebrow and tapped her finger on her lips.

'I'm dying to hear this one.'

'Una, you could stay cloaked for hours without even trying.'

'That's no great shakes.'

'It *is* great shakes. I do it for five minutes and I feel like I'm suffocating.' Grace turned to the rest of them. 'There are six of us and we've got any number of skills between us. We're practically an army.'

Rachel still looked unconvinced.

'None of that would matter if we went up against Murdrina. If she practically finished off Bob in one swoop, she'll make mincemeat out of us.'

'Only if we went head to head with her without a plan.' Grace unfolded a large sheet of paper and smoothed it out on the table. 'But we have one more thing going for us. We're smart.'

'Speak for yourself,' said Una.

'Stop thinking of it as a straightforward fistfight where the strongest wins, because it doesn't have to be that way. Think outside the box.'

'I'm sorry,' Una said, 'my brain is lodged firmly inside the box. What are you saying?'

'We have one awesome weapon that Murdrina knows nothing about. And it's right outside that door.'

'The P block?'

Grace sighed, exasperated.

'What's *in* the P block?'

'Oh, em... ooh, ooh, ooh, the demon well!'

'She doesn't know it yet, but that's where Murdrina's going.'

'Wait,' Adie said. 'Murdrina's inside my mum. You're not sending my mum down the demon well.'

'No,' Grace replied, 'we're taking her out of your mum first. And then we're chucking her down the well.'

Jenny grabbed the sheet of paper on the table.

'I'm gonna need to see this plan.'

The demon well was the girls' messy initiation into the world of witchcraft. It was an invisible circle, not much more than a metre in diameter, that was a weak spot in the Earth's spiritual plane. The thin barrier covering this porthole was all that stood between the human race and an entire realm of dark creatures made of black mist that would possess any poor soul they could grab hold of. Una had been one of those poor souls for a while. The girls had unwittingly summoned a demon from the well and spent the next few weeks in terrified limbo, on the steepest learning curve of their lives. It was a baptism of fire but they pulled through, and so had begun their Wiccan schooling.

'We used a Chi orb, remember?' Grace said, going through her plan step by step. 'To collect those lost souls from the stone house.'

'Those poor souls, stuck between worlds?' Adie said. 'I remember. That was awful, and nobody can help them.'

'I know, but it's the orb I'm talking about here. We could use it to trap Murdrina's soul, right Delilah?'

The small girl nodded.

'Yeah, that would work. If you can get her soul out of Adie's mum to begin with.'

'And once it's in the orb, we simply chuck the orb down the demon well.'

'Which is open,' said Rachel.

'Right.'

'And out of which,' Una said, 'many demons are spilling into our world.'

'I'm getting to that.'

'Good, I'd hate to think you'd forgotten about the body-possessing demons.' She shivered. 'I'm no fan of them.'

'I know you're not, Una, but we used these porcelain cups and baggies to keep the demons at bay when we were trying to send your one back down the well, remember?'

'Mrs Quinlan made the potions for those,' Rachel said, 'not us.'

'But Delilah can source those recipes pretty easily, right?'

Delilah nodded again.

'How are you going to keep Murdrina still long enough to get her out of my mum?' asked Adie.

'Delilah, I hate to mention her, but I saw your mother use a net made of smoke once. Did she ever teach you that?'

'I know how to produce a smoke strand from each arm,' the small girl replied, 'but making enough for a whole net takes hours and hours of practice. You can't master it overnight.'

'Would six strands be enough for a net?'

'Probably.'

'Then teach three of us to make smoke strands, and we'll make a net between us.'

'I suppose that could work.'

'Wait a sec,' said Rachel, 'if the well's fully open, there'll be any number of demons pouring out of it. We can't keep them off and trap Murdrina at the same time.'

'Drake,' Jenny said. 'He'll want to help, won't he? Agata, too, if we can get in touch with her.'

'Maybe that doctor you talked about?' said Adie.

'Oh no,' Una said, 'he is the creepiest of creepy creeps.'

'Who was trying to save us from the hex,' Grace reminded her.

'What about Ms Lemon?' Delilah suggested.

'She told us to stay out of the fight with Murdrina,' said Jenny. 'She's not likely to get on board with this, is she?'

'Well, we need her,' Grace said firmly, 'so she can just think again and get on board.'

'Yeow, Brennan. Is this really *you* flouting authority?'

'Yes.'

'Well,' Jenny grinned, 'welcome to the dark side.'

'Thanks very much.'

'So how many demon goalkeepers have we got now?' asked Una.

'Drake, Agata, the doctor, if we can find them, Ms Lemon–'

'Don't forget Bob,' said Adie.

'Bob will be busy,' Grace replied.

'Doing what?'

'Being the bait.'

✷ ✷ ✷

Mr Pamuk's beaming face was at odds with the solemn gloominess of his cavernous shop. Adie could see Delilah shivering and felt an instant chill herself within the damp-stained walls of the underground cave.

'Well, well, little witchlets. All the water-messaging went well, I hope?'

'Yes, thanks, Mr Pamuk.'

Adie bit her lip nervously. Technically the water-messaging *had* worked. Mr Pamuk didn't need to know the confused and grave circumstances that had followed that ill-advised trip to Hy-Breasal.

'We're looking for a few other things today.' Adie pulled a

list from her pocket. 'A Chi orb, some ground locust chitin, a frog's heart... and some other bits and pieces.'

She could see his mind working as he read through the list, his joyful expression slowly disappearing.

'An interesting list,' he said finally. 'I hope all is well.'

'It is, Mr Pamuk. Thank you.'

He watched her for a moment, his smile sympathetic as always.

'Very well. This will take a few minutes, if you don't mind waiting.'

'We'll check out the spell books for a while.'

Adie followed Delilah to the far end of the cavern. There were a few books scattered across the numerous trunks and coffers, but hundreds more were stacked in a little maze of bookshelves at the back.

'An expulsion spell, a strong one,' Delilah said, lifting the cover of one book on a table. 'That's what we need. I'm trying to remember this one book – by Nefarious somebody – the spells were really old, so they'd be very powerful now. And they were all based around movement of objects and places and feelings–'

'And souls?'

'And souls.'

'Can you remember the title?'

Delilah shook her head.

'It had something about movement or motion... I can't

exactly remember.'

'Alright, well we'll just have to go through all of them and see if we can spot this Nefarious person.'

Delilah started at the bookshelf nearest, and Adie went to the opposite end. There were countless books written by various authors with strange names, but she didn't see Nefarious anywhere.

'Mr Pamuk,' she yelled back to the storeroom, 'we're looking for a particular book but we don't know the title, or the author's name. It has lots of spells on movement, or motion or something. We only know the author's first name, Nefarious...'

'*Wiccan Oscillation and Kinetics* by Nefarious Wilderblaum,' the man shouted back without hesitation.

Adie blinked.

'I guess... that sounds right.'

'Weird Science section, back row, top shelf.'

With no ladder in sight, Adie used some larger volumes to make a crude set of stairs, reached the book, and scrambled back down. Delilah took the book.

'This is brilliant,' the small girl said. 'There'll definitely be something in here.'

Delilah plonked down cross-legged in the open space beyond the bookshelves and began scouring the pages. At the counter, Adie could see Mr Pamuk gently placing packages in a brown paper bag. She took out the wad of notes that were the sum of all the girls' savings.

'Would you like the suede-effect gift bag for the Chi orb?' Mr Pamuk asked. 'It's only another €7.'

'No, thanks,' Adie said. 'Just the orb.'

'And a square of violet silk embroidered with catgut, and two stalks of lime grass,' Delilah called from her spot on the floor.

Mr Pamuk looked to Adie.

'Yep,' she said, 'those too. Oh, and the book, of course.'

'Ah, that is a first edition. Quite expensive.'

'Oh,' Adie looked through the small amount of change she had left.

'Let us call the book a loan,' the man said, 'for a favourite customer. You may return it when you have... when you are ready.'

'Thank you, Mr Pamuk.'

'You are welcome,' he said, handing her the paper bag. 'Best of luck, my dear witchlets.'

✵ ✵ ✵

The town was quiet and dark. Dunbridge Park was empty but for one huddled figure sat on a tree stump.

'He's still here,' Jenny said, as she and Grace made their way into the park. 'He must be pretty worried about you.'

'He's worried about all of us.'

'I'll give you a fiver if he remembers my name.'

Drake slipped off the tree stump as they walked towards him and, as the moonlight shimmered across his scaly skin, Grace felt the urge to run forward and hug him. It appeared he almost did the same, but he held back at the sight of Jenny, and there was a cringeworthy moment where they both hurried forward, then both pulled back. Grace thanked the dark for hiding her blush.

'I'm Jenny,' Jenny said, sticking out her hand.

Drake gave her a quizzical look.

'I know.'

'Oh,' Jenny said, smiling at Grace. 'Just checking.'

'Sorry we didn't come looking for you sooner,' Grace said, trying to ignore the growing glow in her cheeks. 'There were a few things we had to do.'

'Where's the straw doll?' asked Drake.

'Our teacher has it. She's locked in her house. We were locked in there too, but Jenny got us out.'

Drake let out a long slow breath.

'I'm sorry about your teacher.'

'We haven't given up, we'll get her out. But we have to deal with Murdrina first.'

Drake looked like he'd been smacked in the face.

'Murdrina? She's here? How? What–'

'Our friends summoned her by accident, trying to find out what the hex was,' Grace said. 'There's no point getting worked up about it now. It's done, and we have to sort it out.'

'I wasn't gonna blame your friends,' Drake said. 'It's 'cos of the hex, it's our fault.'

'Justine's fault, and the ringmaster's. We know what you and the doctor did for us. I'm so sorry I didn't trust you.'

'You didn't have no reason to.'

His eyes were warm and forgiving, and Grace felt a wave of gratitude that he held none of her mistakes against her.

'Anyway,' Jenny loudly broke the moment, 'it's been lovely catching up, but we're actually here to ask a favour. Well, when I say favour, you really owe us. You know, the whole hex thing.'

'Which Drake and the doctor tried to save us from,' Grace said through gritted teeth.

'Sure, sure, tried and failed. But never mind. We need help to send this Murdrina cow to hell. Are you in?'

Before Drake could answer, there was a shriek from across the park.

'Drake! Drake, mein schatz!'

Agata's powerful frame came thundering across the grass. She grabbed the boy with both arms and hugged him so ferociously that Grace could swear his eyes were bulging. Keeping one arm around his shoulders, Agata swept his hair back from his forehead.

'You are okay?'

'I'm good, Agata. You don't gotta worry. I'm sorry I had to break out of there without you, but I had to try–'

'No, no,' Agata dismissed his apology, 'is no need. You are sweet boy, always.'

Drake hugged her back.

'So they let you go, but what about the doctor?'

'They vont to kill him.'

'He's still caged?'

'No, no,' Agata waved her hand again, laughing this time. 'He let go fireworks and blew doors off. It vos funny. He is here also.'

She pointed, and through the dimness Grace could see the unnerving silhouette with the trenchcoat, hat and the burning ember of a cigar glowing in the night. He took his time strolling up the park, silently smoking his cigar.

'Evening, witches,' he said. 'Drake, you're well?'

'Yeah, I'm good.'

'Excellent. Well, since you young ladies are currently without terrible affliction, I must surmise that you did not find the doll.'

'Their teacher's got it,' Drake replied. 'It's locked up her house with her inside.'

'Ah,' the doctor said, taking another puff of his cigar, 'now that is a shame. But one life lost is better than half a dozen.'

'We'll get her out,' Grace said, 'after we've—'

'They've,' Drake cut in suddenly, 'eh, got another problem.'

'Already?' the doctor replied. 'How industrious.'

'Murdrina is here, in this town. They... she was summoned

accidentally. They have a plan to get rid of her.'

'Permanently,' Grace said.

The doctor lowered his shaking hand and Grace saw the cigar fall from his limp fingers and smoulder in the grass.

'Yeah,' said Jenny, 'so we're gonna need your help with that. You all in?'

23

demon goalies

The doctor agreed to take part in Grace's plan, but he said little more before leaving. Agata, at first taken aback by the news, recovered quickly and was soon quizzing Jenny on her progress with the weights. Never one to be modest, Jenny immediately flexed her biceps and described, in minute detail, her training and nutrition plan. Weary of the muscle discussion, Grace wandered off towards the edge of the park. Drake followed.

'That is some scheme you've come up with,' he said. 'You don't even seem scared.'

'I *am* scared. I'm terrified.'

She had said it without thinking, and realised it was true. She was right to set up the new coven, and she had absolute faith in herself and her friends, but there was no denying what they were up against.

'Well,' said Drake, 'just so you know, I'm scared too.'

She nodded, her nose stinging with the threat of tears.

'Okay.'

They stood side by side, shaded from the moonlight by the trees, and a single tear rolled down Grace's cheek. In the dark, she felt his fingertips reach for hers and hold them gently. It helped, so she firmly grasped his hand with both of hers and rested her head on his shoulder.

'Grace,' she heard Jenny call from across the park, 'we gotta go. We've got people to corral and potions to make.'

'See you at the school then,' said Drake.

Grace took a few steps, turned back, looked up into his lovely eyes and kissed him. He was warm, despite the bitter cold, and his skin was so soft she could trace the barely perceptible cracks. Something fluttered madly in her stomach and when she pulled back, he smiled.

'What was that for?'

'For luck,' she said.

She gave him another peck on the lips, making him laugh, then she left the park, her brain spinning with what had just happened and what lay ahead of her.

'Forty-five minutes to go.' Jenny patrolled the desks in the P block lab like a security guard. 'Who's falling behind?'

'Me,' said Adie, urgently scraping at the powder in a metal bowl she had balanced above a Bunsen burner. 'It's all clumping together.'

'It's too damp,' Delilah said, handing her a jar. 'Grind in a little yarrow.'

'Thanks. I'm really bad at this.'

'You're not. We should be ageing these potions over days – this is the speedy version, so it's bound to be a little messy.'

'I'll take over from you, Adie,' Grace said. 'You'll have to go soon.'

'Yeah,' Adie sighed. 'I know.'

The desk at the centre of the room was quickly being covered in a selection of small, cloth bags and porcelain containers.

'We should just keep going 'til all the ingredients are gone,' Jenny said, counting the baggies and cups. 'This whole thing will be for nothing if we run out of stuff to keep the demons under control.'

On the teacher's desk, at the top of the room, Delilah had two potions on the go. Turquoise liquid bubbled in a round-bottomed flask, flashes of pink popping through it as it boiled and, on a thick-bottomed plate, a soldering iron sat propped up with its burning end lodged in the centre of the plate. Rust-coloured powder swirled around the soldering gun like iron shavings around a magnet; once the powder burned orangey red, it moved to the edge of the plate, circled, cooled, and moved back in for another shot.

Grace checked both potions while Adie packed up her things.

'This,' Delilah said, noting Grace's interest, 'is for the expulsion spell. You're going to have to throw this in her face, sorry.'

'That'll make her mad.'

'Yes, but the good news is she'll probably be mad already. And this is the powder that'll guide her soul into the Chi orb. It's really easy to use—'

'I just scatter it around myself and hold up the orb,' Grace interrupted. 'Yeah, I've used that stuff before.'

'Great.' Delilah was delighted. 'Then everything should go smoothly.'

Grace nodded through a brief wave of nausea.

'Right, I'm off.' Adie stood at the door with her jacket on. There was an apprehensive silence. 'Well, don't all wish me luck at the same time.'

There were cries of 'sorry' and 'good luck'. Adie waved them away and smiled.

'Not before four o'clock,' Grace said.

'Not before four a.m. I've got it.'

'Good luck, Adie.'

'You too.'

She disappeared into the P block corridor.

'Right,' Jenny yelled, making the others jump, 'the countdown is at thirty minutes, people, and this table isn't full.'

'Ever consider a career in a sweatshop, Jenny?' Una said. 'You'd be really good at it.'

'Are jokes going to get the job done any faster, Una?'

'They might.'

'I don't think so. Get to it.'

Rachel gave her a mocking salute as Jenny continued her patrol.

✳ ✳ ✳

Moving from foot to foot at the back entrance of the school, Grace couldn't stop shaking. She told herself it was the cold. She stood with Una and Delilah, waiting for the people that would act the part of demon goalkeepers. Ms Lemon arrived first, only minutes after Delilah had called her, looking fit to burst.

'What did I tell you?' she snapped. 'You're to stay out of this, that's what I said. And Delilah, I'm disappointed in you. I thought you were in bed.'

'Miss,' Una said, casually tying her short black bob into tiny pigtails, 'this is happening. You can get on this crazy train and help us out, or you can wait until we're all killed, and then wonder for the rest of your life if it was your fault.'

Ms Lemon opened and closed her mouth like a goldfish, apparently too shocked or angry to speak.

'Ms Lemon, we're decided on this,' said Grace. 'We know

how dangerous it is, but we're already a part of it and we have to try. We'll do it with or without you, but we'd much rather with.'

'So, what do you say?' said Una.

Ms Lemon huffed and stared up at the stars in indignation. Finally, she spoke.

'Well, that doesn't leave me much choice, does it?'

'Cool!' Una clapped. 'Welcome to the plan, Miss.'

'And what *is* the plan, may I ask?'

'I'll go through it,' Grace said, pointing at the figures coming through the back gate, 'when everyone else is here.'

Grace had explained the purpose of the baggies and the porcelain cups twice, and Agata still had a pained look on her face. She pointed to the bags.

'Before or after in de body?'

'Before. Before, that's...' Grace took a deep breath. 'If you see a demon, and it hasn't touched anybody yet, you open the bag over it. The powder will burn it up.'

'Umhmm,' the woman nodded. 'And dis?'

'If the demon touches somebody, it will possess them, but that can take up to a minute. You'll know it's happening because the person's eyes will glow a strange colour.'

'Ja, ja, I see.'

'You smash the cup at the their feet and say–'

'Exitus, exitus, exitus.'

'Yes, that's it. The stuff in the cup will turn to smoke, and you have to make sure the person breathes it in. That's really important.'

'Must breathe smoke.'

'Yes.'

'Ja, okay.'

Grace turned to Drake and the doctor.

'Is that all clear?'

'Yeah, we got it,' Drake replied, though he looked worried.

'I'll go through it with you a few more times,' Ms Lemon offered. 'And Grace, some of these baggies need to be retied with a highwayman's hitch or they're not going to open easily.'

'I'll help with that,' the doctor said.

'Good, thank you. And if you could also take charge of the potions when it all kicks off,' Ms Lemon went on, 'I'll try to watch the well, and track what's happening to everybody's eyes. If I see a demon possession beginning, I'll yell. Between us, we're sure to spot any danger.'

The teacher seemed to have put her anger to one side for now, and Grace was very grateful.

'Here come Jenny and Rach,' said Una as their friends emerged from the woods. 'And look, they got creepy Bob to come.'

'Don't call him that, Una,' Grace chided.

'Sorry. They got nice Bob to come.'

The hood of Bob's black slicker shadowed his pale, withered complexion. He marched towards Grace, with those heavy and purposeful steps that had once terrified her. His expression was stern and his eyes – one blue, one pearly white – focussed fully on her face. He stopped barely a step from her and she could feel his breath on her forehead.

'Where do I stand?' he said.

She was confused for a moment.

'Inside,' she said. 'We'll all be in the P block, by the demon well. You're going to be the bait, you see, Adie–'

'I know the plan,' he said, stepping around her and through the emergency exit into the school.

'We talked on the way here,' said Rachel. 'He's not as gruff as you'd think.'

'I think he's relieved.' Jenny nodded, as the others gave her skeptical looks. 'Seriously, I think he had no idea how to beat Murdrina.'

'So everyone's here now,' said Grace.

'Everyone's here.'

'Then let's get this show on the road.'

Adie turned the key as quietly as possible, she didn't want to wake her father and brothers if she could help it. She shut the door and glanced through the hall where she saw a figure standing at the kitchen window. All the lights were off and Murdrina stood in silence. She looked less like Adie's mum than ever before.

Adie entered the kitchen and cried out. There were three figures slumped at the table.

'Not dead,' Murdrina said, still facing the window. 'Not yet. But they do talk such tedious nonsense, perhaps it would be kinder...'

She turned and Adie put her hands out.

'No, please, I beg you. Don't hurt them.'

'I missed you, my sweet.' The black worm wriggled across the whites of her mother's eyes. 'Your conversation I think I could tolerate, especially when it concerns a mutual acquaintance of ours.'

'That's what I came to talk to you about. Bob wants to meet you. He says he's ready now.'

'Indeed?' That wicked smile that was nothing like her mother's. 'That is good news. After our last rendezvous I was beginning to think I had made a mistake. That pitiful little hut wasn't even charmed for protection, and the man himself? Fell far too easily.' She sighed. 'The tyranny of boredom.'

'I think he was setting you up.' Adie warned herself not to push it too far. 'I think he's much stronger than you think.'

'One can but hope.'

'So you'll come with me?'

'Are you leading me, my sweet?'

Adie snuck a glance at the motionless bodies around the table.

'Yes.'

'Then I'll follow.'

They turned in through the gates at the back of the school and Adie's pulse quickened. Her friends would be in place now, hiding in the shadows of the P block with Bob centre-stage, everything set for the attack. She would take Murdrina in through the emergency exit, the net would be thrown and the spells would begin. In minutes, Murdrina would be down the demon well and out of their lives forever.

'You seem nervous, my sweet.'

She can probably feel my heart beat, Adie thought.

'I'm not nervous. He's in there, through that green door. He's waiting for you.'

'Inside the building?'

'Yes.'

'And what surprise is in store for me there?'

'He told me that's where he'd be, that's all I know.'

'Oh, my sweet,' said Murdrina. 'You know much more than that.'

The woman stepped forward and raised her hands. The walls of the P block began to shake.

'Dark corners hide dark secrets,' she said, her hands moving in rhythm with the block. 'I prefer to battle amongst the elements.'

With a terrible and deafening crash, the walls of the P block exploded outwards. Adie dropped to the ground, debris hissing past her ears. Rubble landed as far away as the football pitch and, when the smoke cleared, there were her friends, exposed and reeling from the blast. Only Bob remained on his feet.

'What is this?' Murdrina's expression was one of delighted surprise. 'Cheerleaders? Or is this adorable little army the extent of your preparation?'

The woman's laughter echoed through the settling dust. She kicked idly at a few loose pieces of brick.

'And yet, I am disappointed. I cannot tell you how much.'

It was a flick of her fingers, nothing more, and lumps of concrete lifted off the ground. They hovered in the air for a moment and then smashed into Bob, sending him rolling back into the building. Where he had stood, Adie could see the scattering of green pebbles over the mouth of the demon well. She knew that when Delilah added a scattering of white pebbles, the well would open. There was little time left.

'Grace,' she hissed at the gaping hole in the school building. 'Where are you?'

✳ ✳ ✳

Grace could hear a clanging bell and, behind that, the crackle of white noise. She clambered to her knees, wiping at the grey powder that stained her skin and clothes. What had just happened?

They had all been in position, waiting for the emergency exit to open, when the whole world had blown up. She was thrown backwards as far as the double doors that led to the C block, her eyes were stinging and she could feel a trickle of blood down her temple. Something sailed past her − a body followed by bricks and rock. Then a sound reached her through the chaos. Adie's voice, urgent.

'I'm here,' she croaked.

Slowly her mind cleared and the plan reformed. She was to help throw the net. Rachel, Jenny and she would throw the net of smoke, and Delilah would open the well. The body sailed past her again − in the opposite direction this time. Bob was fully conscious, and she could feel the wave of power that emanated from the jewelled fly in his grasp.

Let him distract her, she thought. *Get back in the game.*

She focussed on her wrists, cursing the thin strings of smoke that flowed from them on command.

'Come on!' she said aloud. 'Concentrate!'

A billow of smoke made a bulge in one of the strings, but didn't take. Angrily she shook off both strings and focussed again. There, a proper smoke rope was emerging now. She glanced around for the other two, but only Rachel was visible. She looked as dazed as Grace felt, but she caught her eye and, soon, smoky ropes appeared along her arms.

'Where's Jenny?' Rachel mouthed.

Grace felt panic rising. She couldn't see Jenny anywhere – and two wasn't enough to make a net.

24

IN THE RUBBLE OF THE P BLOCK

Adie could see the problem. Jenny lay just to the left of the P block at a funny angle. For one awful second she looked dead, but her arm swung over her head and she jolted awake. She would struggle getting to her feet though, Adie could see that. Grace and Rachel were armed with smoky rope and ready to go. They needed a third.

Adie hadn't materialised rope before, but she had over-heard Delilah teaching the others. Recalling the lesson as best she could, she was startled when smoke immediately puffed from her right wrist. She was on the right track. Three more attempts and the rope from her left arm looked reasonably solid.

There was a smaller, blasting noise and Adie glanced towards Bob and Murdrina. They were battling across the concrete, moving closer to the woods, and she could see a small wound on her mother's face. She instinctively moved towards her, but reminded herself that her mother was not her mother while she was in Murdrina's hold. The only way to save her was to go through with the plan.

She jerked her right arm and a tightly woven rope of smoke burst from her wrist.

'Grace,' she shouted. 'I'm here. Let's do this.'

Grace and Rachel sprinted through the rubble and readied to throw their rope. Bob and Murdrina were spinning now, bouncing painfully off the ground as they tried to twist out of each other's grip.

'Get ready,' Grace said, 'when I say.'

Adie flicked her ropes nervously.

'Nearly,' Grace said, 'nearly... Bob! Let go!'

Bob released Murdrina mid-spin and she was catapulted towards them. Grace and Rachel swung their ropes like giant lassos, they clashed together and instantly bonded, closing around the woman in a loose weave. But Adie's ropes fell short.

She gasped in horror as they missed the net and trailed along the ground. She threw them again, harder. There was a spark as the ends caught the weave, but still they didn't latch on.

'Adie,' Rachel yelled, 'swing them together, like they're one rope. *Now*, or she'll get through!'

Circling both arms over her head at the same time, feeling one shoulder nearly pull out of the joint, Adie fired the ropes with all the strength she had left. They caught, only just, halfway across the net and slithered around to complete the woven trap. But Murdrina's arms wriggled through the squares, and already Adie could see the ropes fraying against her grasp.

Grace had seen it too. Pulling a vial of turquoise liquid from her back pocket, she uncorked it and threw it in Murdrina's face. The sorceress screeched and writhed against the net. From another pocket, Grace pulled a dainty wooden shaker. She sprinkled rust-coloured powder around herself. Then she knelt and caught the Chi orb that Delilah had located among the rubble.

Adie watched the small girl scurry back to the remains of the P block and scatter white pebbles over the demon well. The figures of Miss Lemon, Drake and Agata emerged from the corners of the block, their hands filled with bags and porcelain cups.

This was it. This was the moment.

Grace's heart was racing, and she was gasping for breath by the time she knelt. She was holding the Chi orb in both hands and waiting for that swirl of colour that would mean Murdrina's soul was trapped inside. Inside the smoky net, Adie's mother was twisting and screaming, and Grace willed Delilah's expulsion potion to work. It did. Adie's mum fell silent, her body still as she drifted out of consciousness.

Any second now, and Murdrina's soul would be sucked into the orb. Grace stared intently for any movement, any sign. There was nothing.

She looked to Adie and shook her head.

'Where is she?' Adie cried.

'I don't know.'

Then it hit, like a giant corkscrew burrowing into her back. Something wormed across Grace's field of vision, and everything went black.

✴ ✴ ✴

There was screaming coming from the demon well. Agata had one great hand around the back of Drake's neck, holding him over a thin wisp of smoke that twirled from a smashed porcelain cup.

'Exitus, exitus, exitus,' she cried.

A pink glow faded from Drake's eyes the moment he inhaled, but more black misty limbs reached from the red circle in the ground, grasping for bodies. One of the demons crawled free of the well, and snatched at Delilah's ankles. Ms Lemon pulled a cloth bag apart, showering him with dust that burned through his back in tiny fires. The creature disintegrated, leaving a scorched patch on the ground.

Glancing back at Grace, Adie noticed she was no longer holding the Chi orb. Her friend sat on her heels watching the turmoil taking place in the P block. When she turned to face Adie, a slither of black crossed her eyes.

'No,' Adie whispered.

'Goodness, my sweet,' Grace said, getting to her feet. 'A demon well. I must confess I've never seen one open, in the flesh. They're nasty creatures, don't you think?'

Adie backed away, shaking her head.

'Perhaps a demon possession or two might liven this battle up,' Grace sneered.

She ran towards the well, reaching for the next demon that pulled itself free. Gleeful, the creature ploughed its misty hand into Grace's arm. Her eyes turned a violent shade of red.

'No!' Adie screamed, running. 'Delilah, Ms Lemon!'

Delilah leapt on Grace's back, holding her head back by the hair, while Ms Lemon smashed a porcelain cup in front of her.

'This is much more fun than I expected.'

Adie spun around to find Bob standing over her, the black worm wriggling over his pearled eye.

'Please, please don't do this!'

'Your friends are nothing special, after all,' Bob said. 'But this? This is a game that could go on for hours.'

Bob shunted backward, and Murdrina was gone.

'Where is she?' he growled, himself once more.

'She's moving around,' Adie wailed. 'She could be anyone.'

'Over here, my sweet!'

The doctor grinned at her, black flickering across his eyes. He grabbed Agata by the hair and plunged her head into the open well. The strongwoman threw him off and staggered backwards, a demon curled around her face, sinking into her skin.

'Agata!'

Jenny got to her feet and ran to the woman, but Agata turned on her and swatted her like a fly. Grace, now free of her demon, joined Rachel, Una and Ms Lemon as they struggled to keep Agata's powerful, demon-infested frame immobile. Delilah crushed a cup under her foot and threw herself on top of the pile of bodies pinning Agata to the ground. Still Agata resisted, and it took the addition of Drake before she could be held over the sublimating smoke long enough to inhale.

But too many demons were pouring through the open mouth of the well now. They fought and clawed at each other to get out, and that was the only thing that slowed the spill.

'Shut the well, Delilah!' Jenny cried.

'No!' Grace yelled, 'this is our only chance!'

'We've lost, Grace, now shut the well!'

Adie felt limp with fear and regret.

'Shut the well, Grace,' she whispered.

But no-one could hear her.

Grace rolled off Agata's back, her arms trembling with exhaustion. It was madness. Jenny was screaming for them to close the well, Drake was yelling for help, another demon was grabbing hold of Ms Lemon. Across the concrete, Grace met the black-flickering eyes of Bob, now grinning a grin that was not his own.

We've lost, Grace thought. *Lost.*

But Delilah still stood poised with a silk bag in her hands – the bag that had contained the green and white pebbles that were keeping the well open. She was waiting for a signal, Grace realised. She was ignoring Jenny's calls for the well to be shut, and holding out for Grace's instructions.

One more minute, Grace begged silently. *Give me one more minute to think.*

But there was nothing to think about. The demons were swarming from the well – soon Grace's coven, and every-one else, would be overwhelmed. A black tail flicked across Jenny's eyes, across Una's, across Drake's. In each of the faces, Murdrina's smile grew bigger and more wicked.

'Isn't this fun?' someone hissed in her ear.

Grace shook her head, tears spilling down her cheeks, as she looked at the small girl holding the silk bag…

'Delilah…'

Suddenly Grace was wrenched back by her arm. She spun around to face the doctor.

'Push me in,' he said quietly.

His face, so close to her own, was startling.

'What?' Grace gasped.

'When Murdrina jumps to me, push me in.'

'I can't, you don't understand. You don't know what's down there.'

'I understand well enough.' The doctor pulled roughly on her arm again. 'It ends today. No more, for us or anyone else. *Do it.*'

He dropped Grace's arm and strode over to his place by the demon well once more. Grace stood directly behind him. One push was all it would take. She pleaded with herself to find some other solution. The noise, the screaming, everything seemed to focus her mind, but the clearer it became, the more she realised there was no other way.

Jenny threw Una across the block. She landed in a crumpled heap in the corner.

'Stop,' Grace begged Murdrina. 'Please stop!'

But the cackling moved from Jenny to Ms Lemon, from Adie to Delilah, from Rachel to Agata. That awful screeching laugh so horrible that Grace couldn't take it anymore.

'Delilah,' she said, 'shut the well.'

The doctor turned to her, a black flick in the whites of his eyes.

'Aw, don't let's end the fun just yet.'

'No,' Grace said, as Delilah raised the silk bag. 'It ends now.'

She lurched forward and pushed with all her might.

The doctor's black-flickering eyes flashed in terror as he hurtled into the well – grabbed by dozens of misty, black limbs – and vanished into the vicious red light. It was a split second, no longer, and the well snapped shut.

Every sound seemed to have been sucked into that closed portal; the crashing and screaming and snarling stopped abruptly, leaving only a shocked silence. Everyone fell still; only the wind sweeping through their unkempt hair and clothes caused any movement among them. A scorched circle in the carpet was the sole hint of the horror that lay inside the well. Caught by the breeze, the doctor's wide-brimmed hat rolled slowly into the rubble of the P block.

Grace dropped to her knees. She put her head in her hands and sobbed into the ground.

Grace stood in the cul-de-sac of Wilton Place, gazing up at the boarded windows. She had wondered if Murdrina's hex would die without her, but evidently it hadn't.

'Hey, Brennan.' Jenny clambered through the hedge from the school football pitch looking every bit as beaten up as

Grace. 'Didn't break the hex then.'

'No,' Grace replied.

'We'll get her out. Eventually.'

'Sure.'

Grace was weary and had no tears left. They'd try their best to get Mrs Quinlan out but they'd never be able to get the doctor out. As if reading her mind, Jenny said,

'It was his choice, and you did what you had to do. He saved us all and you helped him.'

'Drake and Agata...'

'They understand.' Jenny sighed. 'They're upset, I know, but they understand. Give them time.'

There was nothing more to say so they stood in silence together, watching the house.

Until it coughed.

The house coughed. The front door opened and stretched like a mouth, the hall rug flipped out like a tongue, and the house coughed.

'Bloody hell,' it snarled, 'it tastes like I swallowed a fistful of cat hair.'

The boards on the upper windows splintered and fell off. The windows blinked like eyes opening, the brickwork bending like rubber.

'What are you two doing standing there? And you. I thought I told you to get lost.'

Jenny gawped for a minute.

'You did. I came back.'

'So what, you're gonna be a model student now? Fat chance. Sod off.'

'Eh, Mrs Quinlan,' Jenny said, 'you're a house.'

The house paused for a moment, as if trying to recall recent events.

'Oh, balls.'

'It suits you.'

'Shut it, you. Where's Beth Lemon?'

'She's trying to sort out things at the school,' said Grace.

'What happened at the school?'

'The P block got blown up.'

'Typical. I go incommunicado for five minutes and you lot are blowing up buildings.'

'It wasn't us–'

'I don't want to hear it. I... *caugh, caaaugh.*'

The house began coughing again, eventually hacking up a large ball of fur that came flying out of the door mouth. The ball unfurled on the lawn and meowed.

'God, Mephis,' Mrs Quinlan said, 'you're like sandpaper with thorns in.' The walls groaned as the house wriggled from side to side. 'There's millions of them in here, all scratching and... Oi! Knock it off or I'll kick you all out.'

'Don't worry, Mrs Quinlan,' Grace said, 'we'll get you out of there.'

'Oh, you lot are on the case. I'll hold my breath, shall I? Any day now?'

'It might take a while.'

'There's a shocker.'

The house wriggled again.

'Did you know I had a basement? There's a basement in here.'

Carved pumpkins glowed in the porches along Wilton Place. Kids in costume called to the doors in groups and stood on the road with their bags held up, comparing their loot. Grace carried a crate of apples and followed a bat, a Frankenstein's monster and a green-skinned witch up the driveway to Mrs Quinlan's house.

'Love the costumes,' Grace said as she knocked on the door.

'Thank you,' the kids chimed in unison.

The door rattled suddenly in its frame and swung open. The hall was dark except for a pumpkin that sat on a console table to one side. As the kids watched, the pumpkin turned, a flame burning inside its gaping mouth, and said,

'Come inside, children. You're just in time.... *for dinner.*'

Its mouth twisted wide in a horrible roar. Grace rolled her eyes as the kids ran screaming from the porch. Una came racing from the kitchen with a large bowl of lollipops and chocolate bars.

'Oh, for God's sake, Mrs Quinlan,' she said, 'those ones didn't get even get any sweets.'

Wheezing laughter shook the walls of the house and Grace carried her crate of apples inside.

'For toffee apples,' she said, planting the crate on the table, 'and that Halloween game. What it's called?'

'Bobbing for apples,' Rachel said, draping a garland of paper spiderwebs around Grace's shoulders.

'What about that one where there's an apple hanging on a string and you have to try and bite it without using your hands?' asked Jenny.

'You cheat at that one,' Una said. 'You jam it up against the door frame.'

'It's called strategising, Una. That's what a winner does.'

Grace pulled a newspaper from inside the crate and slapped it on the table.

'I also found this.'

'What is it?' Adie asked.

'Latest edition of *The Chronicle*. Take a look at that photo.'

She pointed to a fuzzy black and white picture of a man on the steps of a courthouse, under the headline *Insurance Scammer Indicted for Fraud*.

'Isn't that Felix, the ringmaster? He looks weird in a suit.'

'Yep, and check out who's trailing along behind him.'

Una leaned in and gasped.

'Is that Justine?'

'Without the beard. She must have shaved it off when they went down the con artist route.'

'Ha,' Una jammed a finger into the paper, 'how do you like them apples, Justine?'

She grabbed an apple from the crate and chomped on it.

'Good riddance,' Jenny agreed.

'Anyone for a slice of brack?' Ms Lemon began carving the fruity loaf on the counter.

'Be careful of your teeth, Miss,' Adie said.

'Yeah,' said Rachel, 'Una got a little overzealous with the hidden surprises. That loaf is mostly rings and coins.'

'I was making sure everyone would get something,' Una snarled. 'You're all so ungrateful.'

'Trick-or-treaters!' a voice boomed from inside the walls. 'Get there quick if you want to give the brats some chocolate. I'm gonna see if I can make these ones pee.'

Tutting, Rachel snatched the bowl of sweets and hurried to the front door.

'When are Drake and Agata coming?' Delilah asked, wincing as B-brr swung Tarzan-like from her hair, chattering to himself.

'A little later,' Grace replied. 'Agata was all excited about the trick-or-treating, she ordered her favourite sweets from Germany especially. Drake said they looked gross.'

'Do you think we could get Drake to wear a fake tail and jump out at kids like a real giant lizard? That would be so funny,' said Una.

She looked around at the appalled faces.

'What? I want to use my unusual-looking friend to scare small children. What's wrong with that?'

'I brought some popcorn,' Adie said, changing the subject, 'for the movies later.'

'Ooh, I have some brilliant stuff.' Jenny pulled a bunch of

DVDs from her bag. 'You won't sleep for a week after watching these.'

'I don't know,' Grace said. 'Watching scary movies when Mrs Quinlan's bound to try and scare us at the same time? I might not be up for that.'

Jenny snorted.

'She couldn't scare me.'

Reeooooumuw!

A long-haired cat was hurled from inside the wall and landed on Jenny's hair, howling and clawing to hold on. The tall girl screamed, slapping at her head. Mrs Quinlan's snickering vibrated through the floor.

'You're hilarious, old crone,' Jenny said, smoothing her auburn hair.

'You might want to watch your mouth,' the house replied. 'You'll be me one day.'

'Fat chance.'

Rachel returned from the hall and plonked the bowl down on the kitchen table.

'After all the screaming that lot did, I doubt any other kids are coming in. I'd say that's it for the trick-or-treaters.'

'Why don't we take some chocolate over to Bob?' Delilah said, eyeing the still-full bowl of sweets.

'That's a lovely idea,' Adie said. 'I bet he never gets to eat choc-olate.'

'Not if you can't hunt it in the woods,' said Jenny.

'We can have some punch when we get back,' Ms Lemon said.

'It won't take long to make up.'

Jenny and Mrs Quinlan snorted at the same time.

'Punch?' said Jenny. 'We're not in a Jane Austen novel, Miss.'

'I thought we could have a toast for the doctor, when Drake and Agata arrive.'

Everyone was silent for a few moments.

'I'd like that,' said Grace. 'So would Drake and Agata.'

'Oh, good,' Ms Lemon looked relieved, 'I didn't want to tread on anyone's toes, but...'

'It's a lovely thought, Miss,' Jenny said. 'Right, will we head off then?'

'Oh, just sod off and leave me by myself, why don't you,' said Mrs Quinlan.

'We are.'

Jenny scooped up the bowl, gave one of the skirting boards a sharp kick for good measure, and headed into the hall with everyone else following behind. Grace was last to the front door.

'You know, Mrs Quinlan,' she said in the hall, 'Delilah's already found some really in-depth stuff on hexes. Stuff that not even Bob knew.'

''Course she has. She's bright as a button.'

'So I don't think it'll be long at all.'

'I'm sorry, are we having a moment here? Am I supposed to cry and talk about my feelings? Wah-wah-wah.'

'Happy Halloween, Mrs Quinlan.'

'Bah, humbug.'

Grace smiled and pulled the door closed.